"Margaret Maron brings back one of her best characters. . . . A fascinating mystery centered in the fast lane of the world art community. . . . Great atmosphere with subtle and evocative writing."
—**Advocate Magazine**

△▽△

"I found myself reading with glee. . . . The best Sigrid Harald novel."
—**Toronto Globe & Mail**

△▽△

"Good news: Margaret Maron has a new mystery out. . . . Maron writes with humor, truth, and knowledge. Read it, and warm up to Sigrid Harald."
—**Greensboro News & Record**

△▽△

"Bravas for the return of Lt. Sigrid Harald!"
—**Dorothy Salisbury Davis**

△▽△

"Maron reawakens a too-long dormant series with thereturn of Lt. Sigrid Harald of the NYPD."
—**Library Journal**

△▽△

BOOKS BY MARGARET MARON

•

SIGRID HARALD NOVELS

THE DEBORAH KNOTT MYSTERIES

MARGARET MARON

FUGITIVE COLORS

THE MYSTERIOUS PRESS

Published by Warner Books

A Time Warner Company

"Time Does Not Bring Relief," by Edna St. Vincent Millay. From *Collected Poems*, HarperCollins. Copyright 1917, 1945 by Edna St. Vincent Millay and used in cooperation with Elizabeth Barnett, Literary Executor, Estate of Edna St. Vincent Millay.

Il Libro dell' Arte (*The Craftsman's Handbook*), by Cennino d'Andrea Cennini. Translated by Daniel V. Thompson. Jr. Copyright 1933, Yale University Press. Reprinted 1953 by Dover Publications and used by permission of Dover Publications.

MYSTERIOUS PRESS EDITION

Cover design by Jackie Merri Meyer
Cover illustration by Scott Hull

The Mysterious Press name and logo are registered trademarks of Warner Books, Inc.

 Mysterious Press books are published by
Warner Books, Inc.
1271 Avenue of the Americas
New York, NY 10020

Visit our Web site at
http://warnerbooks.com

A Time Warner Company

Printed in the United States of America

Originally published in hardcover by The Mysterious Press.
First Printed in Paperback: June, 1996

10 9 8 7 6 5 4 3 2

This is for Joe,
who still doesn't like mushy dedications:
Without you, my dear,
life (and writing) would be a lot less fun.

Author's Note

Lieutenant Sigrid Harald, NYPD, first appeared in an abortive Raven House edition of *One Coffee With* in 1981. *Futgitive Colors* is her eighth adventure, with each book set in what was—and is—the current "now."

One Coffee With began on a blue-sky sunny April day. Spring gave way to summer, then autumn in New York, followed by Christmans and one of the worst Februarys in the city's memory. (In Sigrid's memory, too, unfortunately.)

For the author, fourteen years have passed. For Sigrid Harald herself, no matter how much internal evidence alert readers may cite to the contrary, it has been only one short tumultuous year.

And now it is spring again . . .

Time does not bring relief; you all have lied
Who told me time would ease me of my pain!
I miss him in the weeping of the rain;
I want him at the shrinking of the tide;
The old snows melt from every mountain-side,
And last year's leaves are smoke in every lane;
But last year's bitter loving must remain
    Heaped on my heart, and my old thoughts abide.
There are a hundred places where I fear
To go,—so with his memory they brim.
And entering with relief some quiet place
Where never fell his foot or shone his face
I say, "There is no memory of him here!"
And so stand stricken, so remembering him.

—Edna St. Vincent Millay

March

She lay motionless beneath the blanket and stared at the ceiling dry-eyed, fighting against doing this to herself again, yet unable to resist.

It was like probing a sensitive tooth to see if it still hurt, Sigrid thought dully. You could almost forget it was there; and then, cautiously, the tip of your tongue lightly explores, barely touches the tooth, and excruciating pain lances through your whole body.

If only this pain were as simple, as *physical*. As treatable. If only there were something to numb inflamed memory . . .

But this aching grief was too deep-rooted for any narcotic. No way to yank out the irreversible cause, no way to deaden the nerves around it.

She closed her eyes and tried to sink back into oblivion, but it did not come.

So far, sleep had been her only release—twelve, sixteen hours a day of uneasy gray nothingness that left her listless and unrefreshed.

Her throat was raw from swallowing unshed tears.

Yet, despite everything, there were flashes of irrational anger that Nauman had reduced her to this. Of all the embarrassing times when he'd bullied her into admitting emotional depths no one else suspected, this surrender of will was the most humiliating. The most shameful.

Hating him and hating herself for a weakness she could not seem to control, she rolled over and opened the drawer of the night table, scalded by the knowledge that she was, at this moment, no stronger than any three-time loser reaching for nirvana in some filthy tenement crack house.

Inside the drawer was a microcassette player that held a long-playing tape from her answering machine. Mechanically, her slender fingers pushed the right buttons.

Rewind.

Stop.

Play.

Oscar Nauman's warm baritone flowed over her, wry and witty, cranky at having to attend a College Art Association meeting on the West Coast, exasperated both by the inanities of some of his colleagues and by his own inability to synchronize the different time zones with her shifting schedule.

She remembered coming home that freezing February night—was it already a full three weeks ago?—to find this message on her machine. As with all the other messages he'd left during those few days, she'd undressed and prepared for bed while the tape unspooled, amused by his fulminations, yet touched by his untoward lapse into genuine feeling just before he broke the connection: *"But the panels weren't a total waste, and the parties were better than I thought they would be. Got to see some of my pictures I hadn't seen in years. Years? Hell, decades! You never forget a one of them, Siga. Funny how they mellow. I hated to walk out of the room . . . was like I might never see them again. . . . Never had that feeling before."*

Stop

Rewind.

Play.

"*. . . like I might never see them again . . . never had that feeling before.*"

Rewind.

Play.

"*You never forget a one of them, Siga . . . hated to walk out of the room . . .*"

Rewind.

Play.

"*. . . never forget . . . never see again . . .*"

Stop.

Rewind.

Stop.

March 16

"Piggy toes, brrr-r!" the toddler told her young mother cheerfully when Georgia Fong stopped in front of the narrow stoop that led up to their three-room walk-up apartment over a hardware store that had already closed for the evening.

Even though there was no way those little toes could be cold inside their woolly socks and sturdy sneakers, Georgia said, " 'Piggy toes brrrr' is right," as she fished for her keys and prepared to lift Julie from her stroller. She pulled aside the fuzzy pink blanket, and her chilled fingers fumbled with the safety-strap catches. "Radio says it's gonna freeze again tonight."

"Fweeze," said Julie. She strained against the strap, eager to get out of the stroller, and her small face, a dimpled copy of Georgia's blond, blue-eyed beauty, was so close to her mother's that she impulsively bestowed a loving kiss on that smooth cheek.

Immediately, Georgia engulfed her daughter in a fierce hug. God, she loved this kid! She could barely remember how she'd existed before Julie. Couldn't imagine a future without her.

"In like a lion, out like a lamb," she told Julie optimistically, but there was nothing lamblike in the biting March wind that whipped down their street, teasing wisps of long blond hair from beneath their knitted hats and turning their cheeks bright red. The wind plucked greasy papers from a litter basket outside the fast-chicken place on the corner and bellied the canvas-and-plastic awnings that sheltered the heaping boxes of fruits and vegetables at the brightly lighted fruit stand next door.

Indeed, as she stooped to swing the child up onto her thin shoulder, the first shot sounded almost like the crack of stiff plastic snapping in the wind. Customers paused from filling their bags with string beans and bananas and looked at each other apprehensively. Georgia heard one of them say, "What was that?"

An instant later the second shot tore into the doorjamb just beyond Georgia's head and showered her with splinters of wood.

"Holy shit!" Georgia yelped. She snatched Julie out of the stroller so quickly that it racketed across the sidewalk and crashed into a car parked at the curb.

Tomatoes and grapes went flying as terrified customers stampeded into the cramped safety of the small grocery, and Georgia and her daughter crowded in right behind them.

April

Joseph Dortches, just off Lexington Avenue in Midtown, is an old New York institution, part bookstore, part art gallery. The ground floor is a maze of narrow aisles and dark oak shelving full of oversized art books. Ten feet up, a wide catwalk circles the interior and looks out over the heads of browsing customers. Here the bookcases are only waist high, and the walls above them are usually hung with moderately priced artworks. The current exhibit featured prints and drawings from the WPA projects of the thirties.

Hal DiPietro intended only to stop by the periodicals at the front of the store for the latest issue of *The Loaded Brush,* a leading art journal that carried an interview with Oscar Nauman conducted on the very morning of his death; but one look had led to another and soon he was happily rummaging through the shelves at the back of the store.

An art dealer—indeed the son of an art dealer as well—DiPietro considered himself thoroughly at home in this store of intellect and international culture. A slender man of medium height, he was only forty-three but his fair hair had been completely white for several years, a hereditary trait he had shared with his late father. Beautifully razored silver locks flowed into a short silver beard that effectively disguised a weak chin and counterfeited a certain saturnine urbanity.

At the very back of the store was a small area devoted to more expensive rarities. Locked wire doors protected these books while allowing customers to read the titles. An elderly woman in a maroon cardigan sat at a writing table in front of the locked shelves, and as DiPietro approached, she peered at him disapprovingly over her rimless bifocals until he came close enough to be recognized. Then her wrinkled face broke into a smile of true pleasure and she rose to unlock the wire doors for him.

"Mr. DiPietro! We haven't seen you here in some time. We trust you haven't been ill?"

"No, no. Just very busy, Katerina." With the slightly arrogant presumption of a customer who knows he is valued, DiPietro reached out to the large book that lay open on her table and turned it around so that he could see the text. Unfortunately, this was written in German, a language he knew only from sitting through an occasional Wagnerian opera. "What's this you're reading? Anything interesting?"

"Oh, indeed! It arrived only last week. Our scouts are still finding so many wonderful things in East Germany. This one is a treatise on privately held collections of Italian primitives in northern Italy. Printed in nineteen-twenty. Look at the illustrations."

She opened the book to a stunning black-and-white illustration of the Madonna and gently smoothed it down against the spine. There was an unusual velvety quality to the image that reminded Hal DiPietro of a mezzotint, yet the details were as crisp as those in an Avedon photograph.

Intrigued, he looked at the Gothic lettering of the title stamped in gold on the spine. He would not admit to the multilingual Katerina that his German was sketchy at best, but he was almost certain that the title translated roughly to something like *Sienese Paintings of the Fourteenth Century.*

"How much?" he asked.

"We didn't realize you had an interest in the Trecento," the elderly clerk said in surprise. "Or that German was one of your languages."

"I'm not fluent," he said with just the right touch of amused regret, "but Victor Germondi is."

The woman glowed her approval. "Signor Germondi is back with us now?"

"He will be next week. I just returned from Rome myself yesterday. Went over for the awards ceremony for his father."

"But surely his father is not still alive?"

"It was a posthumous award for his role in saving so much of Italy's art from Nazi confiscation."

Expansively, Hal described how the senior Germondi, with incredible cunning and bravery and at great personal risk to his own family, had managed to safeguard innumerable works of art. "So the Italian government posthumously awarded him a medal night before last. Part of their ceremonies marking the end of World War II there. The Trecento was old Leo Germondi's area of special expertise, and this would make a terrific gift for Victor when he comes over next week. Lucia d'Alagna is giving a reception here in honor of his father because he saved so many of her family's treasures."

"Ah," she murmured, clearly impressed by his casual mention of the Contessa d'Alagna.

Katerina might speak five more languages than he, but Hal DiPietro was willing to bet this sweet old lady never got to speak them at the sort of glittering international functions he attended as his birthright.

"Let me just check on the price for you." Her knobbed and wrinkled hands reached for the small wooden file box on her table.

Dortches had long since computerized its inventory, but

their oldest clerk continued to keep her own records on index cards, which she meticulously notated in her thin, spidery handwriting. "This is the only copy we've ever seen listed, but the Italian primitive is such a specialized area that it probably has a narrow appeal and shouldn't be too expensive."

Hal DiPietro's expansive mood took a slight wobble as he remembered that he still didn't know how many thousands last week's disastrous mistake at the gallery was going to end up costing him.

But what good was money, he asked himself, if you couldn't splurge occasionally on old friends?

1

*There are those who pursue [painting] because
of poverty and domestic need, for profit and enthusiasm for the profession too; but above all
these are to be extolled the ones who enter the
profession through a sense of enthusiasm and ex-
altation.*

—*Cennino Cennini*
Il Libro dell' Arte, 1437

Spring was back in all its giddy glory, lifting the hearts
of winter-weary New Yorkers with blue skies and vernal
breezes. No more ice and sleet and brutal cold. One of the
worst winters in memory was now itself becoming a memory as the city's bare-twigged trees pushed out tender green
leaves. In every vest-pocket park from Inwood down to the
Battery, forsythia bushes were going off like Roman candles, showering golden blossoms through the black iron
fences with in-your-face exuberance.

Downtown, in one of the shabby old precinct buildings,

Detective Ruben Gonzalez paused in his paperwork to stare dreamily through dirty wire-glass windows at a tree coming into leaf on the street outside. There was a waitress in the bodega near his apartment who had smiled at him when he stopped in last night, a springtime smile that—

The telephone terminated his daydreams, and he picked it up to hear a woman's shrill voice. Something about a murder that was being passed off as a suicide.

"He would *never* kill himself," the woman said passionately. "First somebody tries to shoot our daughter-in-law, and the very next day they shoot our son in cold blood. I *know* they did!"

Sighing, Gonzalez extracted a yellow legal pad from beneath the phone and began taking down names and dates. "Do you recall the name of the detective you talked to before, ma'am?"

He raised his voice and caught Jim Lowry's eye across the squad room. "Ma'am, let me see if Detective Lowry's around, okay?"

He put his hand over the receiver. "Some DOA that Eberstadt worked. The M.E.'s calling it suicide and his mother says it's murder. A Mrs. Angie Fong. Says she talked to you last week. You want to pick up on line two?"

Winter or spring, some things never changed.

On the other hand, now that spring was here, now that pneumonia season was finally over, officers out on the beat could quit hustling street people into shelters to keep them from freezing at night. No dark heavy overcoats and a hurry to get inside for the more prosperous, either. Now it was linen jackets and light sweaters when they, too, lingered outside at lunchtime.

In Midtown, along streets redolent of bus fumes and dirty gutters and perpetually overflowing trash baskets, the fragrance of spring even overrode the smell of frankfurters, sauerkraut, hot pretzels, and popcorn from the pushcarts on every corner. Worker or beggar, urban homeless or suburban commuter, people perched like pigeons on every low wall. They sprawled down marble steps or leaned against tall south-facing buildings to munch on chopped egg or tuna sandwiches that suddenly tasted better, now that food was spiced with sunshine once more.

April again. Passover over, Lenten penitence forgotten.

Diagonally across from Saint Patrick's, in the Channel Gardens of Rockefeller Center, workers were digging up faded Easter lilies and replacing them with vibrant tulips and poppies. Store windows up and down Fifth Avenue bloomed with bright silky dresses and colorful straw sandals. In Cartier's show windows, exquisite jeweled flowers were heaped with careless abandon into white wicker baskets, and F.A.O. Schwarz was awash in baby animals of every size and fabric.

Just off Madison Avenue, in a large second-floor corner office behind the exhibition area at Kohn and Munson Gallery, a summer scent of gardenias overpowered the delicate spring perfume of the paper-whites that sat on a wide glass-top desk. The glass was an irregular slab of sea green, the office walls were painted a deeper shade of green, and two highly chromatic red-and-orange abstract canvases completed a sensuousness that contrasted sharply with the chaste white and pale gold of the narcissus.

Hester Kohn, whose gardenia perfume and dramatic desk and office they were, didn't much care for paper-whites. Too utterly banal for her taste. If Arnold Callahan were perceptive enough to succeed in his specialized niche, she thought, why couldn't he take one look at her and *know* she couldn't be wooed with prissy narcissus?

Passion flowers, maybe. Birds-of-paradise, certainly. Anything as lush and tropical as her own ripe body.

But paper-white narcissus?

Please!

She centered an onyx pen above the lavender-hued legal pad that lay on the green glass desktop before her and said, "I'm sorry, Arnold."

There was very little sorrow in her voice, only obvious patience.

"To mix three or four paintings with dozens of prints and drawings would be like sprinkling pickles over ice cream, Arnold. Are you sure that's the flavor you want to convey?"

Arnold Callahan had a trendy haircut—closely shaved on the sides and a pouf of thick brown curls on the top. With his slender build, narrow features, and alert brown eyes, he looked like an overbred poodle. An unhappy overbred poodle.

Any work of Oscar Nauman's carried importance now, but works on paper were not where the late artist had made his reputation. Arnold suspected that Hester Kohn might be patronizing him, but Kohn and Munson Gallery enjoyed a huge reputation. They had represented Nauman for almost his whole career, so Callahan was not going to take umbrage. Not when so much was at stake. Not when they were letting him take part in what was shaping up to be *the* art event of the year.

When Hester Kohn had broached the possibility back in January, he could scarcely believe his luck. He'd met Oscar Nauman once or twice, had even gushed to the artist over a suite of etchings that complemented his *Tempo* series. More importantly, he had invested heavily over the years in a stock of Nauman's drawings for his own gallery, which was how he'd met Hester in the first place.

"Nauman's finally agreed to a retrospective," she'd told him that snowy winter day as they concluded their latest transaction, by which a portfolio of Nauman lithographs was consigned to his gallery.

"Oh, yeah," he'd said. "Someone told me they'd heard a rumor. But they heard the Breul House." That part he'd discounted. Surely no artist with Nauman's clout would show at that tatty old historical house down in Sussex Square?

"No, the Breul House is out. Elliott Buntrock will be curating it at the Arnheim."

That was more like it. The hottest freelance curator and the best—in Callahan's opinion—museum of modern art in the city.

"Nice for Kohn and Munson," he'd told Hester. "The Arnheim's imprimatur will push Nauman's prices right into the stratosphere. Hmm-m. Maybe I'd better beef up my inventory before the markup."

"With all your holdings?" she'd scoffed. "You could almost mount a retrospective of his works on paper yourself." Then her eyes had narrowed. "How would you like to?"

"Huh?"

They were planning a multi-gallery show here in the building in conjunction with the Arnheim, she'd explained. It was old Jacob Munson's final wish before he withdrew from the gallery, and Oscar Nauman had agreed when Jacob suggested they invite the DiPietro and Germondi galleries to join with Kohn and Munson since they were located side by side up on the seventh floor and occasionally collaborated on exhibits.

"The synergistic effect will be even greater if we have a fourth gallery here in the building to show Nauman's works on paper," she'd said. "I'll have to speak to the others, but can I tell them you're interested?"

"Oh, God, yes!" he'd said prayerfully.

And now that he was in, he wasn't about to jeopardize his position at their first full-blown strategy session.

"I merely thought it'd be fun to use a few of the paintings that were closely related to the drawings in theme or subject," he murmured, fingering the diamond stud in his left ear. "But, hey, if no one else agrees . . ."

"Why don't we wait till Buntrock and Germondi get here? See what they think," said Hal DiPietro, who lounged in a plum-colored chair as if it were a throne and he the benevolent ruler of a small kingdom. His white hair gleamed like a silver crown against the velvety green walls of Hester's office, and he stroked his short white beard with aristocratic delicacy.

"Don't worry, Callahan," he said. "Elliott Buntrock's a genius at staging, and Victor's been coordinating multi-gallery exhibits for more years than you and I have been alive. Which reminds me—did you each get an invitation to the contessa's reception for him next week? When we had lunch together in Rome last week, she asked me for suggestions, and I took the liberty of naming the rest of you."

"So you've told me," Hester reminded him. "Twice."

She had also heard about the lunch in Rome in more detail than she cared to, but Hal took such pleasure in mingling with Victor Germondi's European clientele that she bit off the rest of her sarcasm while he impressed Arnold Callahan.

And Arnold Callahan *was* impressed. This would be his first encounter with the Contessa d'Alagna, one of the wealthiest women in Western Europe, and he'd been awed when the invitation appeared in his mail two days ago, on heavy ivory stock engraved with the contessa's coat of arms. Awed, and a bit confused as well. "I didn't realize Germondi was old enough for the Second World War."

"Not Victor," said Hal DiPietro, pleased to instruct the younger dealer. "Victor was only a teenager when the war ended. It's his father who received posthumous honors last week from the Italian government."

"His father had a gallery, too?"

"He dealt, of course," said DiPietro. "Eventually made quite a nice little fortune at it, when things were going for a song after the war. But Leo Germondi's original reputation in Milan was as a professor of the Trecento. He was the foremost scholar of Italian primitives, had an encyclopedic knowledge of the era. So when the Germans came looting, Leo pretended to be a Fascist and insinuated himself into the bureaucracy as their local art expert."

It was a tale Hester Kohn had heard before from Victor Germondi himself. Like Hal, who was a few years older, she had practically grown up in this building. Her father was dead now, and old Jacob Munson no longer played an active role in the business, but they had begun here, so they'd known Victor Germondi and Henry DiPietro quite well.

Expansively, with all the details beloved by an inveterate gossip, DiPietro described how Leo Germondi had kept secret records of every work of art that passed through his hands.

"He listed who owned it, which Fascist hung it on his walls during the war, or where in Germany it was sent. So many of Italy's art treasures were lost or destroyed, but Leo Germondi was personally responsible for the recovery of an incredible number of confiscated pieces."

"And Victor was a hero, too," Hester added. "He even got shot stealing a Nazi truck."

"Shot twice," said Hal. "Fortunately, both were only flesh wounds and he escaped."

"*Shot?*" Callahan's poodle eyes widened. He had a degree in conservancy and had been a dealer for eight years, but he'd never thought of art as something for which you could actually risk your very life. Art as adventure? Intrigue? Physical danger?

"He doesn't like to talk about it, but yes," DiPietro said, as willing to tell as young Callahan was to listen. "He was only fourteen or fifteen at the time. Near the end, when the Germans evacuated and were throwing everything into trucks and heading north, Victor actually managed to drive away one of the trucks loaded with paintings and sculptures."

"Some of which belonged to Lucia d'Alagna's family," Hester Kohn said, stepping on the punch line of DiPietro's story. "Which is why she's giving a reception for him next week."

"You went to Rome for the ceremony?" asked Callahan.

"Wouldn't have missed it for the world," DiPietro assured him. "Very stirring. And when the president announced Leo Germondi's award, the applause was deafening. I've never seen dear old Victor quite so moved."

Hester Kohn glanced at the crystal clock on her desk. "I wonder what's keeping him."

Hal DiPietro shrugged. "He phoned when his plane was still thirty minutes out from Kennedy. It was cleared to land on time, but he's bringing in a small Giacometti bronze that a very important client commissioned him to buy."

From the look of frustration that flickered across his face, Hester was willing to bet that Victor had been quite careful not to tell Hal who wanted the Giacometti. ("In his mind, in his mouth," old Jacob Munson used to say about Hal.)

"He's probably held up in Customs," she said.

"And you know Victor. He'll start a conversation with a lamppost if it looks interesting. God knows why Elliott's not here yet."

"Maybe he's bringing Miss Harald," Arnold Callahan suggested.

"*Lieutenant* Harald," Hester corrected automatically.

"I never dreamed Oscar Nauman was sleeping with a police officer," he said, "but then, I've only seen her picture in the paper. Is she really that gawky-looking in person?"

"Those were old pictures," Hester said, trying to be fair. "She's cut her hair since then, but no, she's certainly no Francesca Leeds."

"Few women are," said Hal. "Present company excepted, of course."

"Of course," Hester said complacently. Even though Hal was only semi-married these days to that blue-blooded anemic down in Princeton, it was Hester's choice, not his, that they remained friends instead of lovers.

Momentarily distracted by the sexy purr in her voice, Hal ran his eyes appreciatively over her body. From the age of ten, she'd known her own attractions very well, and he was often aroused by the way she dressed to enhance those attractions. Her vibrant purple turtleneck clung to every curve, and a chunk of raw green crystals hung from a heavy silver chain between her perfect breasts.

Nevertheless, Lady Francesca Leeds was easily the more glamorous. The daughter of a minor Irish lord, she moved in social circles that frequently overlapped Hal's, and he was always ravished by her beauty. Masses of burnished auburn hair around a lovely oval face. Golden skin. Mischievous topaz eyes that flashed with wit and amusement. Legs that went from—

"Did Nauman really leave all his paintings to a policewoman?" asked Arnold Callahan, interrupting Hal's mental catalog of Francesca Leeds's physical charms. "Without any restrictions?"

"Paintings, drawings, house, car, *everything*," Hester answered bitterly.

As much for Callahan's benefit as for his own enjoyment of a good tale, Hal prompted, "And she doesn't even like his work?"

"Can you believe it?" Hester lifted her manicured hands in an appeal to heaven for enlightenment. "And Oscar thought it was *funny!* He even laughed about it with Jacob."

"Laughed about what?" asked a voice from the doorway.

Tall and almost skeletally thin, Elliott Buntrock had a stiff-jointed, uncoordinated appearance that reminded many of his friends of a cross between Abraham Lincoln and a long-legged waterbird. A crane or a stork, perhaps. His pleated trousers and nubby wool sweater-jacket were a nondescript gunmetal gray as befitted a responsible, trustworthy member of the establishment, but beneath the jacket was a bright yellow T-shirt emblazoned with a red vinyl pickup truck and the words "LIKE A ROCK."

To Arnold Callahan's disappointment, Buntrock was alone.

"Laughed about what?" he asked again after acknowledging their greetings.

"I was telling Arnold about Oscar and Sigrid and how she hates his work," said Hester. "He told Jacob that it must mean she loved him for himself alone and not because of who he was."

"She doesn't *hate* his work," Buntrock said heatedly. "She just doesn't understand it. She's like ninety-nine percent of humanity when it comes to abstraction. They just don't get it."

"Elliott's appointed himself her personal defender," Hester said bitchily to Callahan.

Buntrock shrugged his bony shoulders. "I wasn't aware that she needed defending."

A born pacer, he moved jerkily toward the windows at the end of the office, and Hal DiPietro shared an amused look with Hester.

"Germondi's not here yet?"

"No," said Hal, "and I vote that we go ahead and get started. We can bring Victor up to speed when he gets here and—"

But through the open door drifted the sound of a masculine voice, then laughter from the receptionist, and finally, in the doorway, Victor Germondi himself. "Hester, *che bella, cara mia!*"

He started to hand her the pot of orchids he carried— three dramatic cattleyas that were dark red with bright fuchsia throats, then stopped as he noticed the paperwhites. "Ah! Someone has already brought you flowers."

"Yes, Arnold did. Aren't they lovely? But one can never have too many. Oh, Victor, these are *glorious!*" She accepted the orchids with undisguised pleasure and lifted her face for his kiss. "You remember Arnold Callahan, of course? Orchard Gallery up on the fourth floor?"

"Of course, of course!" Germondi's large hands enfolded Callahan's slender one. "All those wonderful works on paper. Very clever of you to specialize in postwar American modernists. And such a good space. Unlike my tiny broom closet."

The description was heresy, as they all knew. Germondi's New York gallery on the seventh floor of this same building might be small, but to call it a broom closet was like calling a Cellini casket a jewel box. The space was exquisite, beautifully lighted, and the walls held examples of some of the biggest names in modern European art.

In addition, Victor Germondi owned a large and prestigious gallery in Milan. It had been the southern European outlet for Kohn and Munson Gallery as well as for DiPietro Gallery for almost forty years. And since his gallery here was next door to DiPietro's, the long association had resulted in something very like an uncle-nephew relationship between Germondi and Henry DiPietro's son.

He beamed as he greeted Hal DiPietro with a warm bearhug. Germondi's English was excellent if heavily accented. Clever tailoring, dark hair, and a perpetual tan could not entirely obliterate all marks of age. Now in his middle sixties, years of fine wines and Milanese cuisine had thickened his body. There were liver spots on the backs of his hands and deep lines around his faded brown eyes. But Victor Germondi still carried himself with the vigorous dignity of a civilized man whose family had served the arts since the late seventeenth century.

Buntrock came forward with an expectant smile as Hester said, "And I believe you've also met Elliott Buntrock? He's curating the Arnheim show."

"Of course, of course," Victor Germondi said again.

The two men shook hands cordially, each well aware of the other's status and reputation.

Hester gestured to the plum silk upholstered armchairs that formed an irregular semicircle in front of her desk. Germondi sat, but Buntrock roamed restlessly around the large office.

"So!" said Germondi, who had flown in from Milan early specifically for this conference. "What have you decided?"

"Not a hell of a lot," said Hal DiPietro. "We're still waiting for Lieutenant Harald to commit. I'm starting to wonder if she ever will."

He turned to Hester. "Do we really have to keep waiting

on her? Oscar gave us verbal approval back in January. We could go to court on that if we had to."

"It won't come to that."

"Won't it? If we don't get things firmed up soon—"

"I know, I know!" Hester swiveled in her chair to Buntrock, who paced back and forth along the windowed wall. "Elliott, you're the one with clout. She can't back off from the Arnheim, but you've *got* to make her commit to something definite with us, too."

Elliott Buntrock paused stiff-legged by the window, stared out gloomily, then paced back to Hester's desk. "She's still grieving," he said softly.

Germondi and DiPietro sank back in their chairs, but Hester Kohn rolled her eyes and gave an exasperated sigh. "We're *all* grieving, Elliott. She doesn't have a monopoly on grief. It's been almost two months now. Hell, she only met Oscar when? Last spring? We knew him for *years*. Kohn and Munson have represented him since before Lila Nagy tried to cut his ear off."

Arnold Callahan pricked up his own sharp ears. He was dying to ask questions, but somehow he felt less free to speak since Buntrock and Germondi had arrived. Besides, he seemed to be the only one who didn't know about the incident to which Hester Kohn referred. As the newest member of this elite group and probably here on sufferance, he wisely held his tongue.

Hal DiPietro was less tactful. "Too bad Oscar didn't make *you* his executor after Jacob withdrew, Hester. Why'd he have to go and put everything in the hands of some ignorant female cop, for God's sake?"

"She's not ignorant," Buntrock objected. He was pacing again, wearing new grooves into the hand-sculpted carpet of Hester Kohn's office.

"Ah?" said Germondi with an inquiring tilt of his dignified head.

DiPietro's fingers paused in a downward stroke of his

beard, and mischievous curiosity shone in his eyes. "Is the friendship becoming less platonic, Elliott?"

Buntrock turned jerkily. "You know something, Hal? You're always just a little too damn quick to shoot your mouth off."

DiPietro started to bristle, but Victor Germondi laid a conciliatory hand on the smaller man's arm. "Now, now, Hal. We are all of us on edge. I, too, can wish that poor Oscar had appointed Hester, or even his own attorney, to administer his estate; someone less emotionally involved. But great artists—always they follow their hearts, no?"

"It was supposed to be a temporary arrangement," Hester Kohn sighed. "Jacob pushed him into it. Before he left the business, he wanted all the work legally back in Oscar's hands. You think Oscar'd ever given two thoughts about dying or what he wanted to do with his pictures? Even with the Arnheim committed to this exhibit? Jacob insisted he had to *start* thinking about the problem, so that's why Oscar had Marc Livingston draw up a simple everything-to-her will. He promised Jacob he'd sit down and do a proper one when he got back from California."

DiPietro started to grumble, but Hester cut him off. "You'd better be grateful he did this much, Hal. If you think dealing with Sigrid Harald is difficult, imagine the complications if Oscar had died intestate."

"He talked about his will on the flight out," said Buntrock, who still felt guilty. If he hadn't badgered Oscar into attending that conference in L.A., he thought despairingly. If he'd kept Oscar from taking their rental car for a quick spin out to the desert . . . If, if, if!

"The Getty. MoMA. The Guggenheim. They've been after him for years. He knew his pictures were going to have a life of their own after he was gone, but he hadn't given it much thought until he agreed to the Arnheim show."

The Arnheim had been Oscar Nauman's favorite museum in New York. Not only was it within walking distance of Vanderlyn College but it also embodied what he called "the nonideological side of the modern spirit," which for him meant that it was open, inviting, serious, and above all fully attentive to the human scale. Both an optimist and an unreconstructed humanist, Nauman loved the Arnheim's felicitous blend of marble, glass, and steel—building materials which had flowered at distinctly different times in mankind's journey and which were now brought together so harmoniously in this building and in this age.

The permanent collection, installed on the second of its three floors, consisted of individual works assembled with great care and intelligence from the middle third of the twentieth century and was centered on smaller masterpieces by modern European and American artists. Matisse shared space with Arp and Rothko, Miró with Carl Holty and Burgoyne Diller. Several late Picasso "archetypes," brimming with liquid urgency, had a room to themselves.

"Planning this Arnheim show made him start thinking for the first time of his own mortality."

Depressed, Buntrock hooked his bony fingers into the lapels of his loose gray jacket and pulled on them so hard that his long neck bent forward under the pressure like a lassoed ostrich.

"What he might have done no longer matters," Hal DiPietro said heartlessly. "Here and now we need decisions. Answers. If you're the only one she'll listen to, then you've got to make her understand that something like the Arnheim doesn't come along every day. It's going to really hype investors. Everybody wants an Oscar Nauman. But they want it *now!* Who knows what his market will be next year? If she screws us up—"

"Nauman isn't a fad," said Hester Kohn. "Interest won't evaporate."

Arnold Callahan shifted uneasily in his chair, wondering if the faint sarcasm he heard in her voice was for that conceptual artist whose recent fifteen minutes of fame had actually fizzled in eight, before DiPietro Gallery could recoup the money spent on promotion.

Fortunately, Prince Hal was too focused on their present problem to reflect on his own gallery's immediate past.

"You can't bank on it, Hester. The whole art market's still bearish. If she holds us back now, it may take five or six years to jack Nauman's prices up this high again. We've *got* to make her focus on the bottom line."

Elliott Buntrock shrugged and started to turn away, but Hester reached out and pulled his sleeve.

"Do sit down, Elliott," she said patiently. "It may be difficult for her, but Hal's right. Oscar *did* commit to us. When you talk to her next time, you have to encourage her to keep that commitment. Make her see that she owes it to Oscar's memory. She has to let us carry out his last wishes."

"A memorial?" Buntrock wrapped his long arms around his thin body and came to rest in a chair beside her desk. "Very good, Hester. That may well be the right approach." He nodded in growing approval. "Yes, I do believe that may just reach her."

Victor Germondi laced his hands across his broad stomach and relaxed in his chair. Arnold Callahan held his breath. Even Hal DiPietro was content to watch Hester Kohn in action.

"So we'll proceed as if we have her full cooperation?"

Murmurs of assent from the men.

Hester flipped open a laptop computer, and her bright red fingernails flashed across the keys as she began to make notes. "Okay. I have an inventory of everything we handled over the years. I appreciate that you'll want first choice for the Arnheim, Elliott, and I can give you a list of the collections that hold most of the major pieces, but Victor and Hal and I will need several important oils for each of our galleries."

Her fingers hesitated on the keyboard. "What about your

friend at Turin's Moderno, Victor? Think they'll let you borrow *Tempo I*? That's such a key work."

"*È possibile,*" Germondi answered. "An exhibit of this scope enhances everyone's holdings."

"And then there are the private collections. Insurance is going to be a bitch."

"Not if Miss Harald is selling," murmured Victor Germondi.

"She'll sell," said Hal DiPietro, who had already calculated his potential commission to the nearest ten-thousand. "How else can a cop find the money to pay inheritance taxes?"

Unable to remain seated, Buntrock glared at him, but elected not to get into another pointless face-off. "So who's going to show what?"

"Arnold gets the works on paper," said Hester. "That much is settled."

Arnold Callahan sat up alertly, eager to join in and say something of importance, if only to make another pitch for two or three of the small paintings that related to the drawings, but Hester had already swept on. "Victor and Hal will work together as usual?"

Victor Germondi smiled at his colleague. "*Ma sicuro.*"

"We'll have to find a manageable way to categorize the rest into three parts. What about *Youth, Coming-of-age,* and *Maturity*?"

"BOR-ring," said Hal.

"You have a better suggestion?"

"We could simply do it by years," Victor Germondi interposed smoothly.

Hester looked over at Buntrock, who had started to speak and then abruptly resumed his pacing instead.

Anybody could hang pictures on a wall, but Elliott Buntrock was a brilliant and innovative curator, a fact acknowledged by the Arnheim when that great museum asked him to curate the Nauman retrospective. His conception and installation of exhibitions became artistic statements in and of themselves, even though he scorned the arrogance of curators who hung absurdly bizarre shows and claimed that they "painted" with artists. Yet Hester Kohn could see that he'd suddenly thought of something intriguing. Something that would electrify the Arnheim. Something that could very well mean lines of eager viewers streaming through their own galleries, each with checkbook clutched in hot little hands.

Her hazel eyes were quizzical and her voice like honey as she coaxed him. "Elliott? How will *you* define Nauman's periods?"

"I—" He suddenly shook his head. "No," he said. "It's too exploitive."

"What is?"

When he paused in front of the windows, the bright April day outside turned his thin figure into a dark silhouette. "You think she's a dumb cop, and yet she saw something none of us ever saw. Not even Oscar."

"What?" they asked.

He hesitated, remembering . . .

He and Oscar had both missed lunch, and the flight to Chicago offered only peanuts or chocolate, so they'd skipped drinks. Then they were stacked up so long over Chicago that they'd barely had time to trek from one end of O'Hare to the other. At least the rest of the trip was first class, so as soon as the stewardess asked if she could get them something right away, they both opted for Bloody Marys.

"Lunch," he'd said.

"Healthier," Oscar had agreed.

Although a good twenty years younger, Elliott had admired Nauman's work for years, had written several critiques for various journals and magazines, had exchanged pleasantries with him at openings, and had even gone out for drinks with him after the occasional symposium over the years; but it wasn't until that debacle in December, before the Arnheim deal when Nauman was still considering a major exhibit at the Erich Breul House, that they had become real friends. Even then it might not have happened if he and Sigrid Harald hadn't discovered a mutual fondness for Gilbert and Sullivan.

A freelance curator hears all sorts of art world gossip, and while he was no Hal DiPietro, ready to speculate on every love affair that crossed his path, in this particular instance, Elliott Buntrock had been as frankly curious as Hal. Oscar Nauman could have had almost any woman he chose, so why this cold and humorless, starkly efficient police lieutenant?

It was his accidental allusion to *The Pirates of Penzance* which let Elliott see that coldness was her defense against an almost crippling shyness, that her unsmiling exterior concealed a wide streak of dry humor, that her luminous gray eyes saw with quick intelligence. He made her laugh, and her laughter so pleased Oscar that he'd impulsively taken Elliott along to a small tree-trimming party at the apartment she shared with an old family friend. That evening marked the end of casual acquaintance between the two men and the beginning of true friendship.

Now, as they raced the February sun to California, one drink became three and both were just sloshed enough to let down some of the barriers that keep older males separated.

"Doesn't really like my things," Oscar confided below the steady hum of the jet engines.

"Who doesn't?" He'd sat up belligerently, ready to take on the ignorant philistine who could scorn his friend's work.

"Sigrid."

"Oh. Well." Elliott relaxed back into his seat because by now he knew that her taste in art, such as it was, gravitated toward the works of artists like Mabuse, Dürer, and Holbein. Intellectually, she could appreciate Oscar's cerebral use of line and color, but emotionally she was drawn to the exquisite individuation and austerity expressed in those north European portraits of the early fifteenth century.

"Nothing personal," he assured Oscar.

The older man nodded. "Ironic as hell, though, that she's the only one to see."

"See what?"

"That last article you did for *The Loaded Brush*. You talked about my winter period, my spring, my autumn?"

"Just labels. More about the colors on your palette than anything."

"That's what I mean. You see color seasons. Riley Quinn saw mind-sets. Sigrid sees the women."

"Huh?"

Oscar shook his head ruefully. "Here's everybody—me too, just as dumb. Intellectualize about volume and line and negative spaces and mathematical permutations, and damned if it's not gonads when you get all the way down to basics."

Abruptly he pulled down the flap of his left ear and thrust his head toward Elliott. "See that?"

The thick white hair was clipped short there, and Elliott saw a jagged scar beneath the hairline. It followed precisely a curved line where the ear joined his head.

"Never heard about it?" Oscar asked him.

"Never. Too much van Gogh?"

"Too much Lila Nagy. Lived with her when I first came to New York. Rudy Gottfried let us share his studio. All those black and purple pictures? Lila. God! The fights— And this . . ." He touched his ear again. "Real, her talent, but had to pull from her soul. Said it came too easy for me. Said I didn't suffer enough for my art. Whack! Thirteen stitches. Bled like the devil. Prison for the criminally insane now."

He was lapsing into the telegraphic speech so familiar to his friends, when thoughts and memory tumbled through his brain too rapidly for his tongue to keep pace. Fortunately, Elliott was just tipsy enough to follow effortlessly.

"They've kept her in prison for trying to cut your ear off?"

"And Susan's neck."

"Who's Susan?"

"After Lila."

Food finally arrived, then more drinks. And Elliott listened as Oscar spoke of the women who had affected his palette. The violent dark pictures from Lila Nagy's time had given way to a cascade of brilliant color with Susan Seawell. A few years later came Cassandra Palmer and a serene pastel period.

"Not your strongest," Elliott murmured candidly.

"Too restful," Oscar agreed. "She made everything too smooth. Too pretty."

"The *Topaz* series. Francesca Leeds?"

Oscar nodded. "And Siga saw. That picture by the door in my apartment?"

Elliott had admired the small oil painting each time he dropped by—brown and burnt sienna and shimmering arcs of gold. When Oscar realized how much Elliott liked it, he had described in detail its mathematical creation from permutations of inverse Cassinian ovals.

"She said it was a portrait of Francesca."

"I'll be damned! It is, isn't it?"

He'd heard of Oscar's affair with the auburn-haired Irish beauty. Corporate America still loves a lord (and, by extension, a lady) and within two years of her arrival in New York, Lady Francesca Leeds was acknowledged as one of the four best party-planners in the city. She became a free-lance publicist, and her specialty was matching charitable fund-raisers with the appropriate corporate donor. For the two or three seasons that they were together, Oscar put on a tuxedo or dinner jacket at least once a week and escorted her to balls, benefits, and special dinners. And in between dancing and chairing the art department at Vanderlyn College, he painted several complex and richly textured canvases of russet, gold, and brown, a palette he continued to explore even after their affair was over.

Elliott sipped his drink, waiting. And when Oscar remained silent, he said, "So what is Sigrid?"

"I don't know." Oscar held out his hands and looked at them as if he'd never actually examined them before. A few age spots and wrinkles marked the backs, and deep lines grooved the palms; but they remained a craftsman's hands, square and strong and infinitely clever.

"Something's happening, though. Can feel it changing. Less color? More line? I'm playing around with silverpoint." He had shrugged then in self-deprecation. "Who knows? Maybe there's nothing else there."

"Nonsense," Elliott had said forcefully. "You've got years of good stuff ahead of you!"

How could he have known that at that moment it was only four and a half days?

"Elliott?" Hester Kohn was giving him an odd look.

Elliott Buntrock took a deep breath and came back to the moment as Victor Germondi asked, "You have a better idea for categorizing the work?"

It would be irresistible.

Instead of a Blue Period or Pink Period like Picasso, thought Buntrock, it could be the Lila Years, the Cassandra Years, the Susan, the Francesca.

The Sigrid?

She would hate it. Lady Francesca would be amused, flattered even; but Sigrid Harald would loathe having her personal life put on display. On the other hand, there probably wasn't enough post-Francesca work to constitute a change, which would make that particular point moot.

"Let me think about it a couple of days," he told them.

Hester Kohn shrugged, then frowned at the screen of her laptop. "Can you have the catalog ready in time?"

"Of course. There's so much data in my computer I could almost write his definitive biography. I outlined an overview at Christmas. But we'll want to intersperse vignettes—appreciations by some of his contemporaries. What about the guy who gave him studio space when he first came to New York? Rudy . . ." He closed his eyes, trying to fish the name from his memory of that flight to California. "Rudy Gottfried?"

"Gottfried?" said Hester. Her eyes darted toward Hal.

Arnold Callahan frowned in concentration. Somewhere he knew he had heard that name, but memory failed him.

Not Hal DiPietro though. His face was flushed beneath his silver beard. "My God! Is he still living?"

"No, no!" Germondi exclaimed. He patted Hal's arm and leaned forward to frown at Elliott. "Him you must disregard, my friend. Rudy Gottfried is a bitter old man, jealous of everyone who succeeded while he failed. Even if he is cogent, he will only spew venom."

"Why don't you speak to Luigi Bruniera, Victor?" DiPietro hastily suggested. "Wouldn't he be the best European critic for Nauman's impact on the international scene?"

Diverted by an expert of such world renown, Buntrock said, "Do you think he'd do it?"

"If Victor requests it," Hal DiPietro assured him. "No one in the Italian art world would refuse him anything these days."

Germondi shrugged, downplaying Hal's extravagance. "We are old friends."

He heaved himself to his feet and smoothed the faultless jacket across his broad abdomen. "Hester, my dear, I must go now. We have an early luncheon reservation, Hal and I, and then I must sleep a few hours or I shall never get through dinner tonight. Elliott, I will ring you. I don't suppose any of Oscar's colleagues at Vanderlyn can write? Too bad Riley Quinn is dead. A terrible elitist, but he wrote like an angel and he knew such naughty stories."

Reluctantly, Arnold Callahan joined the general exodus. Even though he seemed to have lost his argument for the paintings he wanted, he'd found this whole first session immensely interesting, if a bit rarefied. Orchard Gallery *was* a wonderful space to exhibit, as even the venerable Victor Germondi himself had acknowledged. And when he expanded into this building, he'd brought along an extensive clientele. But he'd never been involved in any project of this magnitude. (*The Contessa d'Alagna!* he reminded himself.)

What luck that he'd invested so heavily in Nauman prints and drawings these past few years. That, even more than his proximity, was the main reason they were letting him participate. That, and because his was the only gallery in the building devoted to works on paper.

Callahan didn't care. He might not belong to their inner circle, but he was still going to be part of this Oscar Nauman retrospective! He knew he was acting like a starstruck groupie. He also knew that they would disdain him entirely if he stood there grinning like a hayseed at his first topless bar, yet sheer delight made it impossible for him to wait sedately for the elevator. Instead he pushed open the door to the fire stairs and raced up the four flights as if they were an escalator, his pouf of brown curls bouncing with the electricity he felt.

"Good meeting?" asked one of his assistants as he bounded through the doorway of his gallery.

"*Fabulous* meeting!" he caroled.

Yet once he was in his own office with the door firmly closed, he remembered that bit at the end. He rather thought there was something unsavory attached to Rudy Gottfried's name, if only he could remember what it was.

He stuck his head back out the door. "Any of you people ever heard of a Rudy Gottfried?"

One young woman looked up from the print she was matting. "Did he used to teach at Vanderlyn? I think my last boyfriend might have had a course with him a few years back."

Light bulbs began clicking in Arnold Callahan's head.

Vanderlyn College.

Where Oscar Nauman had chaired the art department.

And where good old Lemuel Vance still taught printmaking. A superb technician, Lem probably knew better than anyone else working in graphics today how to coax line and ink to perform intricate subtleties. And he could instill these concepts in his students. Unfortunately, he wasn't terribly intellectual. Or artistically creative.

But he was a great raconteur and loved to tell stories. There was an excellent Greek restaurant near the college, thought Callahan, reaching for his Rolodex. Maybe he could tempt Lem Vance to come have a spanakopita.

With Rudy Gottfried for dessert.

2

Take note that, before going any farther, I will give you the exact proportions of a man. Those of a woman I will disregard, for she does not have any set proportions. . . . A man is as long as his arms crosswise. The arms, including the hands, reach to the middle of the thigh. The whole man is eight faces and two of the three measures in length. A man has one breast rib less than a woman, on the left side.

Cennino Cennini
Il Libro dell' Arte, 1437

"Ah! Lieutenant Harald."

From the surprise in Marc Livingston's voice when Mrs. Bayles showed her into his Madison Avenue office at ten o'clock on the dot, not to mention the expression on Mrs. Bayles's face when she first arrived, Sigrid Harald gathered that neither the attorney nor his secretary had truly expected her to keep this appointment.

It would not have been her first cancellation. So much of the past two months had passed in a listless gray fog that she knew there were times when she'd simply gone back to bed without bothering to cancel, just unplugged the phone and not shown up.

She was normally so conscientious about such matters that she was now appalled to think how cavalier her attitude must have seemed. Rationally and intellectually, she knew all about subconscious acts of avoidance, but reason and intellect were poor supports these days, and they could not keep her from dreading this interview.

Ever since Nauman's attorney had explained the deceptively simple terms of the will—that she was both executor and sole beneficiary—feelings of sheer inadequacy had alternated with dreary resentment that Nauman had dumped it all on her and irrevocably complicated her life. She was a homicide detective, a professional solver of crimes, and a good one at that, she reminded herself. What did she know about the efficient disposal of a body of important artworks? Balancing her checkbook and investing in some modest CDs for her eventual retirement were no big deal, but how could she manage an estate worth millions? And of more immediate concern, how much more could she take of this Irene Bayles?

She sat in the comfortable leather chair the woman had given her in front of Marc Livingston's wide desk and tried to hold on to her frayed nerve endings while Mrs. Bayles, fifty and comfortable with it, bustled around playing hostess.

"Now I do remember that you drink coffee instead of tea, but was it one lump of sugar or two?"

"Nothing," Sigrid murmured.

"No sugar *or* cream? Are you sure?"

"Nothing. Thank you."

"But you're so thin, a little cream would probably be good for you."

She *was* too thin. She knew it. But the thought of cream nearly choked her, so she shook her head again and placed her hand over her cup to prevent Mrs. Bayles from pouring her some anyhow.

Undeterred, Mrs. Bayles proffered a cookie tin. "These are what Mr. Livingston's having. Shortbreads. Imported from Scotland. Let me just put a few here on a napkin for you."

Sigrid felt herself starting to lose it. Another two seconds and she would either snap at the woman or else get up and walk out.

Fortunately, Mr. Livingston said, "Thanks, Irene. I'll buzz you if we need anything else."

The door closed behind her. He held a cookie from the tin in his stubby brown fingers, examined it a moment, then disposed of it in two bites. "She really does have a kind heart, you know."

Remorse flooded her. "Was I that obvious?"

"Attorneys get adept at interpreting body language." He smiled. "Police officers, too, I should imagine."

"Yes."

His wiry hair was clipped short and beginning to go gray, but everything else about the big African-American who sat across from her was brown. Skin, eyes, a well-tailored brown suit so dark it was nearly black, light brown button-down shirt, a silk tie discreetly patterned in russet and cinnamon. The smile broadened across his pleasantly homely face. "And you're probably getting a bit tired of being treated nicely?"

She suddenly relaxed into the soft leather chair, took a sip of the steaming coffee, and smiled back at him. "Nauman liked you, didn't he? I mean, more than just as his lawyer?"

"Were we friends, do you mean?" He stirred his own cup as he considered. "Did he ever take you to a place called Madigan's?"

Even if he'd been Nauman's blood brother, there was no way she would reminisce about that first evening when she'd left Riley Quinn's Upper West Side brownstone after trying to interview his widow, to find Nauman out on the sidewalk in front, furious because his car had been towed.

Again.

They had both been tired and irritable and she'd offered him a lift downtown so that she could hear firsthand his speculations as to why Riley Quinn had been murdered.

"Only on condition that we stop for dinner first," he'd said. "I haven't had mine yet, and you probably wouldn't be so bitchy if you'd had yours."

"I'm not a health-food, wheat-germ addict," she'd warned him sharply.

"I had in mind a thick and bloody steak," he'd said.

That had been the start of it—a late supper at a ratty old saloon with sawdust on the floor, chipped mugs of full-bodied ale, the best steak she'd ever eaten.

"Yes," she told Marc Livingston. "We went to Madigan's a few times."

"I met Oscar because I'd done some outside work for Kohn and Munson and Jacob Munson was good enough to recommend this firm when Oscar was buying his Connecticut house. Almost twenty years ago. He suggested we meet at Madigan's to discuss it. I think Madigan's was like a test."

"If you weren't too squeamish to eat there, if you didn't worry all evening about ptomaine or botulism?"

Entirely against her will, a small trickle of amusement bubbled up through layers of grief. "The place should have been closed up years ago. Some health department inspector's probably getting paid off with free steaks and porter."

"If they ever get cited, I'll defend them pro bono," said Livingston. "I love that place. Oscar and I used to meet there for lunch or supper every couple of months or so. I won't say we were old drinking buddies exactly, but yes, our association was certainly more than business."

He set aside his cup and saucer, and his hands hovered over several thick manila folders that lay in the center of his neat desk. "Speaking of which . . ."

Desperately, Sigrid said, "Did anyone ever say what happened to Nellie?"

"I beg your pardon?"

Sigrid set her half-finished coffee on a nearby stand. "I don't know her last name, but you must have heard of her, being an attorney. She was the sweetheart or wife of a man who died out west. Maybe after the Civil War. I think he was a prospector during the gold rush and he'd actually filed claim on a mother lode. He was in an accident or something, dying, and no way to make a proper will."

"Ah, yes," Marc Livingston nodded. "So he scribbled on a piece of paper 'Everything to Nellie,' and it was held to be a valid instrument."

"She was probably some poor illiterate farm girl he'd left behind back east," Sigrid said haltingly. "And suddenly there she was with all that he'd worked for and no way to know what he might have wanted her to do."

"No strings, either," he reminded her.

"I just wonder what became of her, that's all," she said in a small voice.

"Everything to Sigrid," Livingston murmured thoughtfully. "Feeling overwhelmed?"

The look she gave him was almost hostile. "Should I not be?"

"You're no illiterate farm girl." He squared the thick folders so that their edges were aligned with the edge of his polished walnut desk.

"And I didn't just fall off the watermelon truck, for that matter." His mouth was suddenly grim, and a scowl furrowed dark lines between his eyes.

"There is absolutely nothing in Oscar's will to prevent you from retaining another attorney, Lieutenant. The verbal agreement we made the day I read it to you is also nonbinding since it could be argued that you spoke without sufficient consideration and while under great emotional stress."

Shocked that he would ascribe her dismay to racism,

Sigrid held up her hands. "No! That's not what I meant at all. Why would I want a different attorney?"

"Beats me. Oscar thought I was pretty competent." As suddenly as it had disappeared, his smile was back. "Look, I know this is all unfamiliar territory, but trust me. It's just *stuff*. We can do it. And if I don't know all the technicalities, there are experts we can call on. One step at a time. The main thing we have to do right now is get permission to liquidate some of the assets so that we can protect the rest of the estate while the will is being probated and you decide what you want to do."

"Liquidate? You mean sell?"

"Right." He selected one of the files. "Now, the inventory and appraisal for tax purposes are—"

"But I don't want to sell anything," Sigrid protested. "I want it all to stay the way it is. I want . . ." She looked at him helplessly as she felt her control crumble.

"You want Oscar not to be dead." His voice was gentle and infinitely sad.

"Yes." she whispered brokenly and buried her face in her hands.

For several moments there was no other sound in the room. He didn't try to stop her. He didn't call for Mrs. Bayles. He just sat silently. Eventually, when the storm subsided, she heard him open a drawer and slide something across his desk.

A box of tissues.

Gratefully, she blew her nose and wiped her streaming eyes. "I'm sorry. I keep thinking I'm over it. That it'll quit hurting."

"It'll never quit hurting," he said bluntly. "Time will help a little. Time can dull the sharp edges, but even a dull knife will cut you."

She stuffed the damp, wadded-up tissues into her pocket, and her gray eyes widened in unspoken question.

"It's been twelve years. Sometimes I go as much as thirty-six, hell, maybe even forty-eight hours at a stretch without thinking about her." He tilted his head toward a nearby door. "That's a lavatory, if you want to splash cold water on your face."

"No, I'm fine now." She took a deep breath and lifted her chin. "What do you mean when you say we have to liquidate in order to protect the estate?"

"It's straightforward math," he explained. "We won't know exactly how much everything is worth till we finish the appraisal. Acting as your agent, I've hired an expert to make an independent evaluation in case the tax people come up with an overinflated final figure that we'll have to challenge in court, but we do have to be realistic. Oscar carried the usual insurance on both his real and his personal property, and that included his pictures. The minute he died, though, his policies no longer covered their value. I've already spoken to the insurance company and to experts in the field. They both agree. The fact that there will be no more Oscar Nauman paintings means that the paintings he did leave have probably skyrocketed in value. There simply isn't enough cash on hand to pay for full insurance coverage.

"We won't know for several months exactly what it's all worth, but the figures fluctuate, depending on who's giving the ballpark estimates, from a low of eight million up to—"

He paused, abruptly aware that she was shaking her head numbly.

"It's okay," he said soothingly. "It's just money, with a few more zeroes at the end. And the government's probably going to take most of it, one way or another, anyhow. We just have to protect the assets until final disposition."

"But I can't afford insurance on that scale," Sigrid said.

"Yes, you can. The law allows you to draw against the estate as long as there's strict accounting. Now, I've been in touch with Oscar's gallery about this upcoming show he was planning when he died. If you'll agree to let the show go forward, Hester Kohn and her associates will agree to set the prices according to our appraiser's suggestions, and you'll have final say if there are any particular pictures you do *not* want to sell at this time. Is that agreeable to you?"

Sigrid nodded.

As Marc Livingston continued to talk and explain and propose, she felt a small stirring of confidence. His matter-of-factness was reassuring. Maybe, just maybe, with his help, she'd be able to deal with this after all.

She signed the necessary applications; then he handed her a sheaf of papers. "These are the inventory sheets. As you see, they merely list the items, not the value of those items, that were in his apartment here and in his house up in Connecticut. I'm expecting another offer soon on the house, and what about the apartment? The lease still has about seventeen months to run. We can sublet it, if you like."

Let a stranger use Nauman's possessions? Inhabit his space?

"We would have to put everything in storage," she said, trying to match his objectivity and willing her voice not to wobble.

"Oh, of course," Livingston agreed. "We don't want anyone walking off with souvenirs. If nothing else, the pictures should go into storage as soon as possible, too. That should help hold down the insurance premiums. And that reminds me . . ."

He made another note to himself on his yellow legal pad, then took a manila envelope from his desk drawer and handed it to her. Inside was a set of shiny brass keys, each neatly tagged.

"I took the liberty of having the locks in Connecticut changed, and I really wish you'd let me do the same for the apartment."

Guiltily, Sigrid remembered that this was another of the many things he'd tried to get her to act on, or at least allow him to take care of, but she still didn't see the urgency. "There's nothing there worth worrying about beyond the bare furnishings, some books, and a few pictures and things."

"Oscar may have treated it like a hotel room, but some of the artworks that wound up there have appreciated considerably over the years, and I have the impression that he was rather free about handing out keys to the apartment when friends wanted to stay in town overnight."

"Friends," she said, turning to the inventory of the apartment. "Not thieves." Yet even as she spoke, she remembered several not-so-subtle phone calls and notes from some of Nauman's self-designated "friends."

"I told Elliott Buntrock that he could take those gallery people to look at the pictures."

"And this Buntrock has his own key?" Livingston asked disapprovingly.

She smiled at the absurdity of Elliott taking even a matchstick from the apartment. "He was in the habit of stopping by after class two or three times a week to discuss the Arnheim show. Nauman never knew if he'd be delayed by students or colleagues, so he told Elliott to go ahead and let himself in and fix himself a drink if he got there first. I know what you're thinking, but Elliott Buntrock would never—"

"I'm sure he wouldn't," said Livingston, "but how many other Elliott Buntrocks are out there with keys?"

Surrendering to his logic, Sigrid agreed to let him call a locksmith. "But not till after Buntrock's finished."

"Just so long as he knows *we* know what's there," Livingston said magisterially.

They spoke together a while longer, and he'd covered several pages of his legal pad with scrawled notations by the time one of his associates tapped at the door and reminded him that they were due down at NYU for lunch.

"Can we drop you somewhere?" Livingston asked.

Sigrid glanced at her watch. Sooner or later she was going to have to do it. Why not now?

"If it's not out of your way," she said, giving them the location of her station house, "you could drop me at work."

3

*And keep [the formula for making ultramarine]
to yourself, for it is an unusual ability to know
how to make it properly. And know that making it
is an occupation for pretty girls rather than for
men; for they are always at home, and reliable,
and they have more dainty hands.*

Cennino Cennini
Il Libro dell' Arte, 1437

At eleven-thirty, Detectives Jim Lowry and Elaine Albee
were seated at a table in one of the squad's interview rooms
with Mrs. Georgia Fong.

From the case file on Todd Fong, they knew that she was
twenty-three and had a two-year-old daughter, but with her
long blond hair caught up in a ponytail, skintight black
stretch pants, and an oversized sweatshirt hand-painted in
swirls of colors, she didn't look a day over seventeen.

Georgia Fong snapped the lid off a cup of peach yogurt
and stirred it with a plastic spoon. "You sure you don't

mind if I eat? Like I said, I only take forty minutes for
lunch. That's so if I want to run do something for my
daughter, the boss can't yell. Not that he would. I'm the
best artist he ever had." She wasn't bragging, just stating
what was—to her, anyhow—an obvious fact.

"What is it you do?" asked Jim Lowry.

The young woman grasped the sides of her pale blue
sweatshirt and stretched it taut so they could appreciate the
shimmering rainbow that began on her right shoulder and
arced through fluffy gold-rimmed clouds to her left hip. "I
painted this one yesterday," she said, "and three customers
have already tried to buy it off my bod today. I'm a designer at the Topp Shopp on West Fourteenth. I do a lot of
Tees and sweats for expecting moms. New babies, too.
Maybe you've seen some? Blue clouds for boys and pink
for little girls, and their names in gold?"

"With gold stars?" asked Elaine Albee.

"Yeah, 'cause they're new little bundles from heaven,
right?"

"I *have* seen one," said Albee. "One of the vice officers
had a baby shower last month, and somebody gave her one.
She loved it."

"Hundred percent cotton, and all my paint's nontoxic,"
Georgia Fong said proudly.

They smiled at each other, and Albee said, "We really do
appreciate your taking time to come in."

"Well, Angie and Doug. They're still all tore up about
Todd, and they *are* my daughter's grandparents, right?
They're both good people. Never gave up on him even if he
was a jerk. If they want me to talk to you, then I told 'em
I'd come and talk to you. And now that I think about it,
could be they're right, you know? Maybe Todd didn't kill
himself." She took another spoonful of the yogurt before
adding bitterly, "He'd never do anything that useful. Too
bad on him. He wouldn't pay child support, and now Julie's
getting his Social Security."

She pulled a picture from her purse and they saw a little cutie with hair as blond as her mother's.

"Not much Fong in her, is there?" asked Elaine.

"Because of her hair?" She laughed. "Nobody in the family looks Chinese. Todd's great-grandfather came over back around 1900 and married a German girl. Doug—that's Todd's dad—Doug says Fong men always liked blondes. You'd never know they had a drop of Chinese blood in 'em, they've got such blue eyes and white skin. Todd's first two wives were blond, too."

"Your mother-in-law said you'd been shot at?" Jim Lowry prompted her. If Georgia Fong didn't come to the point soon, her lunch hour was going to be over and they still wouldn't know if this was something they really ought to investigate.

"Yeah. Let's see. This is April? It was the sixteenth of March. The day before Todd got shot. It was already dark and the streetlights were on. I was taking the baby out of her stroller. She's in day care just down the block. Anyhow, her jacket got caught on the handle and I'd just bent down to get it loose and I heard like a pop-pop, then two bullets zinged over my head. One of 'em chipped the brick beside the front door, and the other one went right into the doorframe. Scared the you-know-what out of me."

"Did you see who did the shooting?"

"You kidding? Who stays to watch? I just grabbed Julie and ran next door to the fruit stand and stayed there till the cops came."

"What'd they say?" asked Albee.

"What's to say? It's not the world's greatest neighborhood, okay? Two crack houses at the end of the next block. I figured first it was something to do with them. Then, after Todd died and Angie started saying he didn't shoot himself, we got to wondering if maybe somebody did have it in for him. Somebody as maybe didn't know we'd split up and thought they could get back at him by hurting me or the baby, you know?"

She finished the yogurt and dropped the empty cup in the wastebasket beneath the table.

"Who would have had it in for him?"

She shook her head. "Whoever he last pissed off." With one eye on her watch, she rattled off several names.

A few minutes before noon, Captain McKinnon, NYPD, stood on his balcony and surveyed his personal kingdom with misgivings.

Grizzled now, he was still a large brown bear of a man and his bulk made the small balcony seem even smaller. As it was, there was barely room for a round glass-and-steel table, four of those ubiquitous white resin chairs, and a narrow wrought-iron bench that held a hibachi and three pots of bright flowers that McKinnon had lugged upstairs from the market less than an hour ago in honor of the occasion.

Small though it might be, the balcony was high on the third floor, overlooked some lavishly planted Greenwich Village gardens, and shared airspace with a tall tree whose name McKinnon had never learned, despite having watched it grow from a sapling to full-blown maturity. Later in the summer, when those delicate young leaves had thickened, the tree would cloak the balcony in cool green shade until sitting there was almost like sitting in a treehouse, sheltered and private. At the moment, welcome sunlight streamed through the branches and sparkled on the two pilsner glasses.

Mac stared at the glasses dubiously and wondered if it was too late to rinse off the dusty wineglasses atop his china closet and run downstairs to the corner deli. He was still relearning her tastes after all these years. Maybe she preferred wine now rather than the ale he and Leif always drank?

He straightened the blue place mats on the glass-topped table, realigned the plates and utensils for the fourth time in twenty minutes, and then realized what he was doing.

Making a big deal out of Anne Harald's casual spontaneous phone call—that was what he was doing.

The last time they'd talked, he'd griped about the delays and mess and endless hassles with the carpenter who was ripping out his drafty old sliding glass panels and replacing them with weather-tight and very expensive new French doors.

The carpenter had finally cleared out yesterday, and the painter had just snapped the lid back on a bucket of white latex enamel, folded up his dropcloths, and was waiting for Mac to finish writing out his check when she called.

"I'll be in your neighborhood around noon," she'd said. "Want to have lunch?"

"Sure." Then, impulsively, "Why don't you come here? It's a warm day. We can eat on the balcony. Inaugurate my new doors."

"A picnic? Lovely. I'll bring the sandwiches. Sauerkraut and pastrami on pumpernickel, extra mustard, right?"

"Right," he'd said, irrationally pleased that she remembered.

But why wouldn't she? he asked himself now as a light breeze ruffled the tree leaves. God knows they'd split enough sandwiches right here on this same balcony back before she married Leif Harald, back when he and Leif were partners. After all, this neighborhood had once been hers, too, a wide-eyed kid up from the South to study photography at NYU and hang out in Washington Square and walk the crooked Village streets with her camera pointing in a dozen different directions at once.

He'd had to miss their wedding. A cop's salary didn't stretch to road trips and rented tuxes in those days, and besides, he'd lent Leif every cent he had in the bank so Anne could have a real happily-ever-after honeymoon. Instead of shouting "Me, damn it! ME!" when the preacher asked if any man had reason why these two should not be joined, Mac had pulled double shifts that weekend, and Leif's uncle Lars had driven down from Brooklyn to be best man.

The ceremony had taken place in North Carolina. That was the only way Anne's mother would bless the wedding of a daughter still in her teens to a Yankee cop, even though the Yankee cop was clearly on the fast track. Even though the Yankee cop could have been born in the heart of Dixie the way he'd charmed his way into Mrs. Lattimore's good graces.

A truck's air horn blared impatiently from two streets over, and Mac straightened the chairs again. He no longer wondered how life might have turned out if he'd seen Anne first. Would it have made a difference? He was big and slow-tongued. Leif had been quicksilver and laughter. What woman had ever noticed him if Leif Harald noticed her first?

And when Leif was killed, shot down in that shabby hotel off Times Square, she'd blamed him.

Well, that was natural under the circumstances. He'd been there. He'd walked away unharmed.

Guilt.

Blame.

And grief.

They'd all been so young. Leif dead at twenty-eight, Anne widowed at twenty-three, McKinnon somewhere in between, abruptly cut off from both of them.

And then, out of the blue, their daughter had been assigned to his command, and all at once there was the possibility of Anne back in his life. He'd tried to go slow, build Sigrid's trust, gradually reveal the past, but those plans had exploded in his face on a snowy rooftop in February. Even so, this time, Anne hadn't drawn back. This time she was willing to let him help. He wasn't going to push it. If her acceptance was only because he was Sigrid's boss now, well, he could live with that.

He'd waited this long. He could wait a bit longer if he had to.

As if to reward his patience, the doorbell rang.

B'Nita Parsons looked up as her boss entered the gallery with an older gentleman. Despite integration, civil rights, feminism, *and* a degree in art history, that was how Mrs. Parsons, reared in Alabama by God-fearing grandparents, still instinctively thought of men, black or white, who bore themselves with Victor Germondi's mannered dignity. Gentlemen.

What she thought of Hal DiPietro was more ambiguous.

What he thought of her, she could only guess. Not much, would be her guess. A B.A. in art history from a branch of the University of Alabama wouldn't rate high with him. He probably thought she was grateful he'd given her the job.

Which she was, of course. Paid more than her last two jobs, even though it was only a three-quarters part-time position. The other quarter was held by a couple of part-time art students who understood about papers and tutorials and who were therefore flexible about filling in. As long as the gallery was manned full-time and nobody screwed up the computer, Mr. DiPietro didn't seem to care who his administrative assistant was.

And he was probably glad he didn't have to go through a formal search process when his last one quit on him. Not that her leaving was unexpected.

"I was totally up front with him," that young woman told B'Nita Parsons when she landed a better-paying position with the Metropolitan Museum last month. "I said, 'First good offer I have of a full-time job with full benefits, I'll have to take it. I've got a baby and no husband, and my parents won't help me.' "

"You have to do what's best for you two," agreed B'Nita, who'd once, briefly, had a husband and then two disastrous love affairs but never a baby. As for parents, they were both dead before she could walk, and they had left her nothing but her father's notebooks and her mother's beauty as a buffer against her mother's dutiful but cold parents.

She never quite understood why her grandparents hadn't

disposed of the notebooks with the rest of her parents' things, unless it was a superstitious reverence for the written word; but when she found them packed away in the bottom of her grandmother's cedar chest and realized what they were, she had hidden them in her own dresser and devoured them page by page. Part sketchbook, part journal, they gave her the mind of a man who had known himself an artist but who had died before he could make the world agree with him, and they gave B'Nita the vision of a world beyond a small wooden house in Alabama, beyond the mediocre college she'd attended. Eventually, they sent her north to the art world of New York.

While pulling split shifts as a salesclerk in one of the street-level stores in the building, she'd spent her lunch hours roaming through the art galleries on the upper floors, always coming back to the DiPietro Gallery. A white leather bench opposite the reception desk made a comfortable place to sit and gossip on those days when she had no classes and didn't feel like trudging back to Brooklyn between shifts. She'd even held the fort for her new friend a few times when there was an emergency with the baby, so when the job opened up at the Metropolitan, the young mother had recommended B'Nita Parsons in glowing terms.

"Is it BuhNyeta or BuhNeeta?" Hal DiPietro had asked, stroking his neat silver beard as he read through her abbreviated application form.

She hated it when white people acted as if the lovely liquid names southern black women gave their daughters were totally unpronounceable.

"Oh, don't bother about that, Mr. DiPietro," she'd drawled pleasantly. "Mrs. Parsons will do fine."

His head had come up at that, but her dark brown eyes had met his bright blue ones with more firmness than she actually felt. She'd guessed right, though, and he'd given her his best boyish grin.

"Crisp and professional," he'd said. "I like that."

Indeed, he liked it so much that as he introduced her now to Victor Germondi he almost believed that calling her Mrs. Parsons had been his own idea. His father, whom he'd alternately feared and adored, had always addressed his staff like that, as old Victor still did. In his younger, hipper days, Hal used to think their formalities artificial and passé. More and more these days, as he settled into middle age himself, he realized that Victor and his father had been right.

Manners.

Dignity.

Class!

"Charmed, Signora Parsons," said Germondi as he gallantly kissed her hand.

Pleased, DiPietro noticed that she accepted his tribute with a graceful smile. None of that tittering embarrassment his last assistant had exhibited when Victor kissed *her* hand.

Really, Mrs. Parsons was working out very well, he thought, leafing through the message slips she'd handed him. She was knowledgeable about art, efficient, accurate—that last a real bonus, considering how absentminded he seemed to be these days *(God! That mix-up with the price list!)*—and damned attractive, too. A pure blend of African and Anglo ancestry. Skin the shade of maple sugar, a cloud of soft brown hair with undertones of red, almond-shaped brown eyes, high cheekbones, thin nose, generous lips, a nicely rounded figure. And on top of all that, a soft southern drawl that clearly enchanted old Victor as she congratulated him on the medal the Italian government had awarded his late father last week.

How clever of Mrs. Parsons to pick up on the one thing guaranteed to make Victor adore her forever, Hal thought. Of all the recognition Victor himself had achieved, nothing had ever pleased him more than the current honors his father was receiving. Hal was glad he'd flown over for the ceremony, part of Italy's commemoration of the end of World War II. It was the first time in his entire life that he'd seen Victor at a loss for words, so choked by emotion that he could only stand helpless on the podium and murmur, *"Grazie, grazie,"* to the tumultuous applause.

A small pang of jealousy had ripped Hal then as Victor stood in the spotlight. Both of them were the sons of larger-than-life fathers; but all his life, Victor had walked in the reflected glow of his father's heroic altruism, while Hal knew there were those in the art world who still judged him by *his* father's mercenary expedience.

Now Hal waited for a break in their conversation, then instructed Mrs. Parsons as to which calls she should return with what answers. His gold fountain pen gleamed as he scribbled a few words on each message slip.

"The cases of champagne arrived while you were out," said Mrs. Parsons. "I had Mr. Levitz stack them just outside the storeroom. We'll put them in the refrigerator before closing time."

DiPietro no longer had to think twice to remember that she was talking about the gallery's gofer and deliveryman, and he could even tell her to ask "Mr. Levitz" to do something; but face-to-face he was still unable to call Donny anything but Donny. But that reminded him: "Did Mr. Levitz pick up the catalogs?"

DiPietro Gallery was having an opening the next night— Buck David's newest works. And Buck's rich girlfriend had agreed to underwrite a glossy eight-page catalog with a color reproduction on the cover instead of the usual photocopied list.

"Catalogs?" Mrs. Parsons's eyes widened as she looked at him in bewilderment. "But you canceled the order."

"What?"

"When they sent the proofs over," she said firmly. "You said their price quote was highway robbery, and then you canceled the order." She pulled a folder from the neat stack to one side of her work space and began leafing through the papers inside. "They were rather huffy about it, too," she added.

"It *was* highway robbery, but I didn't cancel," DiPietro insisted.

Instead of contradicting him, she handed him one of the pink routing slips he'd initiated years ago when less efficient help had to have everything spelled out for them. One was attached to every piece of paper that needed further action. At the top of this one, printed in her neat block letters, was "David Catalog." He could have sworn he'd X-ed the *Approved* box. Instead, there in his trademark brown ink was his own firm *X* in the *Cancel* box and his own scribbled initials underneath.

He swallowed an expletive as he pictured Buck David's arrogant and outspoken girlfriend arriving tomorrow night with some of her equally moneyed friends and what her reaction would be when she didn't see the glossy catalogs for which she'd already given him a check.

"She'll have my head," he groaned.

"You must call the printer," Victor Germondi told him. "Perhaps they did not destroy the proofs."

"I kept a copy of the first rough draft we sent them," said Mrs. Parsons. "It's not complete, though," she warned. "You made changes."

"You're a lifesaver!" He gathered up the material. "I'll correct it in the cab. Victor—"

The older man dismissed their suddenly canceled lunch with a wave of his hand. "No, no. Of course you must attend to business first. We can talk tomorrow."

DiPietro dashed out the door. As Germondi made a leisurely farewell, a slender gold tube gleamed in Mrs. Parsons's hand.

"Oh, dear," she said, her soft southern voice worried. "Mr. DiPietro *is* getting absentminded. He's gone off without his pen."

Later, when Victor Germondi had departed for his own gallery just down the hall, B'Nita Parsons uncapped the expensive gold fountain pen and drew a line across her notepad. From her own purse she took another pen, this one a much cheaper version that had a tendency to leak. She wrapped a tissue around the barrel so that the brown ink wouldn't stain her fingers and drew a second line on her pad. As she thought, the broad nib on her pen matched his exactly.

Smiling, she made a bold *X* with her pen and scribbled his initials. It was no different from calligraphy, she thought. Try to copy something exactly and the lines would waver. Think the shape, do it without hesitation, and you achieve a confident panache.

She recapped her pen, crumpled the page into a ball, and hid both of them deep in her purse. Then she went into the lavatory, emptied the ink from Mr. DiPietro's pen, washed away all traces of brown from the white porcelain, and left the pen on his desk. Perhaps he'd be in the middle of writing something for an important client when it ran completely dry.

Only a minor embarrassment, of course. She'd be the first to admit it. And nothing to compare with her first coup when she so cleverly manipulated those price lists that went out to the gallery's best customers.

But as her grandmother used to say, "Many grains of sand will a mountain make."

"I can't believe you've kept the same place all these years," Anne Harald said, handing McKinnon the deli bag that held their lunch. The smell of fresh paint lingered in the air as her gray eyes swept around the spacious room, noting changes in the apartment. (In the past two months, she'd already noted the physical changes in him.) "You knocked out a wall there?"

"I didn't need three bedrooms after I made detective," he reminded her.

She remembered. Five cops sharing three bedrooms and one bath and Leif one of those five. She herself had been living in the women-only residential hotel decreed by her mother as a condition of studying photography in New

York. It was more like a dormitory than a hotel: two women to a room and a four-shower communal bathroom on each floor. The hotel had been torn down years ago, yet this apartment remained basically intact.

She heard herself chattering, exclaiming, cooing as Mac gave her the fifty-cent tour of everything except his bedroom, which he claimed was too messy to show. She always talked too much when she was nervous, and she hadn't realized how unsettling it would be to walk sedately up the same four flights of stairs she'd raced up so many times to get to Leif during their whirlwind courtship.

After their wedding, home had been a basement sublet a few blocks down the street, so this apartment had remained familiar territory. And after the other guys moved out and Mac stayed on here alone . . .

She jerked away from those memories and moved toward the sunlit balcony, burbling about the graceful new French doors, the charming place mats, that heavenly tree. She couldn't seem to stop her runaway tongue and risked a quick glance.

There was a dazed look on his face.

Oh, God, she thought. He must think I've turned into a blithering magpie.

She made herself sit quietly as Mac brought out two bottles of ale.

"I could go get some wine if you'd rather," he offered.

"With pastrami?" She laughed and shook her head. The dark ringlets flashed threads of gray in the sunlight. "Ale is perfect."

They clinked glasses, and suddenly everything became normal.

She loosened the paper around her sandwich and breathed in the wonderful aroma of warm spicy meat, melted cheese and dark mustard on fresh-baked bread. "I'm starved! All this exercise. I walked thirty blocks today, and we swam *miles* yesterday."

Mac bit into his own sandwich. "We?"

"Sigrid and I."

"You've got her swimming? That's good, isn't it?"

"I think so. Anything to get her out of bed, out of the house, and really moving again. I told her I needed help on my crawl."

"And being a dutiful daughter . . . ?" he asked.

"Siga *is* a dutiful daughter. From the time she was little, she had me questioning who was more mature. She takes responsibility seriously. You know that."

He nodded.

"If she didn't blame herself so much for that officer's death, she might not have gone so completely to pieces over Oscar's."

Anne and Mac had been over it and over it in the past two months, but Anne's heart still sank every time she thought of how she'd delivered that second hammer blow to her daughter.

It'd been a chill February night, and for some reason, Anne had decided to make a pan of fudge, singing along with Mary Chapin Carpenter on the kitchen radio as the sensuous sweet smell of boiling chocolate filled the apartment. She had just finished beating the cooling mixture to a proper consistency and was stirring in the walnuts when the music stopped for headlines at the top of the hour.

"The Mideast . . . Haiti . . . the president says . . . the Knicks . . . more snow on the way . . . and this just in," the announcer said. "In California, noted New York artist Oscar Nauman died in a car crash this afternoon, north of Los Angeles. California state troopers say—"

The phone interrupted the announcer's calm voice, and it was Roman Tramegra, her old friend and Sigrid's housemate for the past few months. Elliott Buntrock had just called from California, distraught, incoherent, and frantically trying to locate Sigrid.

"It's true, then?" she whispered.

"Oh, my dear, my dear," he answered sadly.

Blankly, she left the fudge to harden in the pan and

started calling all the places Sigrid might be. No one seemed to know where she was.

But less than ten minutes later her doorbell rang and there was Mac, awkward and tense, with his arm around her daughter in solicitous support.

One look at the naked anguish in Sigrid's eyes, and Anne had burst into tears and murmured, "Oh, Siga, honey, I'm so sorry."

Even though Sigrid was half a head taller, Anne managed to enfold her with the motherly comfort of her body.

Bewildered, Mac asked, "You heard?"

"It was on the radio," she said, accepting his presence after so many years of denying his existence. "And Roman just phoned. Elliott Buntrock called there trying to find Sigrid. Oh, baby——"

Sigrid pulled away from her at that. "Elliott? The radio? What are you talking about, Mother?"

"Why, Oscar, of course." Now it was her turn to look at them in bewilderment. "It was on the radio . . ." She faltered. "A car wreck near Los Angeles. That's not why you . . ."

For the first time, she noticed her daughter's disheveled appearance, her wild hair, a button ripped from her coat, broken nails on her scraped and dirty hands. "You didn't know he was killed?"

Sigrid's face went so bloodless that a faint bruise over her right eye stood out in bold relief. "Nauman? Dead?"

A soft moan escaped her lips, and before either of them could catch her, she crumpled to the floor.

Maternal adrenaline kicked in.

"Call nine-one-one!" Anne said, on her knees, cradling her daughter's head. "An ambulance—the emergency room!"

"Now, now," Mac said, and his rumpled solidity calmed her down. Indeed, he'd barely lifted Sigrid to the couch before she came to and demanded to hear every detail Anne knew.

Roman had left a number to call out in California in case Anne should hear from Sigrid first; and Sigrid listened dry-eyed as Elliott Buntrock told her again. By then, she had started to shake, though. And she was unbearably cold.

Somehow Anne got her to take two sleeping tablets and to lie down in her bedroom. But even beneath three blankets Sigrid couldn't get warm. She was still shaking as the barbiturates finally took her under. When Anne returned to the living room, Mac was waiting as patiently and as solidly as one of the creek boulders of her childhood.

They talked long into the night as Mac described the traumatic evening—how Sigrid had stalked a killer who took her hostage and how she'd nearly been killed in the shoot-out that left one of her own men dead.

"Oh, Mac," Anne grieved. "No wonder she fainted. What's going to happen?"

"Coming over here, she agreed to take a leave of absence till the departmental hearing on the shooting. The D.A.'s office will have to file a report, too."

Anne stiffened protectively.

"That's just a formality under the circumstances," Mac assured her. "It wasn't her gun that killed him, but there'll be psychological counseling."

"If she'll go," Anne said doubtfully.

"She won't have a choice. It's mandatory in cases of this nature."

Knowing her daughter's reluctance to discuss her personal emotions, Anne could only hope she'd cooperate. At best, counseling might somehow lessen Sigrid's grief; at the least it should surely keep her subconscious from thinking that Nauman's death was some sort of cosmic retaliation for her part in a subordinate officer's death.

Both were careful to draw no parallels to that earlier shooting of thirty years ago when Leif was killed; and by the time morning came, Anne Harald and Mac McKinnon had established something very like their first early friendship. This time, though, Sigrid was the bridge between them, not Leif.

Valium and sheer willpower got her daughter through the official hearings and through Oscar's memorial service, too. But when his attorney told her the simple terms of his will that made her sole executor and beneficiary and explained that she was now an exceedingly wealthy young woman, Sigrid had retreated to her own bed, pulled the covers around her, and started sleeping eighteen hours a day.

For the first two or three weeks, she seemed to leave her room only to drag herself to the counseling sessions. She'd quit after the required minimum; and if they'd done her any good, Anne couldn't see it.

"Thank the Lord for Roman Tramegra," Anne said now, as Mac refilled her glass. "If she still lived alone . . . Well, a mother can do just so much nagging. A housemate's *there.* All the time."

"What about the lawyer?"

"Him, too," she conceded. "And the gallery people. They're starting to bug her for decisions. There's so much unfinished business when a person dies unexpectedly."

Abruptly, it was their own unfinished business that hung between them. She wanted to speak, to brush it away, but her throat seemed dry and her uncooperative tongue chose that moment to go mute.

"Anne?" He leaned toward her across the small table and his craggy face was dead serious. "Isn't it time we talked about Leif? About us?"

Guilty denial swept over her. "There *is* no us," she said sharply.

Mac's shoulders slumped and the big man drew back, almost as if she'd spat on him.

Instantly, she was contrite. "I'm sorry, Mac. That wasn't fair. Or honest."

His brown eyes were wary.

"It was so long ago," she said. "So much has happened."

"Yes."

She laid her small sturdy hand on his clenched fist. "One step at a time?"

Slowly, his fist relaxed and turned beneath her hand until their palms met.

This time she did not pull away.

A few blocks north, Roman Tramegra reluctantly turned away from the new computer he'd installed in the sitting room on his side of the apartment he shared with Sigrid Harald and answered the telephone ringing at his elbow.

"No, I'm sorry, she's not in. May I take a message? Ah, Elliott! I didn't catch your voice. Yes, it's quite remarkable. I think Sigrid's really coming out of it. She went swimming with Anne yesterday, and this morning, when she went off to see her attorney, I told her I'd try out that interesting new recipe for tomato and tuna chowder for our lunch. But she called about an hour ago and said she was going to work.

"I say, Elliott? You wouldn't know about computers, would you? I was hoping Sigrid would show me how to make a directory and she— Elliott? Are you there?"

He frowned at the phone, replaced the receiver and was instantly reabsorbed by the computer. Now was it Ctrl-Alt-Del you pushed if you needed to reset or Shift-Ctrl-Alt?

4

Man [after the Garden of Eden] pursued many useful occupations, differing from each other; and some were, and are, more theoretical than others; they could not all be alike, since theory is the most worthy. . . .

It is not without the impulse of a lofty spirit that some are moved to enter this profession, attractive to them through natural enthusiasm.

Cennino Cennini
Il Libro dell' Arte, 1437

Elaine Albee spotted her first.

She and Jim Lowry were sifting through the Todd Fong jacket again, looking over statements taken by a former colleague and discussing how soon they could reasonably expect a crime scene unit to go dig that bullet out of Georgia Fong's doorway. The front of Albee's desk butted the front of Lowry's, which meant that she was looking over his shoulder and straight at the frosted-glass door when someone hesitated in the hallway outside. As it swung open, she stopped talking in mid-sentence and stood up so abruptly that the others in the squad room turned to see who'd entered.

Jim Lowry immediately came to his feet. Even Sam Hentz, who'd headed up the detective squad this past month and who hoped he might get the job permanently if Lieutenant Harald did resign, as had been rumored, found himself standing.

Dinah Urbanska tried to rise, but somehow her leg got hooked in the telephone cord. Her impulsive gurgle of welcome turned into a dismayed wail of "Oh, gosh, no!" as telephone, three file folders, and a half-empty coffee mug went crashing to the floor.

Hentz shook his head at his klutzy partner and protégée. "The Polack poltergeist strikes again."

By the time they picked up the phone, mopped coffee off the scattered papers, and restored momentary order to Urbanska's desk, the first awkwardness had passed.

There was even a ghost of a smile on Lieutenant Harald's lips as she acknowledged their greetings and moved through the big shabby room to her office. Tillie started toward her, but she shook her head. "Give me ten minutes," she told him and went inside and closed the door.

Ruben Gonzalez, who'd transferred in only a couple of weeks ago, looked over at Hentz in surprise. *"That's* the Lieutenant?"

"Yeah." Hentz deliberately turned his back and resumed his interrupted phone conversation with a potential witness.

Detective Gonzalez raised an eyebrow at Elaine Albee. She gave a friendly shrug to show he shouldn't take Hentz's snub personally.

Gonzalez went back to the report he was supposed to finish before lunch. As one of the new kids on the block, he was still getting a feel for the department and knew he hadn't quite figured out all the nuances. Hard to, though, what with the lieutenant on extended leave of absence the whole time he'd been there and with speculations flying over whether or not she'd even come back at all now that she'd inherited a bunch of money from the guy she'd been sleeping with.

Not the fox he'd expected from some of the things the others had said. Good eyes, but too skinny. No boobs. Uptight lines in her face. Of course that could be because her man was dead.

He gnawed the eraser on his pencil and shot a covert glance at his new colleagues around the long cluttered room.

Albee and Lowry had their heads together with Tildon and were talking too low for him to hear. Hentz was punching in another number on his phone pad, and Dinah Urbanska sat staring at the closed inner door with a sad expression on her face.

It hadn't taken Gonzalez more than two days to realize that Tillie was totally dedicated to the absent lieutenant.

Albee and Lowry? Probably.

Hentz? Doubtful.

Dinah Urbanska was the most junior member of the squad and seemed to like everybody, so she was no help.

Gonzalez wondered what Kevin Jackson, the other new guy, would make of Lieutenant Harald. Jackson had transferred in around the middle of March and hadn't met her either, but one of the civilian aides downstairs was a close friend of Jackson's wife, and she'd filled Jackson's ears with a lot of chatter that Captain McKinnon had omitted from his official briefing.

All they'd been told was that one detective from this squad had been killed, that his partner had requested a transfer out, and that Lieutenant Harald had been there when the officer was shot.

The aide described who did what, when and why, and said maybe Harald had even pulled the trigger herself.

Shortly after he came, Gonzalez had heard Jackson ask if

that was the real reason the lieutenant was on such an extended leave?

"What happened in this department before you got here is none of your damn business," Sam Hentz had said. "But for the record, no. The shooter was an officer from the Six-four in Brooklyn, and he was completely exonerated. So was she."

The other detectives had looked at Jackson like he'd just dumped a load on the squad room floor, so the subject of Lieutenant Harald was pretty much dropped after that.

Across the room, Albee and Lowry were trading papers back and forth. With a troubled glance toward the lieutenant's door, Tildon returned to his own desk.

The hell with the report, Gonzalez thought. He snagged his jacket and headed for lunch. Jackson had gone on ahead and was supposed to be holding a burger and fries for him at a grill two blocks away. The report could wait another hour.

Walking through the squad room was the first hurdle, Sigrid Harald told herself. Next would be calling Tillie in for a quick briefing. Then talking to Hentz and the others.

Not yet, though.

She stood for a long minute with her back against the closed door and gazed around the small boxy office. So much had changed in her life that she was vaguely surprised to find everything here exactly as she'd left it that chill February night when she and a Brooklyn detective had rushed out to trap a killer.

The rest of the building's interior was mostly in tones of blue; but sometime in the past, this small boxy office had been painted white, and she had moved in without once thinking of giving it a softer look. A fluorescent light, recessed behind frosted glass overhead, shone down harshly on the usual assortment of file cabinets, bookshelves, mismated chairs, and a standard metal desk. A computer terminal had replaced the old electric typewriter she'd found there when she arrived a couple of years ago, but everything else in the room was decidedly low-tech.

The psychiatrist they'd forced her to see after the shooting in February would probably make something out of the lack of personal effects here. No snapshots beneath the glass top of her desk, no photographs or diplomas on the walls. Just a map of the five boroughs divided by precincts, a map of the city itself, and an administrative flowchart. Nor were there any potted plants on her windowsill or hanging baskets of vines or ferns.

The only objects not issued by the city were a green desk lamp, a large brass-bound magnifying glass, a little bowl that held her collection of puzzle rings, and a blue-green coffee mug.

She picked up the mug and ran her slender fingers over the smooth surface. In the time she'd owned it, she'd never given it a second thought. Today it suddenly triggered the memory of a homicide victim's husband. The man had been stoical until someone unthinkingly handed him coffee in the victim's favorite cup, a silly pink-and-white china mug with a handle whimsically shaped like a flamingo. One sight of that cup and the husband had smashed it against the nearest wall, yelling in anger to keep from crying. "It sucks that *things* last longer than people! Why should glass be stronger than flesh? Oh, God, *why?*"

Sigrid swallowed abruptly and tried to blank out that memory, willing herself not to be pulled back into the dark abyss of her own grief.

It was nearly two months now. More than time enough for any normal person to have stopped choking up over things like stupid coffee mugs.

Carefully she set the mug back on the desk, straightened her back, and opened the door to the squad room.

As with most things, the doing was easier than the dreading; and stepping back into this world wasn't nearly as harrowing as she'd anticipated. The worst was having to ignore the curiosity that no one in the squad room had the nerve to voice, and to accept the sympathy that they awkwardly tendered.

In accordance with Nauman's wishes, his body had been donated to a medical school in the Midwest, so there had been no funeral rites, no ashes to scatter—just a memorial service up at Riverside. Sigrid knew that several of Nauman's peers and colleagues had spoken eloquently of his life and work and how he'd influenced them, and for all she knew, every officer in the precinct could have passed through the reception line afterward, but that day was mostly a blur in her memory.

She thanked the detectives again for their expressions of sympathy and then asked Tillie and Hentz to bring her up to date with the current caseload.

One comforting thing about police work was its sameness. The names of victims and perps changed, of course, particulars differed in every crime, there were even some seasonal variations, but otherwise the department was clocking along pretty much as she'd left it.

Except for Gonzalez and Jackson, who came in toward the end of the meeting.

As Tillie introduced them, Sigrid was reminded all over again that two detectives from her squad were now gone for good. Their careers in this department had ended on the roof of a sleazy hotel a few blocks north. When Bernie Peters was killed, his partner, Matt Eberstadt, had transferred out as soon as he could; and these were the replacements.

Ruben Gonzalez was a slender five-nine, Hispanic, late thirties, and divorced. Kevin Jackson was white, midforties, and maybe an inch taller, but much wider and more muscular. Married, four daughters who ranged in age from ten to eighteen.

Small talk did not come easily to Sigrid, but she somehow managed to say the right things to the two men before slipping back into the routine of a normal briefing session.

"—so if we get lucky today," Elaine Albee said, "the

crime scene unit could maybe go ahead and find the bullet and—"

The phone rang sharply and Tillie answered. "For you, Lieutenant."

Without thinking, Sigrid took it. Instantly, she wished she'd told Tillie to take a message.

"Ah! Ms. Harald!" said the caller. "This is Irene Bayles again, Mr. Livingston's assistant."

As if she had to be told, Sigrid thought wearily. Sometimes she felt as if the woman's relentlessly chirpy voice had been in her ear at least once a day for half a lifetime.

"How may I help you?" Sigrid said coolly.

But Mrs. Bayles in her solicitous mode was not to be deflected. "I'm sure it'll be better for you now that you're back at work again."

"Did Mr. Livingston want something?" Sigrid asked desperately.

"Oh, yes. You've had another offer for the Connecticut property. They've raised it another fifteen thousand."

The Connecticut property.

Nauman's country home. His studio. The East Side efficiency near the college was little more than a place to change clothes and sleep during his four-day work week. Connecticut was where he actually lived and painted.

Unbidden came a rush of memories. Images of sledding down the ravine behind the house, lazy Sunday afternoons in front of the fire, the clean smell of turpentine that permeated even the sheets in his bedroom so that when they made love in that king-size bed—

She suddenly became aware of their looks. There was concern on Tillie's round face, naked curiosity on Jackson's.

"No!" she said sharply.

"Pardon?"

"Tell Mr. Livingston I absolutely do not wish to sell at this time."

"But, Ms. Harald—"

"I'm sorry," she said. "I really must go now."

And hung up.

Her voice and hands were both steady as she picked up her notepad and said to the younger blond detective. "Sorry, Albee. You were saying . . . ?"

Obediently, Elaine Albee and Jim Lowry sketched in the known facts about Todd Fong's death.

"He was forty-two, separated from his third wife, and there's a little two-year-old girl," said Albee.

Sigrid listened as they described a violent, shiftless man who could, nevertheless, con anybody out of anything if he set his mind to it. Look at how his parents kept cleaning up behind him. Look at how women fell for him. Look at Georgia Fong, for God's sake. A street-smart kid but she was still barely half his age when he died. Todd Fong had been an alcohol abuser and an occasional petty drug dealer, but not a heavy user himself.

"What's his rap sheet look like?" asked Sigrid.

Jim Lowry handed it over. "No actual jail time, but lots of petty fines and warrants."

The last marriage looked like one more attempt to straighten up; one more failure in a long string of failures, they told her. His father got him a job driving a delivery truck and helped them with the security deposit on an apartment, which they lost after Todd got drunk and punched out two walls in January.

"He also punched out Georgia, and she took the baby and left," said Elaine Albee.

On March 17, one week before his daughter's second birthday, Todd Fong was found in a room his parents had rented for him near their apartment. There was a .22 in his hand and a bullet in his head. He'd been shot at close range, but tests were inconclusive as to whether he'd fired the gun himself. The investigating officer had put it down as a probable suicide and the M.E. had confirmed.

At first, Fong's parents had gone along with that verdict, but now they were screaming murder.

"So," said Jim Lowry, "if the bullet that nearly hit his wife turns out to match that gun . . ."

Sigrid nodded. The trail was cold on this one. Common sense and experience said if you couldn't pinpoint the perpetrator within forty-eight hours, you probably never would. All the same, they seemed to be carrying a fairly light caseload at the moment.

"Take a couple of days and see what you come up with."

As she rose to return to her office, she caught Sam Hentz's eye. "See you a minute?"

Hentz scooped up a stack of folders, followed her into her office, and laid them on her bare desk. Symbolically, he was handing the reins of office back over to her, and she acknowledged the gesture with a grave nod.

"Thanks, Hentz."

He shrugged, not giving anything away. At forty, Sam Hentz was in good physical trim, his dark hair just beginning to go gray at the temples. On most detectives, jacket sleeves always looked tight; on Hentz, suits and sports coats hung so beautifully that they almost looked tailor-made. Adding to his dapper appearance was his fondness for shirts with French cuffs and square-toed cowboy boots. Divorced, no kids. A thoroughgoing chauvinist and somewhat aloof from the other detectives on her squad, yet he'd taken klutzy young Dinah Urbanska to raise and was patiently teaching her more than the basics.

From Sigrid's first day on this job more than two years ago, she understood quite clearly that he resented taking orders from a younger female and that he thought he should be sitting behind her desk. Nevertheless, as long as he continued to perform well and wasn't overtly insubordinate, she could put up with his attitude. Nothing in the rule book said they had to like each other.

She waved him to a chair and touched the folders. "Any time bombs here I need to know about?"

"No, it's all pretty straightforward." He continued to stand, but did lean against the door, legs crossed, one hand in his pants pocket so that the handle of his gun showed beneath his dark gray jacket.

"You're back to stay?"

"Yes."

"Even though you don't need to work now?"

She looked at him with level gray eyes, and he shrugged again. "It's all over the house. Big-time artist. Left you a few million. You don't need this job."

"Do you?" she asked curiously.

He straightened.

"I read your personnel file last year," Sigrid told him.

"So?"

"So you listed an aunt as next of kin. Lizzie Stopplemeyer from some little town upstate."

He became very still.

"Aunt Lizzie," she mused. "Now there's a sweet old-fashioned name. Nobody in personnel would think twice about an Aunt Lizzie. But a Mrs. Irving Meyer Stopplemeyer? Stopplemeyer pastries are in every grocery store from Pennsylvania to Florida. Irving Meyer Stopplemeyer was on more television commercials than Colonel Sanders. And you're his widow's favorite nephew."

"You had me investigated?" he asked harshly.

Her tone matched his. "I saw you on the GWB one day. You drive a very expensive sports car, Hentz. You wear expensive clothes."

"So you automatically thought I was dirty."

"I don't automatically think anything. Things may be coming apart all over the department, but not in *my* squad!"

He jerked his head toward the squad room. "Anybody else know?"

"Not from me."

Hentz looked at her for a long silent moment. "You're different," he said at last. "Not just your looks, either." He hesitated. "I guess I was wrong. You do need this job, don't you, Lieutenant?"

Empathy?

From *Hentz*?

To her horror, her throat began to close up again, and tears prickled her eyelids.

"That'll be all," she said brusquely and swiveled toward her computer, willing him to just go.

After half an eon, the door opened and then closed again.

5

And if you find anyone protests to you against the verdigris, on the ground that it might eventually corrupt the gold, just listen patiently; for I have found by experience that the gold lasts well.

Cennino Cennini
Il Libro dell' Arte, 1437

Very little of the grandeur that was Greece graced the Vanderlyn Akropolis Restaurant. The Aegean vistas painted on its grimy plaster walls were cracked now and stained with years of cooking oil. The faded plastic vines that twined on the rickety latticed booth dividers, the three imitation amphorae, and the two imitation marble statues were so dusty they could have used a quick dunking in the Aegean. Worse, if Arnold Callahan could judge by the loud-talking college kids sprawled in the booths around them, the most popular dish seemed to be a bastardized pizza with feta cheese.

When Arnold tried to order spanakopita, the fat proprietor shook his head. "You gotta get here before one to get any of that. How about some moussaka? We got lots of moussaka left."

Capitulating, Arnold had ordered the pizza and now sat across from Lemuel Vance in a booth whose cracked plastic cushions had been mended with sticky duct tape.

"The whole department's shot to hell since Nauman's gone," Lem Vance said, digging into his moussaka with relish. From his barrel-shaped build, it was clear that he was no picky eater.

Arnold tried not to notice the printmaker's stained fingers and the half-moons of black ink beneath his fingernails. "Who's the new chairman?" he asked.

Vance gave a rueful grin. "Me. You believe it?" He took a deep drink of his Mexican beer. "Actually, I'm just acting as chair till the search committee and the president come up with someone for the fall. I thought it'd be fun to have some power, but these last few weeks? You couldn't pay me to keep my balls in this vise. Nauman made it look easy. Of course, he had Andrea Ross acting as deputy chair after Riley Quinn got poisoned. She's a historian, not an artist, but she's damn good at administration and that's who they should give the job to."

He drained his glass and looked around for a waiter. "Never happen though. She's only an assistant professor and still pretty young."

Vance, on the other hand, was fifty and an associate professor. And maybe he wasn't an intellectual, but he was nobody's fool either.

"So what's this about, Callahan? You're not buying me lunch to listen to how the art department's going down the slop chute. And it's certainly not because you sold out my last edition, is it?"

Despite his joking tone, Arnold saw the sudden flash of hope in Lem Vance's eyes: *Did somebody like my work? Did they buy me?*

The artist's validation.

For a moment Arnold was tempted to say yes. But then he calculated how much money that would cost him, because even though Lem's last edition was technically exquisite, only twelve of the seventy-five prints had sold thus far.

"Sorry," he said. "No, I was just looking for a little bit of background. A name came up today, and I thought you might know him. Rudy Gottfried?"

"Gottfried? Sure. One of Nauman's charity cases. What'd you want to know?"

"Charity case? I thought he was a painter."

Lem Vance took such a large forkful of moussaka that a string of melted cheese ran down the corner of his mouth. He wiped it away with a paper napkin, swallowed, then waved his empty glass toward the fat proprietor, who came over with a refill.

"He was. Still is, for all I know. I'm talking what? Twenty, twenty-five years? That's when no gallery would touch him and he must have been pretty desperate, I guess. Anyhow, he and Nauman were tight 'way back, so even though the city had a hiring freeze on then, Nauman bent the rules, gave him a couple of classes when people were on sabbatical. And then he arranged an adjunct position in the continuing ed. division so Gottfried could get benefits, maybe even a little pension, for all I know. Probably kept him from starving."

Something Lemuel Vance was in no danger of doing, thought Arnold, watching him slather butter on his sesame roll.

"So what does he paint?" he asked. "And if he's been around all these years, how come I never heard of him?"

"Don't be a jerk-off," Vance said. "Of course you've heard of him. He was one of the guys in old Henry DiPietro's bargain-basement sale."

A wave of sick comprehension swept over Arnold Callahan. "Oh, shit."

"Yeah," Vance agreed, licking butter from his ink-stained fingertips.

By late afternoon, Hal DiPietro was ready to make a novena to the Virgin for sending him an assistant as efficient and tactful as B'Nita Parsons.

Hanging a show is always a delicate matter of tradeoffs, he thought. Which picture works well with which? Do we aim for dynamic tension or collegial interplay? Should we begin with the visual impact of the most stunning work or strive for a gradual buildup to a huge climax? Should they be hung at eye level or slightly above? And then there's the lighting—direct, indirect, off-center, dead on? Does the intensity of light *there* balance the angled shadows over here?

After several hours of this, everyone usually gets a bit short-tempered, and matters are never helped if the artist's lover feels entitled to give her opinion, too, on every judgment call.

Having paid for slick full-color catalogs of the show, Valerie Braydon, Buck David's short-tempered lover, was vocally unhappy that the printer had not yet delivered them; and her discontent was beginning to affect his concentration.

Cleverly, Mrs. Parsons kept finding small make-work jobs for the woman. While Hal and his other assistants worked with Buck David, he noticed that Mrs. Parsons kept shunting the Braydon woman off in different directions. Could she do something with the guest register? Where did she think the caterer should set up? Could she help load the champagne into the refrigerator to let it start chilling for tomorrow night?

Eventually everything fell into place, the artist declared himself reasonably satisfied, Donny Levitz returned the ladders and tools to the workroom, and everyone left for the day.

"We can fine-tune tomorrow," DiPietro said wearily when they were alone.

"Why don't you go on home?" said Mrs. Parsons. "You look exhausted. I'll finish putting things away, then run the vacuum and close up."

A jewel, DiPietro told himself again, too tired to demur.

B'Nita Parsons carefully locked the door behind him, tidied the gallery, and vacuumed away all traces of wire snippets, bits of paper, and other debris. By the time she finished, DiPietro and the others had been gone over a half-hour. More than long enough to have remembered a forgotten item if they intended to return tonight.

She stowed the vacuum in its corner of the workroom and then pulled the boxy old refrigerator away from the wall. Loaded with heavy glass bottles of champagne, it was at first reluctant to move on its castors. But years of summer farmwork had left her stronger than she looked and slowly the refrigerator yielded to her determination.

When it was far enough from the wall, she slipped behind, unplugged it, and, using a screwdriver from Donny Levitz's workbench, carefully removed the rear cover without smudging its layers of accumulated dust. The inner workings did not look very different from the refrigerator that had given up the ghost shortly before she gave up on her marriage back in Alabama. "See that little pinhole?" the repairman had told her. "That's how you lost all your Freon."

Donny Levitz's workbench also provided a tack hammer and a thin framing brad. She chose an inconspicuous location and, after two sharp taps of the hammer, immediately felt the pressurized gas escape past her fingers. A twist of the brad made an even larger hole in the soft metal. When she could feel no more escaping gas, she replaced the rear cover, plugged in the cord, and pushed the refrigerator back into its niche.

The motor continued to run, but B'Nita Parsons knew that the interior temperature would soon begin to rise.

The warm spring day had given way to a clear cool evening. It was really too early in the season to sit outside; but the café here near Sheridan Square in the Village had a few outdoor tables sheltered by glass partitions for hardy souls like Elliott Buntrock, who'd been on the telephone all afternoon and was tired of interiors. Even so, Buntrock appreciated the fleecy sweatshirt he wore over his jeans and shirt and rather wished he'd brought along a jacket.

He had almost finished his cappuccino when Sigrid Harald slid into the wire chair opposite his. She was thinner than ever and her black hair needed reshaping, but she wore a royal blue jacket with dark plaid slacks and a white cotton jersey. Lipstick and eye shadow couldn't quite disguise the vulnerability he saw in her face.

"Do you have one of those?" she asked, smiling at his sweatshirt.

He looked down and saw that the riotous design commemorated a motorcycle rally at Myrtle Beach. "God, no! My sister has a perverted sense of humor. She sends me these things when she's on business trips. Goes back to our sandbox days when I ran over her with my tricycle. She thinks I'm a lousy driver."

Instantly he gave himself a mental kick in the jeans, but she didn't seem to notice his blunder.

"Cappuccino?" he said hastily. "Caffè latte?"

She shook her head. "But take your time. I guess we're in no hurry?"

"He said any time after seven. Are you sure you don't mind?"

"No, it's fine," she told him, as he drained his cup and stood up.

She did mind, though. She minded enormously. But somehow, when Elliott called her this afternoon and spoke of the Arnheim, of the galleries, of the projects to which Nauman had agreed, she was suddenly ashamed of herself for being so weak for so long. That was why she had listened when Elliott told her about this old friend of Nau-

man's, this Rudy Gottfried. And that was why she hadn't
hung up when he admitted that he'd used her name to hook
the man's interest.

"He wasn't going to talk to me. Said he was through
talking with anybody. But your name came up, and he said
if I wanted to bring you along, he'd let me come. It's an
imposition, I know, and if you—"

"I'll come," she'd said quietly.

So here she was, walking along beside this tall, ungainly
curator on this cool April night.

For Nauman's sake, she thought.

Wearing a bright blue jacket, lipstick, blush, and eye
shadow.

For Nauman's sake.

Making light conversation when she'd rather be home in
bed with the blanket drawn up to her chin, staring into the
darkness.

All for the sake of the man who had shaken up her life
like a child's glass snow dome and then left her to drift
down the rest of it without him.

Vehicular traffic was still heavy as they crossed Christopher Street and walked down Seventh Avenue. At Bedford
Street, she glanced up the block to the 9½-foot-wide house
where Edna St. Vincent Millay had once lived.

Now, there was someone who'd had her heart broken at
least a half-dozen times over, thought Sigrid; and out of
that heartbreak and reckless appetite for life had come great
lyric poetry. She wondered if the sixth time was any easier
than the first. And bleakly decided it didn't matter, because
(a) she wasn't a poet, and (b) it was never going to happen
to her again. *Never!*

They passed a group of laughing teenagers outside a
brightly lighted clothing store. Many windows along the
way were dark, although enough bookshops, cafés, and
convenience stores were open to keep the sidewalks lively.

As they crossed Houston, Sigrid barely heard Elliott's

words. She still wasn't clear exactly who Rudy Gottfried was. She'd never even heard Nauman mention him.

But then, there was so much he'd never had time to mention. She had met him only last April while investigating the death of his colleague at Vanderlyn. He was almost twice her age, yet they had become lovers in November and in February—almost two months now—he was dead. No time to exchange all the stories they should have told each other in the long years to come.

Morbidly, she realized that by next month, he would have been in his grave longer than he'd been in her bed. Except that there was no grave she could haunt. No place where all that was once physical of him—

No! she told herself. She could not, *would* not let herself think of his body somewhere on a dissecting slab in some medical school. Not when her own body ached for him, not when she hungered for his hard masculinity in her bed, his hands, his mouth—

She wrenched her thoughts back to Varick Street's shabby storefronts, to the ugly lampposts plastered with lost-pet notices, offers to sell, offers to rent, and said, "Tell me about this Rudy Gottfried."

"I don't know that much about him myself," Elliott admitted as they automatically swerved to avoid the panhandler who stuck out a filthy paper cup.

"That's okay. That's okay. We all Lord Buddha's chickens," the man mumbled as they passed.

"Lord Buddha's *chickens*?" Laughing, Elliott turned back, dug in his pocket for loose change, and dropped it in the cup.

Still chuckling, he caught up with Sigrid and continued, "I had to call around a few places before I could find anybody who knew where he was. Oscar said that when he first came to New York, Gottfried let him share his studio. Gave him a place to stay while he was getting started. I think Gottfried was an abstract painter, too. Back in the late forties, early fifties, he was in there with the big ones, but for some reason, he never quite made it."

They paused until a stoplight went from red to green, then crossed in front of a phalanx of taxi headlights.

"The young guy I talked to this afternoon says he's suspicious and sour. Drinks too much. Just the same, he's the only one left who remembers Oscar from those early days, and I think his memories are worth having for the Arnheim catalog I'm putting together."

They arrived at the cross street where Gottfried lived, and Elliott stopped under a corner light with his hands jammed deep in his pockets. His tall, angular body cast a stick-figure shadow across the sparkly glassphalt sidewalk. "My friend also said he's a foul-tongued man with a short fuse."

Sigrid looked up at him, and her gray eyes were dark pools of amusement in the glow of the streetlight. "I'm a police officer, Elliott. I've heard all the words."

He grinned. "There're always new combinations."

They turned into the deserted side street. Both sidewalks were lined with cars that looked as if they were parked for the night. The street itself was the usual schizophrenic New York mix of industrial and domestic. On the south side stood a corner eatery and a line of anonymous brick warehouses. Hieroglyphed with black, white, and red spray paint, their steel doors were rolled down and locked, and everything was dark. On the north side of the street were trees and a row of four-story red brick houses, some dating from the early 1800s. Polished brass knockers and bell plates glinted from shadowy doorways, lamplight glowed behind closed drapes and gauzy curtains. In one second-floor window, an enormous bearlike dog amiably cocked his head at them as they passed.

Elliott's gloomy mood began to lift. "I've been on this street before," he said. "Leontyne Price lives in one of these houses. Someone brought me to her party here."

He thought it was a house at the end, but couldn't quite

remember. Nearby was the address they wanted. A wrought-iron gate opened onto four shallow steps that led down to a basement door with a locked iron gate beneath the high front stoop. No outside light, just the streetlamp two doors away. No light inside, either, that Sigrid could see.

Elliott rang the bell. After a longish wait, a faint glow appeared behind the front window shades. Another moment and the inner door jerked open. A thickset man with a brushy salt-and-pepper crew cut peered at them through the iron grating.

"Yeah?"

"Mr. Gottfried? I'm Elliott Buntrock, and this is Sigrid Harald."

The man grunted and unlocked the gate, motioned them through and then relocked it.

It was like entering a tunnel, thought Sigrid. The dim passageway was narrow, and the rounded ceiling so low that Elliott had to stoop slightly. Unframed canvases lined the hall, but beneath them were brick and stone walls that had been roughly slathered with plaster and then painted white. Exposed pipes ran along the upper corner.

Elliott touched the wall appreciatively. "This looks like the original masonry."

"Eighteen-twenty," the man said brusquely and squeezed past to lead the way down the hall through a doorway so low that all three of them had to duck.

The first two rooms they passed through were too dark for them to distinguish much. Sigrid had an impression of clutter and an unmade bed. Just as she was wondering how an artist could live and work in such cramped, cavelike quarters with no light, they entered a large airy space that had apparently been added on to the original structure at the back of the house. Glass covered the entire rear wall and half of the upward thrusting ceiling. In daytime, this studio would be flooded with natural light. Leaves brushed the glass outside, and there was probably some sort of garden out there.

All the familiar smells of a working studio assailed her nostrils: paint thinners, various oil paints, the very odor of fresh new canvas. For a moment, the walls tilted and swirled and she was wrenched with a grief so sudden and overwhelming that she wanted to run back through the dark warren of rooms, back into the night. Then she became aware that Rudy Gottfried was staring at her, and she gave herself a mental shake.

After Elliott's phone call this afternoon, she had made Nauman a private promise that she would not disgrace him before his friends and colleagues. Now she held her head high and stared back.

Rudy Gottfried had to be in his mid-seventies, but his brushy crew cut contained more black hairs than white, and he was built like his steelworking forebears. His chest and arms bulged within his dark green coveralls, and his neck was as wide as his head.

An empty whiskey bottle lay atop an overflowing waste-basket, and Gottfried waved a half-empty fifth in their direction. "Drink?"

As he seemed to be taking it straight with neither mixers nor ice, Sigrid shook her head.

Buntrock accepted though, and the artist muttered something about glasses before disappearing back down the darkened hall. From the front of the apartment came the bang of cabinet doors opening and closing.

While they waited, Elliott prowled about with undisguised curiosity.

The studio held the usual assortment of easels, shelves of dry pigments, multi-size paintbrushes jammed into coffee cans like bunches of flowers, rolled-up tubes of oil paint, and a box of rags for wiping brushes. Dozens of pictures, six or eight deep, leaned against the walls. Overhead, suspended by chains festooned with dusty cobwebs, were four long fluorescent lights. They gave a harsh white glare to the room.

One tall easel stood with its back to the center of the room so that natural light would fall on the front from the windows and skylight during the day, and Sigrid followed Elliott around to look at the uncompleted canvas.

She saw a crimson shape, large and amorphous, like a half-melted sun, that floated slightly left of center upon a light gray-green background. The edge of the shape was fuzzy, but the dull crimson sharpened and intensified as it pulled away from the edges until the concentrated center seemed to glow and vibrate with burning intensity. Although Sigrid seldom remembered individual pieces of abstract art, something about it seemed familiar.

Elliott was examining the artist's palette, in this case a sheet of window glass that held dabs of wet oil paint. He lifted a jelly jar half filled with a yellowish viscous substance and regarded it approvingly.

"An egg emulsion?" Elliott asked, showing off a little as Rudy Gottfried returned with an inch of amber liquor in a dusty-looking juice glass.

"My mayonnaise," the artist grunted.

Startled by the term, Sigrid turned to him with a smile. "That's what Nauman used to call it," she said.

"Yeah?" Gottfried did not smile back. "I gave him the recipe."

"Here?" she asked, looking around as if there would still be traces of him after all these years. "Is this where you worked when he came to New York?"

"Not here. Over on Prince Street."

He sat down heavily on a bar stool covered in torn blue vinyl and set his glass on the drafting table in front of him.

There were only two other places to sit in the cluttered room: a wooden armchair with thin spindles over by the windows, and a solid straight-backed mahogany side chair, its bottom cushioned with stained and tattered purple-striped upholstery, a battle-scarred survivor of someone's formal dining room suite.

Although Rudy Gottfried had not offered her a seat,

Sigrid pulled the straight chair over closer and sat down, determined to make Nauman's old colleague unbend, even though small talk had never been one of her strengths. Irrelevantly came one of her southern grandmother's strictures. "Just let it flow, honey. Men don't really care what you say as long as it's about them."

"Are you originally from the Pittsburgh area, too?" she asked. "Is that how Nauman knew you, or did you meet here in the city?"

But Gottfried was watching suspiciously as Buntrock started to look at some of the paintings leaning face inward against the wall. "Hey, pal. If you don't mind, those are private."

"Sorry," Buntrock said, immediately releasing the picture. "It's just that I'm impressed. Your work has great power, Mr. Gottfried."

"You think so?" Gottfried drained his glass and immediately poured himself another.

Buntrock dragged the wooden armchair into an open space and folded his long bony frame into it. "Where are you showing now?"

"I'm between dealers at the moment." With a brusque jerk of his head that included them both, he asked, "So what exactly do you want from me?"

"As I told you on the phone," Buntrock replied, "I'm curating a memorial retrospective of Nauman's work at the Arnheim and I hoped you would write something for the catalog. A reminiscence of his early days in New York. He told me you gave him studio space when he first came over from Pittsburgh."

"Yeah. We shared the same loft, screwed the same—" His eyes flicked toward Sigrid, and he swallowed the rest of his remarks with another swig of whiskey. "Yeah, I gave Nauman a lot more than my mayonnaise."

"Primarily, we'd want your artistic recollec—"

Gottfried interrupted Buntrock harshly. "Tell me, Lieutenant Harald—it *is* Lieutenant, isn't it?"

Sigrid nodded.

"I read you inherited everything he owned? The whole shebang?"

"Yes."

"Tell you what I'll do. Nauman and I exchanged some things back when. I'd like to see mine, if he kept any of it. Maybe take some slides?"

Buntrock's head swung around. "You have some early Naumans?"

"Had. They're long gone. Had to sell them when— Never mind. Nobody's damn business why I sold them. So what do you say, Lieutenant?"

Nauman's voice was suddenly in her ear again: *"Got to see some of my pictures I hadn't seen in years. . . . You never forget a one of them, Siga."*

"Lieutenant?"

"Yes," she said. "Yes, of course you may see them. I can look at the inventory sheets tonight and tell you what's in Connecticut, but I'm fairly sure there's at least one small picture similar to these in his apartment over near the college. We could arrange something."

Unable to remain seated, Buntrock had unfolded his gangly length and was roaming the studio again. "I don't want to push you, Mr. Gottfried, but we're on a tight schedule with the catalog. Do you think you could possibly get me a first draft by the end of the month?"

The older man dismissed any problems with a wave of his hand. "Hell, I've painted whole shows in ten days." He turned back to Sigrid. "Just tell me when I can see my stuff."

She gave Elliott a questioning look. "Didn't you plan to look at the pictures in the apartment this week?"

"DiPietro and I," he said with a nod, and to Gottfried he added, "Would day after tomorrow suit you, too? Give me a call. Maybe you could meet us there."

He drew out his wallet and a pen. "Here's my card. One

of those numbers will get me. And I'll write down the address of the apartment."

"Don't bother. If it's that same place on the East Side, I've probably been there more times than you. My picture's hanging beside the window. Least, that's where it used to hang." He hesitated and, with the most interest he'd yet shown, asked, "DiPietro, you said?"

"Hal DiPietro, from DiPietro Gallery. You know him?"

"Used to bounce him on my knee."

"Really?" Elliott cocked his head at the image that conjured up. "Has he seen your work lately? You know, it might appeal to him. And since you're between galleries right now . . ."

He saw Gottfried stiffen and gave a conciliatory shrug. "He's having an opening tomorrow evening. Why don't you drop by? Everybody connected with Nauman's gallery shows will be there. Maybe we can all talk?"

Gottfried reached for his bottle. "I might just do that."

A light rain was falling as they emerged from Gottfried's basement studio and walked toward Sixth Avenue to catch a cab uptown.

"Will he come, do you think?" Sigrid asked.

"Probably. From the amount of stuff he's got there, I'd say he's been between galleries for years, poor old guy. Artists like Gottfried are always looking for one more show, one more chance to click with the right people, one more chance at the brass ring."

"What do you really think of his work?"

"What I saw looked pretty solid. A bit too redolent of the fifties perhaps, but it has a mature economy and a hell of lot more serenity than you'd expect from a guy with his attitude. Who knows? DiPietro might like it, too. These late bloomings of underground reputations can have considerable appeal."

Without warning, he let out a sudden piercing whistle and waved wildly to a cruising cab, which immediately plunged across two lanes of heavy traffic and squealed to a stop on the damp pavement in front of them. Buntrock opened the door and Near Eastern music cascaded from at least four speakers as they got in out of the rain.

"Christopher and West," he shouted above the music.

Nodding, the driver dived back into the surging traffic and accelerated up bumpy, potholed Sixth Avenue so fast that they were tossed around on the back seat like two sailors in a hurricane.

Alone in his studio, Rudy Gottfried stuck Buntrock's card into the breast pocket of his paint-stained coveralls and walked unsteadily over to a cluttered corner. He had to move stretcher frames and several rolls of canvas to clear space in front of an old green curtain. Behind the curtain was a shallow recess crammed with dust-covered paintings. The light was poor in that corner, and liquor so befuddled his senses that it took him a few minutes to find the picture he wanted.

Eventually he pulled one out, wiped it off carefully back and front with a paint rag from his back pocket, cleared his large studio easel of the work in progress, and set it up there.

He could not remember the last time he'd looked at this picture, and his surly face became almost tender as he studied it for some minutes, reconnecting with its familiar swirls and rhythms. Then he lurched over to the drafting table. His glass seemed to have disappeared, but he didn't care. He tilted the bottle straight up and drank deeply.

The picture. One of the maligned ones.

He went back to it, touched it gently, as a father might touch the cheek of a beloved son.

"Damn you, DiPietro," he muttered. "God *damn* you! I hope your stinking soul burns in hell."

6

. . . and run the style over the little panel so lightly that you can hardly make out what you first start to do: strengthening your strokes little by little, going back many times to produce the shadows. And the darker you want to make the shadows in the accents, the more times you go back to them.

Cennino Cennini
Il Libro dell' Arte, 1437

To their utter surprise, a crime-scene technician got back to Elaine Albee and Jim Lowry first thing the next morning.

"I'll send the report over, but I thought you'd want to know you got lucky with that slug we dug out of the Fong woman's doorjamb," she told Elaine Albee.

"It's a match to the one that killed her husband?"

"Well, now, I wouldn't want to have to get in the burn box and swear to *that*," the technician hedged. "But it was definitely fired from the same twenty-two that was in Fong's hand when he died, and it's also consistent with the slug the M.E. took out of his head."

"Come on, Dotty," wheedled Jim Lowry, who was on the extension. "Only 'consistent'? You can do better than that."

"For you, doll?" Dotty Vargas was a forthright brunette from the Bronx who'd been hitting on him half humorously for a couple of months now. "Ditch Albee and meet me at Pepe's when you get off, and I'll show you exactly how much better I can do."

"Lay off my partner, Vargas," Elaine Albee growled, and she, too, was only half kidding. "There really were no matching striations?"

"Not on the first slug. The wood on that door's a lot softer than the bone in Fong's head, so the one we got yesterday wasn't messed up as bad. But look on the bright side. Both slugs came from a twenty-two, and the one in the door matches the gun at the scene. Unless the shooter— Fong or whoever—got a twofer deal on twenty-twos, odds are good the same gun shot both bullets. I just don't have any pretty pictures I could show a jury to prove it. Sorry."

But Jim Lowry had picked up on the ambivalence in her tone. "You said 'Fong or whoever.' Does that mean you saw something not totally consistent with suicide?"

She hesitated. "Well . . ."

"What?"

"For you, sweetie, and only because you've got such a cute tush, I went back and reread all my rough notes. If it's starting to feel like a homicide to you guys, there are two points that I *can* swear to. Number one, the barrel wasn't right up against his head. Powder burns show it was fired from a distance of at least two or three inches. I don't have to tell you that most suicides jam the barrel right into their flesh."

"Most, but not all," he agreed. "So what's number two?"

"The gun was wiped clean."

"Wait a minute, Vargas," Elaine objected, leafing

through the papers in the case jacket. "Your report said it had a clear set of Fong's prints."

"It did. *One* clear set. No smudges on the barrel, no partials on the stock. You got the pictures there in front of you?"

Jim spread them out on his desk, and Elaine went around to look over his shoulder, the cord of her telephone stretched taut.

"See how he's lying there on the sofa? Everything all nice and neat? His ankles crossed like he's taking a nap? No sign of a struggle, but no sign of a handkerchief, either. I suppose he could have wiped it with his shirt or something—we didn't think to check it for grease—but people getting ready to shoot themselves usually hesitate and think about it a little first. They'll turn the gun over and over in their hands, they'll break it open, check to make sure a bullet's in the chamber. But we're supposed to believe this guy polishes it clean and doesn't smudge it at all when he aims it at his head and pulls the trigger?"

"What about his hand?" asked Elaine. "Any powder residue?"

"Inconclusive."

"You *did* test him, didn't you?" Elaine persisted.

"Listen," Vargas said defensively. "Maybe we weren't as thorough as we could've been, but everybody was treating it like a suicide, pure and simple. Ask Eberstadt. He wasn't bugging us about powder residue."

Yeah, well, they told each other after Elaine had thanked Dotty Vargas and Jim had diplomatically turned down her offer to buy him a drink after work. The only trouble with asking Eberstadt anything was that he didn't work here anymore and somehow neither of them wanted to reach out and touch him at his new posting over in Brooklyn.

They batted it back and forth, reread all his notes, and concluded that Matt Eberstadt had only been going through the motions till his transfer came through. He certainly wasn't looking to turn a suicide into murder.

"And we still don't know if it *is* murder," they reported to Lieutenant Harald. "But somebody could've shot Todd Fong at close range, wiped the gun, then stuck it in his hand. We thought we'd go talk to his wife again, see his parents, then try to hunt up some of his friends."

"Fine," Sigrid said, already reaching for yet another report from the stack in front of her.

It was astonishing how much paper could pile up in two months, thought Sigrid. Ever since the Mollen Report came down, there'd been nothing but ramifications: more guidelines and procedures from the commissioner intended to curtail police corruption and strengthen the integrity of the whole department citywide, more propagandizing "fact sheets" from the Patrolmen's Benevolent Association, "white papers" from Internal Affairs, the mayor, the City Council.

God knows the department's problems needed addressing, but did every assistant-Assistant have to put out a position paper?

She could suffocate beneath their smothering weight. They pulled oxygen out of the very air she breathed, sucked all the moisture from her lungs, would turn her into something equally dry and brittle if she sat here and passively let it happen.

Reacting automatically to survival instincts, Sigrid pulled her wastebasket closer and began to dump in everything that wasn't pertinent to her squad. Out went the polls and surveys and public approval ratings, the self-study results, the self-serving position papers. Yet even when she'd finished, there was still too much paper on her desk. Was this why she'd become a police officer, why she'd worked so hard for her gold shield, why she'd wanted to make lieutenant? So that she could become an administrator who pushed paper through the system all day?

Restless and frustrated, Sigrid leaned back in the chair

and immediately became aware of someone in her open doorway.

Captain McKinnon.

She sat upright and started to rise. He waved her back. "Don't get up. I was just passing. Heard you were back and thought I'd see how it's going."

Uncomfortably, Sigrid knew it was supposed to be the other way around. She should have been in his office yesterday to let him know she was ready to resume her duties.

Her paper-pushing duties.

McKinnon's bulk filled the doorway. A big muscular man with grizzled brown hair and sleepy brown eyes, he could look like a benevolent teddy bear, then tear the hide off you with a few well-chosen words.

This was their first one-on-one meeting since before Nauman's memorial service. In the two years she'd worked for him, he had always made her self-conscious. Nothing new there. As long as she did her job and knew she was doing it competently, she had been able to ignore the feeling that maybe there was something more than boss/subordinate in the tension between them.

But the deck got reshuffled back in February and the cards were now stacked in a different order. McKinnon was no longer merely her boss and nothing more. She had known since October that he had been her long-dead father's partner. In February she'd finally learned that he was also her mother's ex-lover.

Present lover, too? Anne hadn't said and Sigrid wouldn't ask. They were friends again now. That much she knew. In truth, it was all she really wanted to know if she and McKinnon were to maintain any semblance of a working professional relationship.

"Not overdoing, are you?" McKinnon's voice was gruff, as if he, too, were awkwardly searching for a middle ground.

"Just hoping to catch up."

He looked from the overflowing wastebasket to the

mounds of paper still on her desk. "I thought computers were supposed to turn us into a paperless society."

"They'll have to shoot all the copy machines first," Sigrid said bitterly.

He smiled at that and turned his gaze on her. "Don't try to do it all at once, Harald. Maybe you ought to let this stuff ride a little longer and get out on the street for a few days."

Surprised to hear an echo of her own dissatisfaction, Sigrid relaxed unwittingly. "Do you ever miss it?"

"It's why I became a cop."

For a moment, a tentative affinity flickered between them. Then he was gone.

Sigrid sighed and swept everything from Internal Affairs, the PBA, the mayor's office, and the City Council off the edge of her desk onto her already full wastebasket. Paper slid over the sides and puddled around her feet, but she didn't care.

Finally she could see bare glass.

It was a start.

At the back of the Topp Shopp on Fourteenth Street, sweatshirts in varying stages of completion hung from pegs around Georgia Fong's workroom. The young designer had her own assembly line going with cans of spray paint and silk screens. An exhaust system was working overtime to carry off the fumes, but judging from the acrid smell, Elaine Albee doubted if it would meet OSHA standards.

"Switch on the fan if it bothers you," said Georgia Fong, who continued to work after the two detectives arrived. The sweatshirt she wore today was pale green. Baby woodland animals peeked through darker green leaves and colorful flowers to where a fuzzy, genderless human infant lay upon the grass with a yellow butterfly hovering above it.

"I'd take a break, but I need to leave early. The baby's got a little fever, and Todd's mom is keeping her for me. I hate to leave her at day care when she's sick. So what's up?

They know anything about that bullet they took out of my door?"

Elaine nodded. "Looks like it was fired from the same gun that killed your husband."

"Yeah? So Angie's right? Somebody did shoot him?"

"Or he shot at you first," Jim Lowry told her.

Her blond ponytail swung sharply as she jerked around. "Todd shot at me? You serious?"

"You don't think he would?"

She thought about it a minute, then went back to outlining clouds with a fine line of gold metallic paint. "Maybe. Cross him and he could fly off the handle. I even saw him shove Angie once. His very own mother. But go looking for somebody with a gun? And why me? He didn't want us back. Not really. Yeah, he was mad when I walked out, and he was mad when I told him I'd cut his ugly face if he tried to stop me, but jeez! To shoot at me? Maybe hit Julie? Jeez Louise!"

The more she thought about it, the angrier she seemed to become. "If I really thought—"

"Was the gun his?" Jim interrupted.

She was still steamed. "He had a little handgun when we got married. I made him get rid of it when Julie started crawling and climbing up on things. He said he sold it."

"You two were still legally married when he died," said Elaine. "Did you have any sort of marital property that he'd get if you were dead?"

"Not unless you call a couch and a television and a bed I bought and paid for marital property."

"What about insurance?"

"Not a penny." Despite her obvious agitation, she gave the blue cloud she was painting a delicate spritz of gold mist. "I used to have fifty thou on me, but things were so tight back in January, I didn't have the money to keep it up, so I cashed it in."

"What was the name of the company?"

Her pretty forehead furrowed in thought. "Pilot-Life, I

think. But if that bastard . . . ! When I think how really scared I've been since then, worried what'll happen to Julie if I get killed and no insurance to help out . . . My mom's dead, and my sisters, neither one couldn't feed another face without more money. Yeah, Angie would take her, I guess, but they're getting old, and—"

A short fat man halfway down the crowded narrow shop called out, "Hey, Georgia. You got a maternity top for a Mrs. Pratelli?"

"Yeah, Freddy, right here," she called back and lifted a T-shirt from a hook.

Freddy scowled at the two detectives as he took the garment she had personalized with a pink stork that looked more like a flamingo. "Ain't forgetting the lady with the twins is coming back after lunch, are you?"

She put her fist on her hip, and her small chin jutted at an aggressive angle. "So tell me when I ever forgot, okay?"

He went away muttering about socializing on the job, but young Georgia Fong wasn't intimidated. "Ignore him. He just likes to be the big boss."

"We're almost finished anyhow," Jim Lowry told her. "Just for the record, when did you last see your husband?"

She thought hard. "Maybe two weeks before he did it. It was a Saturday. Angie kept Julie so I could do some shopping, and he came by when I was picking her up."

"Did he say anything to you or his parents that might have made you think he was in trouble or thinking of taking his own life?"

"Nothing." Of that she was positive. "He brought Angie a pair of pants he wanted her to hem up for him. And he was bragging that he and Randi—that's his second wife—were getting it on again. As if I gave a damn."

Elaine Albee pretended to look at her notes. "Let's see, now. Your husband was killed between seven-thirty and midnight of March seventeenth. Were you at home that night? Did he try to call you or anything?"

She shook her blond head vigorously. "Nope. Julie and

me, we got home about six-fifteen, and I scooted right in and locked the door and didn't stick my nose out again till after Angie called me the next morning. I was still shook from getting shot at."

If Georgia Fong realized she was being asked about a possible alibi, she didn't show it. Indeed, she paused with her airbrush in mid-stroke. "You really think it was Todd?" They told her it was too soon to know what to think and maybe they'd know more after they talked to Todd's parents.

"Good luck," Georgia said. "Angie and Doug, they both know how Todd never gave me a dime for Julie, never cared whether he saw her or not, but they'll never believe he'd take a chance on hitting Julie."

With the sun so bright and the breeze up from the Hudson so mild, lunch indoors was singularly unappealing. Instead, the two detectives grabbed a couple of burritos at a nearby quick-food window and munched their way westward through the bazaar that Fourteenth Street had become, carefully stepping around street vendors who all but blocked the crowded sidewalks and spread their wares next to the curb on folding tables, on colorful blankets, or on sheets of cardboard laid flat on the filthy sidewalk itself.

Incense and scented oils, remaindered children's books, wind-up plastic teeth and battery-operated dogs, trays full of shiny necklaces and earrings—all were tended by watchful entrepreneurs, many of whom were Third World immigrants striving toward a fingerhold on the still shiny American dream. In colorful ethnic garb, with one eye on potential buyers and the other eye on their particular array of goods, they leaned against signposts and chatted with each other in a half-dozen different languages.

The sidewalks were further obstructed by tall stepladders that overlooked most of the open-fronted shops offering housewares, linens, and cheap clothing. A storekeeper's son or nephew perched atop each ladder, stationed there to spot shoplifters and keep the narrow profits from going home in someone else's pockets.

By the time Jim Lowry and Elaine Albee reached the corner of Eighth Avenue, it seemed silly to take a bus for only ten short blocks. Besides, the siren voice of ice cream was calling to Lowry from a stand on the corner.

"Come on, Lainey," he coaxed. "One little cone. You'll have it walked off before you finish eating."

Elaine Albee wasn't totally persuaded that ten blocks equaled two scoops of maple pecan, but who could resist on such a beautiful spring day?

The Penn Station South apartment complex where Doug and Angie Fong lived was on the southwest edge of the garment district and was part of an urban renewal cooperative underwritten by the International Ladies' Garment Workers Union.

"I was a cutter for forty years," said Doug Fong, when Elaine asked if they'd ever worked in the industry. "And Angie was a presser. We met at an ILGWU rally. She's always been my little union maid."

His wife smiled at them from the hallway beyond the living room even though she'd probably heard the ancient pun a thousand times.

"And this must be Julie," said Elaine, crossing to get a good look at the lovely blond child who lay on Angie Fong's shoulder and looked back at her with fever-heavy blue eyes.

"I was just going to see if she's ready for her nap," Mrs. Fong said and continued on down the hall, crooning to her granddaughter as Mr. Fong invited them to sit, and what about a nice cup of tea? Angie had just brought his in, and he was sure it wouldn't take but a minute to get the kettle boiling again.

"No, thank you," they said.

They knew he was almost seventy, but he was still a handsome man. A little stooped in the shoulders, his button-down collar was loose around his stringy neck as if he'd shrunk some since buying the faded blue shirt he wore; but the bones of his face were good, and his thin white hair retained a few strands of gold.

Although the apartment was scrupulously tidy, everything looked so old and shabby and the walls were so badly in need of paint that Elaine found herself wondering irrelevantly just how far her own union-negotiated pension would stretch in that distant future when she retired. And just as irrelevantly, she wondered again if Lieutenant Harald really had inherited the millions that rumor said she had.

Angie Fong slipped back into the living room and joined her husband on the worn sofa. Slender if no longer supple, blond hair faded to a sandy gray, deep wrinkles around her mouth and eyes, she still carried herself like a woman at ease with her own beauty. Automatically Doug Fong's hand reached for hers, and in that instant the two detectives caught a glimpse of how attractive the couple must have been in the flush of their youth.

"Georgia called us a few minutes ago," said Mrs. Fong. "We're so grateful that you're investigating Todd's murder."

"Now, wait a minute," said Jim Lowry. "We don't know yet that it *is* murder."

"But Georgia said that whoever shot at her used the same gun. Doesn't that prove it?"

"No, ma'am. Didn't your daughter-in-law tell you that there's still the possibility that your son fired both shots?"

From the way Mrs. Fong's shoulders suddenly slumped, they knew that the Fongs had indeed been told.

Doug Fong patted his wife's hand and faced them defiantly. "If you won't do your job, then we'll hire a private investigator to do it for you. Todd didn't shoot at Georgia and Julie, and he didn't shoot himself, either."

Elaine Albee's voice was gentle. "Mr. Fong, I know it must hurt to think your only child could do something like

this, but look at it from our perspective. His third marriage
was down the sewer, he'd been fired from his job, he
seemed to be going nowhere. There was alcohol in his
bloodstream, the gun was fired at close range, and his were
the only fingerprints on it. I'm sorry, but these really are
the classic elements of suicide. We have to go on more than
just your feelings as parents. Did your son have enemies?
Was he mixed up in something dangerous? Why are you so
sure he was killed?"

Husband and wife looked at each other a long moment;
then Mrs. Fong began to speak, haltingly at first, then with
shamed self-recrimination.

"Todd didn't—He wasn't—He was such a beautiful
baby. And even after he was grown—did you ever see a
picture of him?"

Elaine shook her head, unwilling to tell his mother that
the only picture she'd seen of Todd Fong was taken after
he'd been dead several hours.

Mrs. Fong immediately rushed over to an array of
framed photographs atop their old-fashioned television con-
sole. "This is from when he and Georgia got married."

Elaine tilted the frame so that Jim Lowry could see.
"Very handsome," she said.

And he really was, she thought. Georgia Fong was a
pretty young woman, but despite her clear-eyed youth and
brash freshness, her husband had been more attractive. Nature had taken the best of his parents' features and com-
bined them to make one sexy-looking hunk. His smile was
warm and open, his blond hair was much shorter than
Georgia's, but fell in softer waves. Hard to believe that he
was almost forty when this picture was made. Except for a
jaded puffiness around his deep blue eyes, he looked closer
to thirty.

"He was such a beautiful little boy and could be so
sweet, I guess we must have spoiled him. He liked to have
his way, and if he didn't get it— He wouldn't mean to be
naughty but he was so high-spirited he couldn't seem to

help himself. He'd lash out with his mouth or his fists without thinking. He'd always be sorry afterward. Sometimes I think it was all my fault for not staying home after he was born."

"Now, now," said Doug Fong, patting her hand.

"No, it's true." Hopeless tears filled her eyes. "I know it's true. But back then we thought we'd be better off with two paychecks. We wanted to give him so much, and it seemed like the more we gave, the more he needed. In the end we couldn't give him enough."

"He got in with the wrong crowd," said her husband.

"Started taking things—"

"Got in fights—"

"The first time he was arrested for drugs, my heart was in my mouth."

"He never spent a night in jail, though," Doug Fong told them with something very nearly like pride. "We always managed to get him off with fines and warnings."

"Oh, but the lawyers!" Mrs. Fong moaned. "It's a sin what they charge. Worse than doctors. We're still paying for that last time."

"That bitch Randi!" muttered her husband.

Bewildered, Lowry and Albee stared at them.

Angie Fong clucked at his choice of words, but not his assessment of her ex-daughter-in-law. "When Todd and Georgia broke up, Randi wanted him to move back in with her. She's no good, that girl. She's the one who first gave Todd cocaine. Up till then, the only time he got a little high was on beer or maybe smoking marijuana."

"We tried to get him to stay here with us till he could get back on his feet," said Mr. Fong, "but he wouldn't. Afraid we'd be criticizing him all the time. Angie couldn't stand the idea of him moving in with Randi, so we got him a place two blocks over. They call it an efficiency, but it's really just one big room with a bath tacked on."

"And she kept going around there, trying to get him back," said his wife.

"You think she's the one who killed him?" asked Jim Lowry, who was becoming a little impatient at this tale that was going nowhere.

"Oh, no!" Mrs. Fong exclaimed. "They were thick as thieves. That's the trouble. You see, Todd was here late that afternoon to bring his laundry. He'd been drinking. He needed money. I—Doug—we tried to talk to him."

"I lost my temper." Mr. Fong's eyes dropped, as if ashamed of what he had to tell them. "I told him how was he ever going to get a job if he didn't straighten up? I gave him fifty dollars, but I told him that was it. If he didn't give up the beer, he'd never get another cent out of us."

"Of course, he didn't really mean it," said Mrs. Fong, "but Todd lost his temper too. He said if that's what we wanted, fine. He didn't care that much about beer and Randi was bringing over some coke that night and they'd get high on that."

By now she was clutching her husband's hands convulsively, but he didn't seem to notice. Tears streamed down her lovely face.

"I went over the next day to take back his clean clothes. I was the one who found him, you see. I expected to see them both passed out on his bed, but you know what I found." Her voice trembled, and she dabbed at her eyes with a tissue. "It put Randi right out of my mind, and I called Doug."

"First we thought like you police officers," said Mr. Fong, picking up the narrative. "Thought he must have done it to himself. But then about two weeks later Randi came to see us. She'd just heard and she said it couldn't be. She saw him that morning and called him again about seven-thirty that night to tell him she'd got enough coke for them to party all weekend. She said he was laughing, told her to come on over, he'd be waiting for her. But when she got there around ten, she said she knocked and knocked and he never came to the door to let her in."

Mrs. Fong had regained control of herself. "She said she

went back to her own place and she was so mad at Todd for standing her up that she used all the cocaine that night herself. If her girlfriend didn't come in and call an ambulance, she might've died. They sent her to a detox center and it was two weeks till she got out and came looking for Todd and that's when she heard he was supposed to have shot himself."

She stretched out her thin hand and implored them. "Please! Go talk to her. She'll tell you. That's why we know he didn't pull that trigger himself. Not with Randi Jurgen coming to bring him cocaine."

7

And in general . . . you may suit your fancy. For one thing will teach you another, both by experience and by theoretical understanding. The reason is that every profession is fundamentally skilled and pleasant. God helps those who help themselves, and contrariwise the same.

Cennino Cennini
Il Libro dell' Arte, 1437

Late afternoon shadows darkened the nondescript high brick wall on a street of run-down buildings at the western edge of Greenwich Village. Halfway down the block was number 42½, a sturdy wooden gate that could have used a fresh coat of brownish green paint. The brass numbers were so tarnished that they almost disappeared into the dark paint. There was nothing to indicate a private residence here, which suited Sigrid just fine.

She slipped her key into the inconspicuous lock, let herself into the tiny walled garden, then locked the gate behind her.

A paved walk lined with narrow beds of herbs curved past a dogwood tree in full bloom. Beneath the tree sat a small marble statue of Eros that her housemate, Roman Tramegra, had lugged home from somewhere last summer when they first began sharing this apartment at the rear of a commercial building that faced the next street. With days beginning to be warmer, the naked little Eros didn't look quite so uncomfortable as back in February when he'd had snow up to his chin more days than not.

The apartment formed a rough L around the small garden. The kitchen and maid's quarters occupied the short arm of the L, and that was Roman Tramegra's domain. Sigrid had the master bedroom and bath, living room, and dining room. In theory, they were supposed to share only the kitchen. In practice, Roman had not only appointed himself chief cook and bottle-washer, he had also decorated the living room with masses of healthy green plants, and he kept bringing in eccentric dining room chairs that he scavenged from the streets of the city.

Sigrid thought that one such chair was probably quite enough, but since she'd brought home the first one, a massive armchair whose hand rests were carved lion heads, she could hardly cast aspersions on rococo carved grapevines or brass dragon feet. Besides, after a good cleaning and waxing, he gave each chair a deep red velvet cushion so that they all went together amicably enough.

She had hoped to have a couple of quiet hours to herself before dressing to go out again, but as she poured herself a large glass of water, her housemate appeared with a thick computer manual and several arcane questions to which she had no answers.

Roman Tramegra was actually her mother's friend, but in the eight months that they'd shared his godmother's sister's garden apartment, she had become genuinely fond of this large, soft, self-centered man. True, there were times when he treated her rather as an uncle might treat a niece who wasn't quite up to the family standards; but overall, the arrangement was working out much better than she ever expected.

Except when he tried to involve her in his magpie enthusiasms.

Such as now.

No matter how much she denied it, she couldn't seem to dislodge his belief that she was knowledgeable about computers.

"It's like a car, Roman," she explained as he tried to interest her in corn chips and a cayenne-and-artichoke dip. "I turn a key, I can steer and brake, but I don't know what's under the hood and I don't really want to know. All I care about is, can it take me where I want to go? If something as complicated as the Indy Five Hundred comes up, my sergeant runs it for me."

Roman Tramegra brightened. "Do you suppose I could call him and—"

"No," she said firmly. "Besides, you're using a software program that's basically geared for word processing, and mine is a special spreadsheet for statistical data and records."

"But surely all computers must have some elemental procedures in common," Roman persisted. "You're so much better at understanding instructions. We could start at the beginning of the manual—"

"Sorry," she said, hastily swallowing the last of her water, "but I just stopped by to get my gym bag. If I hurry, I can get a good swim in before the evening rush."

Five minutes later she was out the door.

Gloomily, Roman flipped through the instruction manual. It was full of boldfaced *c*'s and *a*'s and colons and backslashes. The index carried a listing for "troubleshooting," but it didn't explain why he could be typing along and suddenly all his words would capriciously reduce themselves to a vertical column of letters along the extreme right edge of the screen.

Sigrid had compared computers to cars. If so, he told himself, then he was probably trying to drive a Jaguar with no more than the mastery of a dirt bike to assist him.

And then he remembered a friend who'd once told him of an automotive class she'd taken at a community college. "They mentioned internal combustion, but basically what we learned was how to check the oil, change the filters, and jump a battery," she'd said. "They called it Powder-Puff Mechanics."

Roman reached for the Yellow Pages. Surely somewhere in this city someone must be offering the equivalent of Powder-Puff Computing.

The day wound down in frustration for Jim Lowry.

After promising Doug and Angie Fong that he and Elaine Albee would certainly speak to their ex-daughter-in-law before letting their son's death stay on the record as suicide, they were unable to put their hands on the woman. They did call the detox center over on the East Side, but they were shunted from one extension to another before someone was willing to dispense with bureaucratic red tape and admit that yes, Ms. Randi Jurgen had "voluntarily" committed herself for treatment on the morning of March 8 after a touch-and-go night in Bellevue's ER.

And yes, she'd been there for exactly fourteen days.

But when they went by her apartment in Alphabet City, she didn't respond to their knock. The two teenagers who were entering the next apartment just shrugged, made a couple of smart-ass remarks, then said they hadn't seen her in a couple of days.

"But it's not like we'd hang out with somebody that old," they said.

The Fongs had told them that Randi was thirty-one.

Which grimly reminded Elaine of time's passage and put

her in a glum mood. It also effectively ended Jim's carefully laid schemes for the evening.

Departmental regulations frowned on in-house romances, but there was nothing that said partners couldn't be friends and catch dinner or a movie together.

He'd hoped to segue from a sandwich after work to an old Jeanette MacDonald–Nelson Eddy movie that was playing at one of the revival houses. Although Elaine refused to let their partnership move into forbidden waters, she was crazy about musicals of the thirties and forties and generally made them an exception to her own self-imposed regulations about after-hours involvement.

Not tonight, though. Tonight, she told him, she was going straight home to start studying for her sergeant's exam again.

Frustrated, he called Dotty Vargas. "Still feel like having that drink?" he asked.

"My place or yours?" she purred.

8

When you have done the draperies, trees, build-ings, and mountains . . . you must come to paint-ing the faces . . . for faces of young people . . . the flesh colors [should be tempered] with yolk of a town hen's egg, because those are whiter yolks than the ones which country or farm hens pro-duce; those are good, because of their redness, for tempering flesh colors for aged and swarthy persons.

Cennino Cennini
Il Libro dell' Arte, 1437

"I don't know why I keep trying to educate your eye," said an angry young man as he stormed from the elevator and almost plowed into Sigrid, who was waiting to get on.

The man wore thigh-high black leather boots, an over-sized black sweater, and a thoroughly annoyed expression. Sigrid heard him say, "Don't you get it? His art reflects the joyless reality of modern New York."

"For God's sake, Justin. I'm a systems analyst," said his companion as she paused to zip up her blue sateen Mets jacket before following him out into the chilly night.

"I live with joyless reality all day," she told amused by-standers plaintively. "Why the hell should we pay eight thousand dollars to hang more of it on our bedroom wall? Would somebody tell me that?"

Belatedly, Sigrid realized that DiPietro Gallery was not holding the only opening in the building that evening. The polished bronze-and-marble Art Deco lobby bustled with the coming and going of art enthusiasts, and her elevator seemed to stop at every floor as gallery hoppers got on and off. Buzzwords and scraps of art chat bounced off the walls like cartoon balloons.

"—so much ambivalence in him, you can't really pin it down."

"Of course, appropriation is only his *interim* strategy—"

"—so superficial? Exactly! But remember: there's more to superficiality than meets the eye."

"—and even a blind man could see the intended symbolism of her flashlights and tennis balls, but it just doesn't sing for me."

"—clearly invites an aural and retinal relationship, a polysemous tissue of codes, if you will, yet the dwarfed dimensions of the physical negate the—"

"It sucks, man. Know what I mean?"

In the seventh-floor hallway, she passed through clusters of laughing, talking people who had spilled over from the galleries on this floor. All of them seemed to hold stemmed plastic champagne flutes and to be munching on whole grain crackers with little chunks of cheese.

As she hesitated in the doorway of the DiPietro Gallery, she caught sight of Elliott Buntrock over by a far wall. His long, bony face brightened when he recognized her, and in that split second, Sigrid's throat closed up.

Nauman had been as tall as Buntrock and she had topped his shoulder, so they never had trouble spotting each other

in a crowd. From the very beginning, even back when she
was still assuring her wary heart that he meant nothing to
her, there had always come that moment of connection
when their eyes locked and she felt the magnetic pull between them.

Swallowing hard, she seized a glass of champagne from
the tray of a passing waiter and drank it quickly, wondering
if the day would ever come when she could step into an art
gallery and not be haunted by the times she'd met Nauman
after work for a quick walk-through before dinner.

The ending lines from one of Millay's heartbroken son-
nets came to her:

> And entering with relief some quiet place
> Where never fell his foot or shone his face
> I say, "There is no memory of him here!"
> And so stand stricken, so remembering him.

The champagne was too warm and sweet as ginger ale,
but when Elliott Buntrock reached her side with a second
glass, she accepted it anyhow and drank it gratefully as he
steered her across the gallery, making small talk about the
shows at which he'd stopped on his way up to this floor.

"I just got here a few minutes ago myself," he said, "but
I saw everything when they were hanging it yesterday."

Sigrid almost never made friends easily, yet Elliott had
become as comfortable to be with as a slightly precocious
cousin. She found him intelligent, knowledgeable, amusing,
and kind. Moreover, because he'd been Nauman's friend
and had been with him those last few days in California,
she could speak to him of Nauman without feeling raw-
nerved and self-conscious. But tonight what she really appreciated was how an acknowledged art expert with such
free-wheeling eclectic tastes could accept her preference
for the late Gothic without condescension or questions.

He did not offer to tour her past all the large paintings
that filled the walls. Unlike Nauman, who never quit trying

to bring her into the twentieth century before it became the twenty-first, Elliott felt no need to proselytize.

"Do you want to meet the artist?" he asked, gesturing toward a hairy young man surrounded by people at the far side of the gallery. "He's a jerk, but his stuff pleases the crowd, and some of it's quite clever within a narrow range."

Sigrid glanced about her. Buck David's pictures had been given the largest of the three rooms. They were full of images appropriated from the past and reassembled in satiric juxtaposition, but at least the works seemed to be paint on canvas and not rows of hanged teddy bears dangling from yellow police barriers such as she'd glimpsed when her elevator stopped at the sixth floor.

"Oh, let's not bother him," she murmured.

Elliott grinned. "Right. But you do see how nicely this space works?"

Sigrid looked, not really sure what exactly she was supposed to see working. DiPietro's three rooms weren't quite as large as Kohn and Munson's but otherwise this gallery seemed much the same as the other to her. Same off-white walls, same light oak flooring, same track lighting.

"The traffic pattern for moving from room to room is well thought out," Elliott said. "Of course, they've been right here for a thousand years. You're bound to learn something about viewer flow-through in that length of time. Now come and let me introduce you to DiPietro and—"

"Ms. Harald?" A muscular middle-aged man of Japanese descent approached with toothy smile and outstretched hands.

"Kenji Itoyama. We met last autumn at Piers Leyden's exhibit." His smile faded, his voice became solemn. "And again at the memorial service, but you will not remember me among so many who were there. Such a loss for you. For all of us."

His hands remained clasped around hers.

"Thank you, Mr. Itoyama."

Unable to place the man, she glanced at Elliott, who came smoothly to her rescue.

"Ken's curator of sculpture over at the Friedinger Museum," he said.

Sigrid smiled and tried to extricate her hand, but Itoyama continued to pump it.

"So sad too that a man of Oscar Nauman's talent never turned to sculpture."

"Oh, but he did," she said.

In Nauman's Connecticut house was a wall that caught the morning sun at an angle. A narrow ledge held small metal sculptures welded or cast by his friends, and Nauman had hung the wall above with a dozen or more deeply carved plaster prints that were three-dimensional variations on some of his favorite abstract etchings. As sunlight moved across the wall, the planes shifted and changed and played their own variations on the works.

"Of course, you may not consider plaster prints the same as sculpture?" she asked doubtfully.

"Yes, yes, yes!" He squeezed her hand with even more enthusiasm. "And the Friedinger would be honored to preserve and exhibit them."

At that, Sigrid pulled her hand away and glanced up at Elliott. "You must excuse us, Mr. Itoyama," she said pleasantly. "I'm afraid we're keeping some people waiting."

"Certainly. It was a privilege to see you again." He reached once more for her free hand, but she had tucked it into the pocket of her deep purple skirt and firmly kept it there.

"Sorry about that," Elliott muttered in her ear as they moved away from the man.

Her gray eyes looked up at him wanly. "People know everything Nauman ever did, don't they? Even his peripheral work?"

"I'm afraid so. He wasn't particularly reticent about his interests. He probably mentioned the plaster prints in passing and Itoyama filed the information away for future reference. Guys like him don't forget. Fact of life."

"I know I shouldn't keep being surprised." She handed her empty glass to a waiter and shook her head when he offered to refill it. "He's not the first vulture to come circling. I suppose he won't be the last. I just haven't gotten used to them yet."

"Some society offenders who might well be underground?"

"They'd none of 'em be missed," she agreed, succinctly mimicking the Lord High Executioner's precise tonal inflection.

"Well, the people here will be different," he promised, pleased that he'd made her smile. "I've warned them they'd better be on their best behavior or I'd put *them* on the list."

He scanned the crowd which had begun to thin a bit as the dinner hour approached. "Ah, there's Hester. Perhaps she knows where the others are."

Hester Kohn was stunning that evening in a deep red paisley silk suit corded in gold. Her dark hair was brushed back from her face and clusters of gold stars swung from her ears.

The two women had first met just before Christmas, during the investigation of a murder at the Breul House. Had it been six months earlier, Sigrid knew she would have been utterly intimidated by the woman's style and verve and blatant sexuality. But by then she was acquiring a smattering of verve herself, not to mention a sexual appetite she hadn't quite suspected until Nauman came along. After the investigation was over, it seemed silly to maintain formality when Nauman constantly referred to each of them by her first name.

At the time of his death, they had spoken once or twice on the phone, but this was their first meeting since the memorial service. Happily for Sigrid, who still had difficulty with public displays of affection, Hester didn't make a big deal out of it.

With a quick air kiss as she touched her cheek to Sigrid's, Hester said, "You look great—purple is definitely your color!" She chortled when Elliott asked where Hal DiPietro was.

"Hiding out in Victor's office," she answered gleefully. "You should have been here for the fireworks when Buck David and his girlfriend arrived. Absolutely everything that could go wrong with this opening has. Hal managed to cancel the catalog order by mistake, and the printer had to do such a rush job that half the titles are wrong. Then sometime after the champagne was put in to chill yesterday, the refrigerator blew a fuse or came unplugged or something and nobody noticed till the waiters got here tonight and were ready to start putting the bottles in ice buckets. They sent out for more ice, but there wasn't time to chill it down properly, and as you may have noticed," she added tartly, "it's not exactly Dom Pérignon. The stuff's undrinkable unless it's ice cold. Valerie Braydon is ready to strangle Hal with her bare hands."

As they neared the front entrance, an attractive young black woman seemed to be making conciliatory noises toward a clearly irate mid-thirtyish white woman.

"More problems, Mrs. Parsons?" Hester asked as the other woman flounced back toward the room where Buck David continued to hold court.

The younger woman sighed. "Ms. Braydon just wanted to make sure Mr. DiPietro understands that she's stopping payment on her check for the catalog."

"That's in case he was the only one in the building who missed it when she was screaming it at seven o'clock tonight," Hester told Elliott and Sigrid. Belatedly, she remembered to introduce them to Hal DiPietro's new administrative assistant, B'Nita Parsons.

Elliott was sympathetic. "Initiation by fire?" he asked when it was his turn to shake her hand. "Too bad your first opening here didn't turn out so hot."

"Oh, it was hot enough," Mrs. Parsons contradicted in a

wry drawl. "That was another part of the problem. Even in Alabama, we know champagne's not supposed to be served at room temperature. From now on, I'm putting that refrigerator in my job description."

They laughed and left her to it.

Victor Germondi's American gallery was at the end of the hall. Even though the walls were hung with representative samples of the best of postwar European art, there was an Old World air to the small gallery itself, a feeling of richness and permanence.

The floor was of dark parquet, punctuated with antique oriental rugs. Instead of the ubiquitous white paint found in other galleries, walls and dividers were covered with ivory linen. The lighting was more than adequate, but somehow softer.

The few visitors who remained spoke in hushed tones as if at a library or museum, and Sigrid felt an instinctual loosening and relaxing of tension as she and Elliott followed Hester Kohn across the room.

With their backs to the open doorway, three men stood before an abstract sculpture on a pedestal. The elder, more rotund man was discussing the piece with elaborate hand gestures while the silver-bearded middle-aged man and a third person with an odd topknot of stiff dark curls gave him their attention.

In their dark suits and pin-striped shirts, the two older men could have been stockbrokers or bankers. The younger was more conventionally arrayed in a formal black cutaway, black satin shirt, white satin tie, and tight black jeans tucked into soft cuffed boots.

A small spotlight in the ceiling made the steel sculpture glow like a piece of polished silver jewelry, and Elliott moved toward it with interest.

"A Brancusi?" he asked. "I'm not familiar with that one."

"Ah, Elliott!" The older man turned and came toward

them smiling and was immediately introduced to Sigrid as Victor Germondi.

"A great pleasure," he said, kissing her hand with such quick grace that there was no time to wonder how to respond before her hand was shaken confidently by the sleek and silvery Hal DiPietro and then, shyly, by young Arnold Callahan, whose alert brown eyes and ridiculous haircut reminded Sigrid of someone, although for a moment, she couldn't think who.

Then she remembered a friendly little chocolate poodle owned by one of her North Carolina grandmother's friends. CoCo had that same thin face and exact coiffure. Put a little pink bow in Arnold Callahan's topknot of wiry dark curls and he and CoCo could pose as brother and sister.

Elliott had assured her that tonight's meeting was less for formal business than to acquaint her with the gallery owners who needed her cooperation and consent if they were to carry out the plans Nauman and old Jacob Munson had begun for ancillary shows in conjunction with the Arnheim's major effort.

Now, as host, Victor Germondi led her over to his latest acquisition. "And Elliott must tell me what he thinks of my Brancusi."

Either Elliott had warned them or Germondi seemed to know instinctively how much she disliked being the center of attention, because the conversation remained amiably unfocused. It bounced from art to Hal DiPietro's jinxed evening and his efficient jewel of an assistant back to art again, and Sigrid was free to join in or not, as she chose.

Germondi's own assistant, a small scholarly-looking man with a frail build and rimless glasses, tactfully herded the last two gallery hoppers out into the hall, closed the double glass doors, then brought out a tray of exquisite canapés and a bottle of dry white wine, perfectly chilled. It was poured into the thinnest crystal goblets Sigrid had ever seen.

"Hand-blown near Pisa," Germondi said when she admired them.

"Do they have a New York outlet? My grandmother will be eighty next year and I've been trying to think of something special to give her."

"Hand-blown *last* century," he amended regretfully.

"Oh," she said, feeling foolish.

"But I know a store in Florence that specializes in antique glass. If you wish . . . ?"

Sigrid shook her head. "It would be much more than I could afford."

"More than you could afford? Ha!" exclaimed Hal DiPietro. "By the time you finish selling all of Oscar Nauman's pictures, one day's interest on the money could probably buy you the whole damn store."

"For God's sake, Hal!" Hester Kohn almost strangled on her wine, Arnold Callahan's curls bounced upright, and Elliott glared at him.

"Sorry," Hal apologized. He looked at Sigrid sheepishly. "Pay no attention to that man behind the big mouth."

Exasperated, Victor Germondi could only shake his head. Always would Hal blurt out whatever popped into his mind. And the *povera signorina,* he thought, standing there so still and straight. Slender as a young willow in a purple skirt and cropped black jacket, short dark hair that brushed her thin face. Incredible silver eyes. Sad eyes, yet eyes that now measured everyone in the room.

And how should they not measure us? he asked himself. Knowing what we want from her, why should she not be wary? From this time onward, always she will have to weigh the words that she hears, the smiles that will shower upon her. Never again will she be sure if the flattering words, the approving smiles, are for herself alone or for the wealth she controls.

He patted Sigrid's arm sympathetically and said, "Hal is not tactful, but he is right, Lieutenant Harald. Life changes for you now."

"Yes."

There was a moment of awkward silence; then she shrugged and, with a glance that included all of them, said, "But just because I'm having trouble learning to live with it doesn't mean I have to keep complicating your lives, too. I'd like for the shows to go ahead at your galleries just as Nauman planned."

They had not expected to win her full consent so quickly. And certainly not this easily. Even Elliott Buntrock had a grin on his face as the others voiced their pleased surprise.

While Hester Kohn immediately began trying to pin her colleagues down for a strategy session the next day, Sigrid wandered around the small gallery, reading the names on the placards beside each modern painting and sculpture.

Through the open doorway of Victor Germondi's office, she spotted a piece of art that was much more to her liking and went inside to look at it more closely.

Enclosed in a flat glass box affixed to the wall, it appeared to be the central panel of what had probably been a small portable triptych. About sixteen inches high and perhaps a foot wide, the wooden panel had two handmade rusty eyelets on either side where the missing panels had been hinged. The edges were chipped and the wood beneath had darkened with age, but the painting itself glowed.

The richly tooled gold leaf had been laid over a red ground that showed on the surface through fine hairline cracks. In the foreground, an austere green-faced Madonna clasped a dark robe to her throat with one hand while holding the infant Christ with the other. In three-quarter profile, her oddly circular head was bent toward the child and her lovely almond-shaped eyes regarded him with a serene love.

"It may have been painted by Duccio di Buoninsegna, a Sienese master of the fourteenth century," said Victor Germondi from behind her, "or if not by Duccio himself, then certainly by a gifted follower."

"I hope I'm not intruding," Sigrid said. "The door was open and I couldn't resist."

"No one can resist her," Germondi said. "She belonged to my father and he would have sold his soul before giving her up."

"It's been in Victor's family almost two hundred years," said Hal DiPietro.

He and the others had followed Germondi into the office. Hester was familiar with the panel, but it was Elliott's first viewing.

"Exquisite," he said, bending for a closer look. "What grace."

At that moment, Hal DiPietro slapped his forehead dramatically. "God! I must be losing my mind! All that mix-up with the catalog—Victor, I bought you a present. Found it in Dortches last week and meant to give it to you at lunch yesterday. Never mind. I'll be right back," he said and hurried from the office.

Victor signaled with his empty glass to his assistant, who immediately lifted a fresh bottle of wine from the ice bucket and refilled all the other glasses, too.

Between DiPietro's bad champagne and Germondi's excellent wine, Sigrid had drunk just enough to loosen her guard. She sipped again, then gestured toward the six-hundred-year-old picture. "I've never understood why so many Italian Madonnas of that period were painted with gray-green skin. It makes them look almost dead."

Victor Germondi was intrigued by Sigrid's naive observation. "I have never thought of it thus. But you are right. The life tones *have* fled."

"What's left is *terre verte*—green earth," Elliott explained and added parenthetically, "When it's freshly mixed, it even smells like dirt. In the thirteen hundreds, Sienese artists used it to model the underpainting with tone and shadows and then overlaid it with a semitransparent layer of crimson so that the eye blended the two and the brain saw a natural flesh color—a technological solution to the problem of how to mix colors without reducing their brilliance. Unfortunately, the *terre verte* might've been permanent but the crimsons were fugitive. They've faded away until all we have left are the shadows."

For a moment Sigrid's own eyes were shadowed.

"And the darker pink on the cheeks," she asked after an imperceptible pause. "Where it looks like undertaker's rouge?"

"A more stable pigment that was less affected," said Elliott, oblivious to her parallel thoughts.

"But what time takes away, the heart can also restore," said Germondi. "My eyes see the dull green, but my heart knows how beautiful she was when she came fresh from the artist's hand—how pink her face and hands, how blue her robe, how brilliant the gold embroidery on the bands around her face. This is not a mere woman the artist has painted. This is the Mother of God. Her face, her head, her halo—three concentric circles that perfectly echo the Trinity. And all bathed in the radiance of hammered gold."

His eloquent hands sketched a cloud of gold around the Madonna's figure.

"Think what effect she must have had back then! The gloomy stone chapel, then the good priest arrives to say mass. On the bare altar, he places the closed triptych—only a plain brown wooden case from the outside. Then he lights the candles and opens it up and the Queen of Heaven glows like the golden promise of salvation in a world dark with ignorance and sin and man's—"

"Got it!" Hal DiPietro's cheerful voice shattered the spell Germondi had woven around them.

Sigrid turned resentfully, but DiPietro was too intent on presenting his gift to notice.

It was a hefty book, about half the size of an average encyclopedia volume, clothbound in buff-colored buckram with brown leather spine and corners, all tooled in thin gold lines. The title, stamped in gold, was *Sienesische Malerei des 14. Jahrhunderts.*

"Ah," Germondi said appreciatively as he opened it at random and a full-page black-and-white illustration of another fourteenth-century Sienese Madonna appeared, almost a twin to his own.

Sigrid didn't read German, but she was willing to bet that the legend beneath the picture identified it with full Teutonic thoroughness.

Germondi turned to the front of the book. "Leipzig, nineteen-twenty," he read. "These illustrations look like heliographs. All tipped in by hand. Ah, Hal, what a wonderful, beautiful book!"

"It was the day after I got back from the ceremony," DiPietro said proudly. "I was browsing in Dortches, not looking for anything special. But then I saw this and—well, you'd just accepted that award for your father and he was such a scholar of the Trecento."

The older man was so visibly moved that he lapsed into Italian, which Sigrid couldn't begin to follow, but she gathered that it was emotional because the two men suddenly hugged and Elliott, who was fluent in several languages, had a foolish, half-embarrassed grin on his face, too.

"But that's not all," said Hal, taking the book back for a moment. "What's so great about it is that there's an illustration of your Madonna when it was still in—I guess it was your grandmother's family chapel?"

With Hester and Elliott looking over his shoulder, Hal flipped the pages, but all the Madonnas were so superficially alike that it took him several tries to find the right one. Eventually, though, he handed the book back to Germondi. "See?"

"*È vero?*" asked Germondi, who had a tendency to revert to Italian when startled or excited.

But before he could verify it for himself, the door of his gallery was pushed open and B'Nita Parsons said, "Excuse me, Mr. DiPietro, but there's a man—I think he's drunk, and he's making people nervous."

Except for the artist Buck David, the still irate Valerie Braydon, and their entourage, few people remained in the gallery and those few were giving Rudy Gottfried lots of space.

When Hal DiPietro arrived, followed by the others, the artist stood in the archway between the two main rooms like a powerful old bull that hadn't quite decided what—or even whether—to charge. He wore a gray tweed jacket with leather elbow patches that had probably been fashionable in the fifties, a maroon turtleneck from the sixties and faded blue jeans from the seventies. His red-rimmed eyes and thick-tongued speech gave evidence that he had been drinking, yet his rage seemed under tight control as he sneered at Buck David's pictures.

His muttered sneers changed to vocal belligerence the instant he spotted Hal DiPietro.

"The little prince!" he roared.

"Rudy?" said Hal in disbelief.

"The little prince has turned into the old king, by God! Even wearing his silver crown."

"C'mon, Rudy, don't be like this. It's been more than twenty years," said Hal, sounding more like an uncertain twenty-year-old than a confident middle-aged gallery owner.

Gottfried shook his fist at Hal and snarled between clenched teeth, "Tell it to the marines. Or better yet, go over to Greenwood Cemetery and tell Morris Wallender. Go find Ben Slocum's wife and kid and tell them."

Even though the man was clearly in his mid-seventies, so much anger radiated from his burly frame that Hal took a couple of steps back.

Elliott Buntrock moved toward him and said pleasantly, "Maybe you should do this another time, Mr. Gottfried."

The older man turned and glared at him.

Behind her, Sigrid heard Mrs. Parsons calmly say, "Go help him, please, Mr. Levitz." And that muscular young man jumped to obey her quiet order.

Together he and Elliott shepherded the unprotesting Gottfried past the others and out toward the elevator. At the doorway though, Gottfried suddenly wrenched free and drew himself up, hands in pockets.

"Bentcock here says you're dealing in abstraction again," he called to Hal.

Abruptly, he turned his pockets inside out and dozens of slides cascaded to the floor. Gottfried kicked several of them toward Hal, and the white plastic mounts slithered across the bare oak. "Looking at slides today, young prince?"

Then he turned on his heel and lurched past Elliott and Levitz. A moment later they heard the elevator chime and the doors open and close.

"Who was *that?*" asked Mrs. Parsons.

9

*[Verdigris] is very green by itself. And it is manu-
factured by alchemy, from copper and
vinegar. . . . Take care never to get it near any
white lead, for they are mortal enemies in every
respect. Work it up with vinegar. . . . It is beautiful to the eye, but it does not last.*

Cennino Cennini
Il Libro dell' Arte, 1437

A little after two-thirty, Gonzalez tapped on Sigrid's
half-open door. She had worked straight through lunch and
was now a little bleary-eyed as she looked up from the
computer screen.

"Sorry to bother you, Lieutenant," he said hesitantly,
"but you got a personal call on line one."

Guiltily, she remembered that Anne had left a message to
call, so she reached for her phone and punched the blinking
line button. Instead of her mother, however, it was Elliott

Buntrock and his words tumbled into her ear as if he expected to be cut off at any second.

"I'm really sorry to bother you, but it's crazy here at the Arnheim today. The director's called an unscheduled meeting that I absolutely can*not* get out of. I phoned Hester, but she already lent the gallery's key for Oscar's apartment to Hal because I knew I was going to be running a little late. I was supposed to meet him there at two, so when Rudy Gottfried called this morning, I told *him* to come at three. Figured it wouldn't take Hal and me more than forty-five minutes to look at the few things there. That B'Nita Parsons woman says Hal left the gallery at one, but nobody answers Oscar's phone."

"So you want me to meet Gottfried?" asked Sigrid.

"Could you?"

"I suppose," she answered reluctantly. "Did you find out what he was so angry about last night?"

"God, yes! He used to be represented by DiPietro's and it ended in a ghastly mess. That's another reason you should get over there. Look, they're yelling for me again. Call me tonight and I'll tell you all about it."

Before she could press him for details, he was gone.

She sighed, checked her key ring to make sure she had the necessary keys, and finished entering some final bits of data into her computer. A one-on-one session with Rudy Gottfried wasn't how she wanted to spend her afternoon, but at least she'd whittled the stack of paper in her in-tray down to a manageable size.

By the time her cab pulled up before the building where Nauman had kept a small apartment, it was 3:12 and she saw Rudy Gottfried behind the locked glass doors, pacing restlessly up and down the small lobby.

"Aha!" he said as he pushed open the door for her before she could insert the key. "That's why Buntrock didn't answer when I pushed the bell."

A camera case was slung over one muscular shoulder

and two dilapidated portable floodlights with frayed cloth cords were parked over in a corner of the lobby. He had rung every apartment, he told her, until someone more trusting than the average New Yorker had buzzed him in.

His mood was much different this afternoon. At their first meeting, he'd acted surly and suspicious, last night he'd been half drunk and pugnacious. This afternoon, he seemed almost genial, as if he'd forgotten that last night had ever happened.

Sigrid explained Elliott's nonappearance and started to apologize for her tardy substitution.

"No apologies needed, Lieutenant. I'm the one infringing on *your* time."

With some awkward maneuvering of Gottfried's tubular (and very collapsible) floodlight stands and trailing cords, they passed from the nondescript lobby into an equally nondescript self-service elevator.

Gottfried immediately pressed the five button, and Sigrid remembered his telling Elliott that he'd often crashed here in years past, so of course he'd know which floor.

As the elevator rose, she felt her heart begin to sink. This was her first time here since early February, and Nauman had been beside her then. His brown paper sack had held a six-pack of pale ale; hers carried little white boxes from a nearby Chinese restaurant. By the time the elevator reached the fifth floor, they had both been ravenous from the warm, fragrant smells of sesame oil and lobster sauce.

That was the last night they'd ever made love. Although she could almost blank her mind against the pain of his loss, she couldn't *not* remember his hands, his lips, the weight of his body on hers.

One thought still comforted her—their lovemaking that night had not been casual and unthinking. The conference in California was scheduled to last a long weekend, and he and Elliott planned to run on down to San Diego for a couple of days afterward.

"I think I'm missing you already," she'd whispered in

the darkness, and he had made slow love to her all over again.

Next day, she'd driven him to the airport to meet Elliott and fly out to California.

She would never pretend that she'd felt a premonition because she knew she had not. But she had known that he'd be gone six days, the longest they'd yet been separated since October. And although she usually shied away from public displays of affection, their parting kiss had been intense and bittersweet before he got out of the car and walked into the terminal.

The elevator slid to a stop and Sigrid picked up one of the floodlights while Gottfried struggled to keep both dangling cords from getting shut in the doors.

As always, it took her a moment to figure out which key turned which of the two locks. Eventually, though, she held the apartment door for Gottfried and his gear. Inside, the curtains were open and late afternoon sun cut through the dusty windows, but the air had that musty, closed-up smell of emptiness.

"Ah!" said Gottfried. "Everything's just where it always was."

He set down the floodlights and went immediately to the abstract blue-and-yellow picture hanging to the right of the windows. "Holds up, don't you think?"

(*"You never forget a one of them, Siga. Funny how they mellow."*)

For all of his faults, thought Sigrid, at least Gottfried wasn't asking her to give the picture back. Some artists had. "It was only a loan," they said, pretending Nauman hadn't given them something of his in exchange. Indeed several people who'd known Nauman personally had actually asked for certain pictures by title. "It would be a memento, something to remember him by," they said blandly. "No harm trying," admitted one cheerful opportunist when she said no, she would not lend him the keys so he could "run up to Connecticut and pick out something that had personal significance."

It hadn't taken her long to start referring all callers to Marc Livingston.

While Rudy Gottfried reconnected with his picture, Sigrid went over to the kitchen alcove, switching on lights as she went. Livingston said that he'd had Nauman's cleaning woman clean out the refrigerator and throw away all the perishables.

And Mrs. Bayles had gone over to Vanderlyn and boxed up everything in his office there. Three cartons now sat beside the kitchen arch next to one of those large reddish brown cardboard portfolios.

She untied the string and looked inside to see a sheaf of prints and drawings.

Something else for the appraisers to put a price on.

She retied the portfolio and lifted a flap on one of the boxes. Framed photographs lay on top. A boyish Nauman and a middle-aged Jacob Munson stood arm in arm with a man she didn't recognize. Hester Kohn's father? Nauman had been so much older than she that this picture could have been taken before she was born.

Here was a color snap of Nauman with a young black woman, a red-haired man, and a younger, stockier Gottfried in someone's studio. More photographs of more strangers, taken in the seventies and eighties, by the looks of the clothes and hairstyles. Beneath the photographs were books and notebooks.

In the next box was his paint-daubed lab coat, and she abruptly closed the lid. She would have to make a decision about his clothes one of these days. Pack them up for the Salvation Army or something.

One of these days.

Not today.

Gottfried began to set up the rickety floodlights, snaking the cords over to an outlet beside the sleeper sofa.

In the hall beside the kitchenette, the bathroom door was

half open. She switched on the light and saw that the cleaning woman had been busy here, too. No crumpled towels or washcloths draped with Nauman's usual abandon over the shower curtain rod, no clutter of toiletries around the sink. Only her own spare toothbrush in the holder, and it hung there alone.

He'd taken his to California.

With blurred eyes, she dropped the forlorn toothbrush into the wastebasket under the sink, then realized that one of the thin cotton robes Anne had sent her from Egypt still hung behind the door next to Nauman's blue terry-cloth robe. She held the nubbly cloth against her hot face and breathed in a faint smell of soap and aftershave and the rich fragrance of his pipe tobacco. For a long moment she gave herself up to memory, unable to resist the pain of knowing that this last lingering bit of the physical him would soon fade, too.

Carefully, even as she told herself that she was being unforgivably morbid, she blotted her eyes on his robe, then wrapped it inside hers and went into the bedroom to find a bag in which to carry them home.

Here too the curtains were open, but except for some books and art journals on the bedside table and pictures on every wall, the room was now as impersonal as a hotel room, which, after all, was how Nauman himself considered this apartment. His real home was in Connecticut; this was just a convenient place to sleep during the week.

The cleaning woman had stripped the bed down to the mattress, then folded the sheets and blankets and big puffy comforter and piled them on the end of the bed, along with the pillows.

At least Sigrid assumed she had left them neatly piled. But the comforter was bulky and had a silky finish that resisted neatness, and it and the pillows had slipped off the edge of the bed.

Sigrid found a bag in the closet for the two robes, then set them on the dresser and went over to pick up the bed linens that had fallen down next to the wall.

As she started to lift the long pillows, the bottom one seemed to be caught on something, and she gave it an impatient yank.

A hand and arm flew up and thumped against the wall.

Startled, she dropped the pillows and jerked back.

In the narrow floor space between the bed and the wall, half-hidden by the bedclothes, someone lay crumpled and motionless, his black shoes toward her.

Male. Short white hair matted with blood.

She pulled back the comforter to see if he was still breathing and a small marble statuette clunked heavily to the floor.

At that point, professional training took over. She dropped the comforter and instead of trying to get to his neck or wrist, she pressed her fingers against the pulse points in his ankles.

Nothing.

Taking great pains to disturb nothing else, she stretched to her full height till she could make out the face that lay on its right cheek.

Hal DiPietro's lifeless blue eyes stared past the baseboard, into eternity.

10

> *We shall next speak about the way to paint a
> dead man . . . do not apply any pink at all, be-
> cause a dead person has no color; but take a lit-
> tle light ocher, and step up three values of flesh
> color with it, just with white lead, and tempered
> as usual.*
>
> Cennino Cennini
> Il Libro dell' Arte, 1437

"What? *Dead?*"

Interrupted in the middle of f-stops and shadowless lighting, Rudy Gottfried almost dropped his camera as he jerked
upright and looked wildly around the living room. "My
God! Who? Where?"

"I'm going to phone for help," Sigrid said. "If you'll just
have a seat on the sofa there and try not to touch anything
else?"

Flabbergasted by the implication of her words, Gottfried
lowered his burly frame onto the couch, but he did not sink

back into the cushions. Instead, every muscle seemed tensed for action as he watched Sigrid maneuver the wall-hung telephone off the hook by touching only the cord.

She deposited it carefully on the kitchen counter so that it lay mouthpiece up with the dial buttons exposed. Then, keeping Gottfried in her peripheral view, she punched in the numbers with the end of a ballpoint pen and placed her face close to the mouthpiece.

Sam Hentz answered on the second ring.

The first uniformed patrol arrived six minutes later.

Upon discovering Hal DiPietro's body, Sigrid's first thought had been to get Rudy Gottfried out of the apartment, locate the building's superintendent to ask if there was a vacant apartment on this floor where they could set up a command post, and then park Gottfried there until she could get around to questioning him in detail.

Her second thought was how best to handle the preliminary investigation so as to avoid even the appearance of impropriety, since she was personally involved.

Now her own people moved in and out of the bedroom, each self-consciously aware of her cool-eyed appraisal as they went about their tasks with less chatter than usual. Their curiosity was well hidden and no one seemed to be obviously sight-seeing, but she was too savvy to believe that they didn't know just how intimate this place was for her.

Even the new guy, Ruben Gonzalez. "Are you all right, ma'am?" he'd asked before going off to canvass the building.

When Dinah Urbanska arrived, trailing Sam Hentz, she had wailed "Oh, gee, Lieutenant!" with such empathy that for one horrified moment Sigrid thought her disheveled young subordinate meant to hug her.

Only Sam Hentz, dapper and competent, possessed enough assurance to treat her with his usual latent hostility as she briefed him on the situation.

"You're putting me in charge of the case? Why?"

"Isn't it obvious? I inherited the lease on this apartment, I have the keys. I've met the victim, I—"

"No, I meant why me? Why not Tildon or Albee or Lowry? One of your pets?"

From puberty, Sigrid had known that she was awkward and inadequate in personal relationships. Possessed of a blond Viking of a father and a socially adept mother whose petite beauty made strangers do doubletakes when introduced to their tall gangly daughter, Sigrid had grown up feeling homely and unappealing. But never stupid. Had not Grandmother Lattimore, herself a famous beauty in her day, told a thirteen-year-old Sigrid just that? "You've got a lot of things about you like your mama and daddy, honey," she'd sighed. "Her eyes, his mouth. Her coloring, his height. Unfortunately, the way you went and put them together . . . well, I guess it doesn't matter. They say you're going to be real intelligent. That's nice."

After her grandmother's brutally honest assessment, Sigrid had turned inward, rarely opening herself to strangers or to colleagues, either, until Nauman came along and, like a curious child when handed one of those Chinese puzzle boxes kept poking and prodding at her cool exterior till he found the concealed latches.

In the past few weeks, however, her emotions had taken so many separate batterings that her nerve endings were frayed and raw. Abruptly, she'd had it with Sam Hentz and she rounded on him with an intensity that left him openmouthed.

"Give it a rest, Hentz!" For all her anger, she kept her voice so low that only he could hear. "I got the job, you didn't. Tough. But you've sulked about it long enough. Either deal with it or put in for transfer, okay? I asked you to handle this because I think you're a damn good detective. Now are you in or out?"

"In," he answered tersely.

"Good."

Curiously, almost analytically, Hentz watched as she took one long, steadying breath and then another. He could almost see her clamping down on her icy anger, regaining cool control of herself. Well, he could match that control, he told himself, stung by her words.

With one of the uniforms baby-sitting Gottfried, Hentz listened dispassionately while the lieutenant explained why she was here, who DiPietro was and why he was here, and how she'd met Rudy downstairs with no other thought but that DiPietro had long since left.

"How well do you know them?"

"Not well at all," Sigrid replied. "I met Gottfried for the very first time at his apartment night before last, then DiPietro at his gallery last night. For what it's worth, though, I haven't told Gottfried who's dead or how he was killed."

"He knew the decedent?"

"Yes."

"And Gottfried was inside the lobby when you got here?"

"Yes."

Sigrid saw Hentz mentally file both pieces of information for future consideration, as if he wanted to get a linear overview of things before being sidetracked by details. That was the way she herself liked to approach a case.

In the bedroom, she described seeing the bedclothes on the floor. "I supposed DiPietro must have bumped them when he fell. No drag marks, so he was probably standing there when someone hit him from behind. A small stone statuette fell out when I moved the comforter. I assume it's the weapon."

The crime scene unit had already bagged it. An abstract marble sculpture that could have fit inside a half-gallon milk carton, it was about ten inches tall with smooth, almost erotic, curvilinear lines.

Hentz hefted the bag. "I'd say about three, three and a half pounds. Yeah, that would do it. Where did your"—he searched for a neutral term—"friend keep it?"

"There on the chest."

They moved back to the threshold. Even though the rooms in this building had been built to generous pre-World War II standards, the bedroom was crowded with enough people already. Cohen, an assistant from the medical examiner's office, stood outside with them, waiting for the crime-scene unit to finish photographing the body so that he could start his own examination. It wouldn't be much longer now. They had taken enough pictures in situ and had carefully shifted the bed so that they could get at DiPietro more easily. Urbanska was already going through his pockets.

"Say he was warm to the touch, Lieutenant?" Cohen asked.

"Cooling, but yes, still fairly warm. I'm told that he left his gallery in Midtown a little before one. I looked at my watch after I found him. It was exactly three forty-six."

Cohen jotted down her times on a pocket-size notepad. "If you could document when he ate lunch, that would really narrow it down."

"Wonder why he was there between the bed and the wall?" asked Hentz.

"Probably to get a closer look at that red painting," Sigrid speculated. "He was part of the planning group for a four-gallery exhibition, and he and Elliott Buntrock are—were—in the process of deciding which pictures should be shown where."

"Only this Buntrock cops out. Coincidence?"

"He called me from the Arnheim Museum," Sigrid said stiffly, not liking the implication. "I'm sure we'll be able to confirm his movements."

"You'd like it to be that someone broke in to toss the apartment and this DiPietro guy interrupted them?"

His tone carried a hint of his usual condescension, but Sigrid let it slide.

"No," she said mildly. As far as she could see, nothing

pointed to such a neat solution. "There's no sign of a struggle or of the lock being forced."

"So if nobody broke in, who else besides you has keys?"

"Half of New York, for all I know. Nauman rented this apartment when he first began teaching at Vanderlyn. During the academic year, he usually had a four-day schedule, so unless he had engagements to keep him in town or when the weather was bad, he'd stay here those three nights and then drive home to Connecticut for the other four. The sofa turns into a bed. If friends came in from out of town and wanted to stay over, he'd give them a set of keys—one to get into the lobby, two for the apartment. Guests were supposed to leave them in that brass bowl over there beside the door, but sometimes they forgot."

She remembered stopping in at a hardware store with Nauman back before Christmas to have a duplicate set made for her and hearing him grumble that he must have bought at least twenty sets over the years. To someone as cautious as Sigrid, his casual trust had seemed foolhardy.

She began to tick off on her fingers the keys she knew for sure: "Mine, of course. The gallery—that's the set DiPietro used." She paused with her thumbnail on the tip of her middle finger and looked across the room. "I wonder if Urbanska's found them yet."

Hentz shrugged. "They'll be evidence, if she does," he reminded her.

"Doesn't matter. We planned to change the locks this week anyhow." She resumed listing with her ring finger. "Nauman's attorney, Marc Livingston. Buntrock. An artist who lives in Seattle, I think his name is Charlie Armstrong. Another artist from Raleigh, Christine Bawker or Baukus, something like that, and a British friend—I'll have to look in Nauman's address book to get you their names and phone numbers. It should be there in the top drawer of the nightstand."

"Later." Hentz jerked his head toward Gottfried. "What about this guy?"

"It's possible. He says he used to stay here frequently several years back when he was teaching night classes at Vanderlyn." She hesitated. "I told you that he was inside the lobby when I got here today. He *says* he rang all the bells till someone buzzed him in."

"What's his connection to the decedent?"

Striving to be totally objective in her account, Sigrid described last night's confrontation at the gallery between Rudy Gottfried and Hal DiPietro. "I don't know what it's about, but Gottfried seems to bear a grudge against DiPietro. Something that happened at least twenty years ago. Elliott Buntrock was going to call me tonight and give me details."

"You'll let me know what he says? See if it matches what the old guy tells us today?"

Before she could answer, Dinah Urbanska stood up and came over to them with a plastic bag that held scraps of paper, a handkerchief, a pocketknife, a key ring, some loose coins, and three keys that Sigrid recognized as fitting the apartment.

"No wallet on him, Sam. No cash or papers, either."

At that same instant one of the uniforms called from the doorway. "Detective Hentz? I just found a wallet in a trash barrel down on the ground floor." He held up a clear plastic bag, and they could see a black trifold wallet inside. "Pushed down under some papers. No money, but all the cards say Henry DiPietro."

"DiPietro?" Rudy Gottfried's grizzled head turned on his thick neck. "*Henry* DiPietro? Impossible. Henry DiPietro was buried at a crossroads with a stake through his heart nineteen years ago." He seemed suddenly weary as he finally sank back on the couch. "So that's who's dead in there. Somebody's killed young Prince Hal?"

Hentz took the wallet from the patrol officer. "Where is that trash barrel in relation to the lobby?"

"There's an unlocked fire door back of the elevator that opens onto the stairwell and goes from there to a locked outer door that'll set off an alarm if it's opened. The barrel was up under the stairs, right next to the lobby door."

Hentz sent the officer back to finish going through the barrel, then turned to Rudy Gottfried. "Sir, if you have no objection, I'd like permission to search your clothing."

"What?" Gottfried set back up again. "Search me?" He appealed to Sigrid. "Can he do that?"

"I'm afraid he can," she said. "It's nothing personal, but you *were* here in the building alone, only a few feet from where DiPietro's wallet's been found. You have the right to make him get a search warrant, but sooner or later you will have to let them search you. Of course," she added, "if he decides to arrest you, then no search warrant will be needed."

With wounded dignity, Rudy Gottfried struggled to his feet and held his arms straight out from his brawny, steel-worker's body.

"You understand that this means you are voluntarily waiving your constitutional right to a search warrant?" asked Hentz.

"I understand," the artist answered stoically.

"Please remove your jacket, sir."

It was the same tweed jacket he'd had on last night. Originally of good quality no doubt, but now nearly thread-bare.

While Dinah Urbanska recorded his findings, Hentz patted Gottfried down, then went through all his pockets. None of the four keys he was carrying matched the apartment's and nothing untoward jumped out at them until Hentz opened his shabby leather wallet. It held four hundred-dollar bills, two twenties, three tens, and six ones.

"You usually walk around with nearly five hundred in cash?" asked Hentz.

"I sold a picture this morning."

"Yeah? Who's your dealer?"

"I don't have one at the moment," replied Gottfried. "I sell directly from my studio."

"For cash?"

"I believe it is still legal to exchange goods for cash," came the testy answer.

Urbanska dutifully wrote down the serial numbers on the bills, then Hentz returned everything to Gottfried.

"When you were waiting downstairs, did you go into the stairwell?"

"I did not." Gottfried put his jacket back on and smoothed the lapels.

"Did anyone come through the lobby?"

"Several people, but nobody I knew."

"Can you describe them?"

"Or sketch them?" Sigrid interposed.

Gottfried slowly shook his head. "I'm afraid I didn't pay that much attention. I was waiting for Buntrock and as soon as someone got off the elevator and fell into the 'not Buntrock' category, I went back to watching the street. But let me think."

He half closed his eyes in an effort to remember. "A thin black woman came in with a fat crying white child, three or four white men left together. One of them might have been wearing a navy uniform; the others were casually dressed. A middle-aged Asian couple came in, then a really beautiful young black woman left just as some noisy teenagers of several races came in. Oh, yes! A UPS deliveryman with a rather large package. I can't remember if he was black or white but I think he arrived immediately before the Asian couple."

He opened his eyes. "There may have been others. I'm afraid I'm not much help."

His lack of specificity did not surprise Sigrid. Until she met Nauman, she'd assumed that all artists automatically noticed details.

Not so.

They'd begin to discuss a movie and he would look at

her blankly. "What fisherman?" he'd ask. "Oh. He was a fisherman?" Or he'd rummage through a utensil drawer for the potato peeler and then grumble that the cleaning woman must have thrown it out, even though he might actually have moved the potato peeler to get at the utensils underneath.

What *would* have surprised her, given Nauman's example, was if Gottfried had started reeling off "sample case with a blue-and-white logo on the side, scar on the left cheek, dreadlocks and amber beads."

And then the exception to the rule demonstrated itself. Gottfried's eyes widened as someone from the crime-scene unit swung past him with a handful of the items they'd bagged.

"Young lady, do you know what that is?" he asked, pointing to the small marble sculpture visible inside the plastic bag.

"Excuse me?"

"I suggest you handle it very carefully. That's a Noguchi. Probably worth about twenty or thirty K."

"Thirty thousand *dollars*?" exclaimed the startled technician.

Gottfried just smiled benignly and the technician continued out the door with the murder weapon cradled to her chest as if it were now a delicate piece of porcelain.

Hentz signaled with a tilt of his head and Sigrid followed him down the hall so that they could confer out of Gottfried's hearing.

"So what's your gut feeling on him, Lieutenant?"

"Offhand, I'd say no. He's strong enough and he seemed to be angry enough last night. But kill someone and then come up with me and calmly start taking pictures? On the other hand," she added slowly, "he was pretty outrageous last night, and today he acted as if nothing had happened."

Hentz thought about it. "So could be he's a good actor, or could be that last night didn't mean anything to him."

"Either's possible."

They stepped backwards into the bathroom so that the gurney could get by with DiPietro's body strapped inside the sheet that covered him.

Cohen followed close behind. "I'll let you know when the autopsy's scheduled," he told them, "but on the face of it, that pretty little hunk of marble looks to be your weapon. The back of his head feels like a ripe tomato. There's gotta be massive internal bleeding. Death was probably almost instantaneous."

Gottfried looked pale and shaken as the gurney rolled past him and out into the hall.

"If you like," said Sigrid, "I could take him back to the station with me and get his statement. Maybe try to jog his memory for more details about the people who passed him in the lobby."

"Yeah, okay. And see if you can get the name of whoever's supposed to have paid him that money."

"Anything else?"

Hentz's half smile acknowledged her deference. "I suppose you could get started on your own statement?"

She nodded, picked up her purse, and went over to Gottfried. His only objection about accompanying her was his concern about the floodlights that he'd lugged over.

"They're not mine. I borrowed them from some guy, and he wants them back today."

Sigrid gave Hentz an inquiring glance.

He shrugged and said, "Okay by me."

One of the uniformed officers was delegated to carry the lights downstairs and find the lieutenant a car and driver.

"I'll finish up here and then I guess someone ought to notify the victim's next of kin. Was he married?" Hentz asked Sigrid.

"I have no idea. You could call the gallery." She looked at her watch and frowned. "Someone might still be there."

She was halfway out the door before she remembered the bag she'd left in the bedroom.

"What's that?" Hentz asked.

"It's personal."

"Something you brought with you today?"

The temptation to lie was almost overwhelming. It chilled her to think of Hentz pulling out her robe and Nauman's for everyone to see and snigger over and make coarse jokes about, but there had been no towels in the bathroom. As an objective cop, she knew it was a distinct possibility that the killer had washed his or her hands and then dried them on Nauman's terry robe. As a grieving woman, she knew that by the time a trial ended and the evidence was released, this last ghostly trace of Nauman's body would be gone, lost to her forever.

It wasn't fair.

But life hadn't been fair to Hal DiPietro either.

She handed Hentz the bag.

"They were hanging on the bathroom door," she said, and turned and left the apartment.

11

Take bone from the second joints and wings of
fowls, or of a capon; and the older they are, the
better. Just as you find them under the dining-
table, put them into the fire; and when you see
that they have turned whiter than ashes, draw
them out, and grind them well on the porphyry;
and use it as I say above.

Cennino Cennini
Il Libro dell' Arte, 1437

The clerk at Pilot-Life's Manhattan office sounded tired and cranky. Evidently it'd been a long day for her and she'd just about used up all her niceness.

Assuming she'd begun with any.

"Look," she snapped. "If the policy's lapsed, we don't keep it in our active files."

"It lapsed less than three months ago," Elaine Albee snapped back. It had been a long day for her as well. "Isn't there a grace period?"

Sulkily, the clerk admitted there was and eventually pulled up the proper file on her computer screen. "So what was it you wanted to know?"

"How much money. Who was beneficiary," Elaine said patiently.

"Let me see if it's still . . . Georgia Fong? Yeah, here it is. Fifty thousand would have gone to her daughter, and since she's a minor, the father would've had the use of it for her benefit."

"Bingo!" said Elaine, and she and Jim exchanged cynical smiles at the thought of Todd Fong giving a rat's ass about his daughter's benefit after killing the child's mother. Every penny would have gone up his nose or down his throat.

"Yo! Lieutenant Harald!" Rusty Guillory, a redheaded stringer for the *New York Post*, circled the edges of the small crowd gathered behind the police barriers and intercepted Sigrid before she could follow Rudy Gottfried and his floodlights into one of the patrol cars. Afternoon sunlight glinted off Guillory's 35mm camera as he clicked off two quick shots of her. "So who's the guy that got himself dead in your boyfriend's apartment?"

"Sorry, Guillory. You want a statement, catch Detective Hentz. He's handling this case."

"Not you? How come?"

The lieutenant shook her head and closed the car door on him. The patrol car immediately edged away from the curb and merged with crosstown rush-hour traffic that was even worse than usual on this street because of the many emergency vehicles blocking one lane. Rebuffed but undeterred, Guillory rejoined his colleagues in front of the apartment building. Sooner or later someone would have to give a statement to the press, and he intended to get in a few questions of his own.

"Am I a suspect?" asked Rudy Gottfried above the chatter of the car radio.

"Witnesses' statements are routine in every investigation," Sigrid hedged. "You were in the apartment when I discovered his body. You may have seen the killer pass through the lobby. It's no big deal. We'll be questioning everybody who's had contact with Hal DiPietro in the last few days."

"Last time I had contact with Hal was over twenty years ago," he protested.

"You were at the gallery last night," Sigrid reminded him.

"For five minutes." He peered at her closely as if to read her face. "Were you there, too?"

When Sigrid nodded, he seemed to deflate a little.

From the staticky radio up front came a dispatcher's monotone request for someone to proceed to First and Twenty-third, where traffic signals were reported to be hung on red in all directions.

Sigrid leaned forward and almost bumped her face on Gottfried's borrowed floodlights, which were jammed in beside the driver's seat. "Officer—?"

"Pokotsey, ma'am."

"Do me a favor, Pokotsey, and turn down your radio."

Instantly the dispatcher's voice became a murmur. Sigrid leaned back and said, "I'm told that you used to be represented by the DiPietro Gallery."

"Aren't you supposed to warn me—what's it called? Miranda-ize me or something—before you start asking questions?"

"Normally we do that only when we place someone under arrest. Although," she added, "strictly speaking, a person is free at any time to ask for an attorney's presence if he feels his statements are going to be self-incriminating."

He frowned. "I can't afford a lawyer."

"The public defender's office will provide one if you request it."

For a moment some of Gottfried's former belligerence seemed to return. "You think I'd put myself in the hands of some old hack who can't do a real practice?"

Sigrid shrugged.

Traffic was so backed up that it was taking three or four cycles of every light for them to move one block. Horns honked impatiently, and Pokotsey was playing mind games with a cab that wanted to move into their lane. He would allow almost enough space for the cab to get over and then, at the last second, inch forward in time to cut the cab off.

"I had nothing to do with this," said Gottfried. "Last night— Okay, last night brought a lot of things back, but if I was going to bop Hal over the head, I'd have done it years ago, not waited till today."

"How did you know he died from a blow to the head?"

Gottfried hesitated. "I heard somebody say it."

Sigrid shook her head, knowing they'd been careful not to discuss the details in his hearing.

"Look," he growled, "I see some kid walking by with a Noguchi marble in a plastic bag, nobody has to tell me. I can add it up for myself."

She conceded the possibility.

"Who were Ben Slocum and Morris Wallender?"

"Pals of mine. From the old days."

"What did Hal DiPietro do to them?" she probed.

"Not just Hal. It was his fucking father that did it to us."

"Did what?" she asked again.

"Cut off our balls."

The blunt words were spoken with a smoldering anger that startled Sigrid.

"Hal was a still a kid when it started. Twenty-six years ago," Gottfried said through clenched teeth. "But he was out of college, working at the gallery by the time it ended."

He began hesitantly; yet, as he worked his way into the

tale, he spoke in bursts of recklessness that seemed fueled by a raw and still bitter pain.

"First me—I was the oldest—and then Ben Slocum. He was a hot-tempered redhead. Always popping off. Morris Wallender. A real sweet guy. Charlie Armstrong came in a lot later. Four of us. We were starting to build decent little reputations. Sales were irregular, not enough to live on maybe, but growing. DiPietro—Henry—decided we were going to be big, so he signed us to exclusive contracts. He'd give us a monthly income and we'd give him so many paintings a year. That was pretty standard back then. Lots of dealers subsidized artists that way.

"The first few shows did okay. Then the reigning pundit of the day issued a proclamation on where American art should be going—*Whither America?*" His words dripped with scornful bile.

"After that we got some bad reviews. DiPietro began to lose interest. Put us on the back burner at the gallery, and we lost our momentum. Finally he decided we were behind the curve, not trendy enough, and he dropped our contracts. That part wasn't bad. Charlie went out to California. Got in with the West Coast crowd. Ben and Morris and me, we found new galleries around town here. Maybe not as fancy. And we didn't have our monthly stipend coming in, and that hurt because my wife was sick. Needed a big operation. Ben and Anita got careless and had a kid about then. Pretty near wiped us both out. Even so, we could've weathered it, only that piece of dog dirt wasn't finished screwing us. He waited till we were starting to get on our feet again."

His jaw tightened and Sigrid could see the muscles in his thick neck begin to tense up again.

"What happened?" she asked.

"It was about eighteen months after he dropped us. Hal had finished college and Henry'd made him a partner in the gallery by then. Might even have been Hal's bright idea, for all I know. You see, Henry still owned several hundred pieces of our work that he hadn't sold, and suddenly the only thing he cared about was unloading them the quickest way he could. So what did the cheap bastard do? I'll tell you what he did. He put us in Macy's bargain basement!"

"What?"

"Full-page ad in the goddamned *Times*." His big raw-knuckled hand blocked out the screamer headlines in broad choppy motions against the back of Pokotsey's seat. "YOUR CHANCE TO OWN AN AUTHENTIC WORK OF MODERN ART! 50-75% OFF THE DEALER'S LIST PRICE!" Gottfried's voice nearly choked with remembered humiliation. "Everything—oils, watercolors, drawings—listed by title, size, artist, DiPietro's list price, and then Macy's sale price. Like we were nothing more than pots and pans or flannel pajamas."

Sigrid was appalled. "What happened?"

"DiPietro recouped most of his money," he said bitterly, "and we went down the toilet. Reputations shot to hell. Morris Wallender killed himself. Ben Slocum was dead of a heart attack within six months. Charlie Armstrong was the only one to escape. He wasn't in to DiPietro for as much, and he managed to scrape up enough cash out there in California to buy his stuff back."

"Your wife—?"

"The second operation didn't work either." If he was trying to sound matter-of-fact, he wasn't succeeding. "I'd probably still be paying off the hospital and undertaker if Oscar hadn't given me a job at Vanderlyn."

Sigrid could not begin to imagine how Gottfried had managed to go on living in New York, much less painting, after being stripped naked like that before the whole art world. The deep personal shame. The ego-scalding disgrace before his peers. No place to hide, no way to cleanse himself of such ignominy.

And then to lose his wife and his friends, too?

No wonder he had shown such rage and resentment last night.

Words were inadequate, yet she said them anyhow. "I'm so sorry. What an unbelievably rotten thing to do."

"Yeah. Well." As if he now regretted that he'd opened up to her like that, Gottfried peered through the window at the unmoving lines of traffic ahead. "We could walk faster than this."

Their driver irrevocably cut off the cab he'd been toying with, and the cabby leaned on his horn in frustration, but Sigrid sat silently through the cacophony, considering the ramifications of Gottfried's words.

For the moment she was reluctant to question him like the usual suspect in a murder case. As always, though, professional need to know overrode her personal feelings. "You do still sell pictures, don't you?"

"Not 'still,' " he corrected her. "*Again.* There was a stretch there when I didn't sell a single picture for almost eight years. Now the buyers have started coming around again. I've lasted long enough that I'm getting to be historical." He shook his head at the absurdity of it. "Young art nerds looking to do essays for the journals or working on their Ph.D.'s. They buy a picture, and they send their friends."

He patted his hip pocket almost cheerfully. "I'd just about given up on this guy, though. I let him take the picture when he'd only paid me half the money. Really thought he was going to stiff me."

Their car finally turned onto Second Avenue and headed downtown. Traffic was still heavy here, too, but at least they had begun to average a full block between red lights. The late afternoon sun bounced off glass-fronted stores. Looking south, Sigrid could see that the sky was actually blue.

"It's taken me twenty years," said Gottfried, "to get back to where I was before I met Henry DiPietro. I haven't got another twenty."

B'Nita Parsons hung up the phone after speaking with Detective Hentz. Because he had worked late last night cleaning up after the opening, Donny Levitz had the day off and Hadley Jones, the other aide, had left at two-thirty, so B'Nita had manned the gallery alone most of the afternoon.

Last night's opening had generated a surge of morning visitors, and three more of Buck David's pictures now sported little red "sold" dots. Several people were wandering around with catalogs when she returned late after lunch; but they were lookers, not buyers, and the last had departed over half an hour ago.

Before she took this job, she had never met Hal DiPietro in the flesh, and she wasn't quite sure if she should weep for his death, stay utterly cool, or become totally distraught.

But since the estranged Mrs. DiPietro was probably learning of his passing at this very moment, thought B'Nita, shouldn't she inform his nearest colleagues here in the building?

First things first, though, she remembered. It took only seconds to slip into the inner office, pick Rudy Gottfried's slides out of the wastebasket where Hal DiPietro had thrown them this morning, and place them in his desk drawer for safekeeping.

That done, she reached for the telephone and dialed.

Down on the second floor in her deep green office, Hester Kohn was just ending her day. She wore a floral silk jumpsuit and brightly enameled gold bangles, and as she reached across her green glass desktop for her orange phone, she looked like some exotic bird plucking an orange flower from a dark jungle pool.

"Oh, my God!" she said when B'Nita Parsons gave her the shocking news. "Does Victor know?"

"I called you first," said Hal's assistant, and Hester thought she heard a tearful note in her voice.

"Wait for me," she told the younger woman. "I'll be right up."

Victor Germondi sat staring at the Madonna, which was hung low on the wall immediately opposite his desk. Technically, the craquelures of fine red lines showing through the gold leaf that surrounded the Virgin were never meant to be. An admiring conservator had once offered to restore the panel to its original state, but Victor had refused. He rather liked that delicate net of red. It reminded him of an anatomical drawing from an old medical textbook. Take away the golden skin and you could view the human form encased in its own net of nourishing red blood vessels.

The panel, painted half a millennium ago, had been so much a part of his life for so many years that there were often long periods when he could almost forget about it, when his eyes would sweep past its specially wired glass case without lingering, much as one's eyes sweep past a light switch or doorknob. One of the reasons he kept it here in his American office was precisely so he would *not* forget. Each time he returned, the Madonna struck him anew with fresh memories of his father, dead now more than thirty years.

He had deliberately turned away from his father's passion—no, not passion; call it by its real name: *obsession*—for Italian primitives and had devoted his own career to twentieth-century art. The treasures Leo Germondi had amassed were now gone, dispersed through a dozen or more private collections around the world.

Only this one, which Leo had loved above all the others, remained. Victor may have kept the Duccio Madonna in his father's memory; but he knew he would not be sitting here studying it quite so intently if Hal's impulsive gift had not revived so many half-buried memories of the Trecento.

Nor was Leo's the only familiar Madonna represented in this rare book. Victor recognized three that were now in public museums, sold after the war to buy food for suddenly impoverished aristocrats. There were several exquisite examples that he did not recognize, but they had been located in places where some of the heaviest fighting had taken place. So much had been lost in bombings and fires, looting, or outright vandalism. It was not wrong, he told himself, to feel pride for what his father had managed to save and protect.

His thoughts were interrupted by a discreet chime that announced the entrance of someone into the gallery. He glanced at his watch. Too late for casual browsers. With a smile, he called out, "Hal?"

Instead, Hester Kohn appeared in his office doorway, followed closely by B'Nita Parsons.

"Ah, Hester, my dear!" He closed the book and rose to his feet in old-fashioned gallantry. "And Mrs. Parsons. Is Hal back yet? We were supposed to—"

His smile faded as he noted the serious expressions on their faces. *"Cos'è successo?"* he exclaimed. "What's wrong?"

"Oh, Victor," said Hester, and tears glistened in her hazel eyes.

By the time their shift neared its end, Elaine Albee and Jim Lowry had talked to a half dozen or more of the marginal citizens with whom Todd Fong had associated. From former neighbors to co-workers at his occasional jobs, not one single person claimed to have noticed any suicidal tendencies.

"Oh, yeah, somebody did say he blew his own brains out," said a couple of loungers at the dead man's favorite bar on lower Broadway. "Last guy you'd expect. Somebody else's brains, yeah, but his own?"

"Surprised the hell out of me," agreed the bartender, who had occasionally ponied up free drinks when he needed Todd's muscles to bounce troublemakers from the bar. "He didn't take no crap off nobody. Dished it plenty, though."

"Ever see him with a gun?" Lowry asked him.

The bartender looked uneasy. "Nah. His fists were big enough. He didn't need iron."

But when they left the bar, one of the loungers was waiting for them around the corner with a different story. For a quick twenty, he was willing to state that he'd seen Todd Fong with a small handgun under his jacket not long before his death.

"Don't ask me what kind, 'cause I don't know. Little, though. Vinnie said for him to put it away or get out of his place. He told Bob and me he was going to shoot his wife."

"Why?"

The man leaned closer and his beery breath wafted over them. "For her insurance is what he said."

"Insurance?" asked Elaine Albee. "She didn't have any. It had lapsed."

"No shit?" He looked befuddled, then brightened. "Maybe *she* shot *him* for his?"

"Did he have any?"

"Well, how the hell should I know?" Miffed, he turned back toward the bar. Their twenty dollars was clenched in his fist. But probably not for long.

"A taker and a user," said Fong's first wife, a faded blond waitress at a café on Eighth Avenue. A recovering alcoholic, she freely admitted that she'd turned an occasional trick before Todd married her. "And when things were tight, he wanted to put me back out on the street."

She swore she hadn't seen him in several months, though, and while Elaine Albee used the office phone to check in with Tillie, the café owner showed Jim Lowry recent pay stubs that seemed to indicate that she'd been on duty the night Todd Fong died.

Lowry dutifully made a note of the pay stubs, but he could tell by the way Lainey jingled her car keys and hustled him out of the café that she'd learned something interesting.

As soon as they were back on the street, heading for the car, she shared her news. "Tillie says the lieutenant found a homicide in her boyfriend's old apartment this afternoon.'

"What?"

"Some Midtown art dealer. Hentz is going to work it, but she's back at the station now, getting a statement from one of the witnesses."

She had parked the car in the only nearby available space, a space which wasn't quite big enough. At least three feet of the front end protruded into a narrow commercial driveway, and the irate driver of a white van was maneuvering to get past. He was inclined to be lippy about it until Lowry flashed his badge.

Albee slid in under the steering wheel and turned the ignition key. "That's not all," she said, pulling out ahead of the van. "One of the beat guys picked up Randi Jurgen and he's on his way in with her."

Like Todd Fong's other two wives, Randi Jurgen had probably once been a pretty fresh-faced blonde. She was seated now in one of the station's interview rooms. Her face was hard, her skin had a sallow tone, and her platinum hair had been bleached so many times that it reminded Elaine Albee of the lifeless acrylic hair on an old Barbie doll. On the other hand, Elaine could not remember that any of her Barbies had ever sported tiny matching Tweety Bird and Sylvester tattoos on her wrists. The yellow bird and black cat flashed colorfully as Randi used her hands to describe how she and Todd Fong had planned to spend the evening he died.

It was pretty much a confirmation of what the senior Fongs had already told them. She did try to say it was a bottle of vodka that she'd procured for their intimate little party, but it was too late in the day for Elaine to play games.

"Oh, come on, Randi. We talked to your rehab counselor at the detox center. You were doing coke that night."

From the moistness of her eyes, Jim suspected she probably had some in her system even as they talked. But she was coherent enough in her insistence that *"Never—never,*

never, never, in a million years would Todd off himself. And especially not on the night we were going to party hearty."

She used both thin hands to push back the haystack of dry platinum hair, and the perky cartoon tattoos contrasted sharply with her haggard face. "Bet it was that bitch."

"What bitch?" they asked.

"Georgia. She was always on him about money for the baby. She probably did it so the kid could get his Social Security."

"Did you ever hear Todd say anything about shooting Georgia?" Elaine asked abruptly.

Before that question, Randi had been fairly open with them. Now they saw her blue eyes dart from one face to the other. Her hands fell back in her lap, but the black and yellow cartoons flickered nervously. "No. I don't know what you're talking about. No!"

By which they knew she meant yes.

But they couldn't budge her on it until Jim said, "Did you also know that Georgia let her life insurance lapse in January?"

"Lapsed?" Her eyes widened and she blurted, "Then it's a good thing he missed, huh?"

Rush hour was nearly over, and it was that halfway point between sunset and twilight when Sam Hentz finally emerged from the elevator and headed across the lobby. Their preliminary canvass had turned up little to confirm or deny Rudy Gottfried's story that he had remained downstairs until Lieutenant Harald arrived to let him into the apartment.

Ruben Gonzalez had located both the black nanny and the Asian couple Gottfried described; they remembered seeing him, but could only guess at the time. No one had been at home on either side of Nauman's apartment at the estimated time of death, nor did any of the tenants who were home recall riding up in the elevator with Hal DiPietro.

At the moment their biggest lead was a crumpled, nearly illegible taxi receipt that Dinah Urbanska had found in the dead man's right pants pocket.

A uniformed officer pushed open the lobby door for him, and Hentz walked out into a thick knot of reporters.

Had he given half a thought to the media, Sam Hentz might have classified the murder of a Midtown art dealer as a quick sound bite on the local news and maybe a brief story that would begin on the front page of the *Post* or the *Village Voice* and then quickly disappear into the back pages. The number of reporters and cameras that descended on him when he left Oscar Nauman's apartment that afternoon and the others who were waiting for him at the station when he arrived effectively squashed that assumption. In addition to the local beat reporters, there were stringers from the international press corps and the wire services, as well as three TV vans.

He made the usual noncommittal statements, but tonight they weren't enough.

Strobe lights flashed in his eyes. Microphones were thrust toward his face. Camcorders and handheld floods angled for better views.

"Detective Hentz, does this have anything to do with Oscar Nauman's death?"

"Were any of his paintings stolen?"

"Detective Hentz! Over here! Would you comment on the possibility that Nauman's death might not have been an accident?"

"Why isn't Lieutenant Harald handling this investigation?"

"Does this indicate that she's a suspect?"

"Detective Hentz, would you characterize—"

"No further comment," said Hentz and retreated to the squad room upstairs.

12

*Then always go out alone, or in such company as
will be inclined to do as you do, and not apt to
disturb you. And the more understanding this
company displays, the better it is for you.*

Cennino Cennini
Il Libro dell' Arte, 1437

As Sam Hentz passed her desk, Dinah Urbanska held out
the taxi receipt she'd found on Hal DiPietro's body. "This
last digit of the medallion number, Sam—does that look
like a three or an eight to you?"

The printing was so light that the figures were nearly un-
readable. The usual slogan was clear enough—I ♥ NEW
YORK—and so were today's date, the time (1:52 P.M.), and
the bottom legend: FOR COMPLAINTS 1-212-555-TAXI.
The fare seemed to be four dollars, but both the mileage and
the medallion number were too faint for him to hazard a guess.

"I'd check 'em both out," he said and handed back the
ticket.

She immediately began to dial the number at the bottom of the receipt and Sam Hentz walked on, mentally shaking his head that she was still naive enough to think that the city's Taxi and Limousine Commission would have a living, breathing person at the other end of a complaint number. When half the cabbies in New York can't speak English and the other half barely know if the Bronx is up or the Battery down?

Even assuming there were workaholics at TLC who lingered at their desks past five o'clock, Urbanska was only going to get recorded instructions either to put her complaints in writing or else "leave your name and number and someone will return your call."

Right.

In your dreams, New York.

Hentz considered telling her how to reach a real human being tomorrow morning, but decided she might as well figure it out herself.

It was the old give-'em-a-fish-and-they'll-eat-today philosophy versus teach-'em-to-fish-and-they'll-feed-themselves-forever. He was beguiled to realize that the theory applied equally as well here in the department as in any undeveloped country.

No sign of Lowry or Albee, but across the squad room, Tillie was straightening his desk before he headed home to Brooklyn.

"She still here?" Hentz asked, nodding toward the lieutenant's closed door.

Detective First Grade Charles Tildon was a husband and father first, a by-the-book policeman second. Early thirties. Until last fall, his open boyish face and cheerful manner could have let him pass for ten years younger; but in October a small homemade bomb had exploded less than three feet from him. Only the thickness of a wooden table had saved his life. Now his face was thinner, less innocent, and lines of pain gave him the pinched look of someone at least forty. In addition to a concussion that had kept him in a coma for several days, his injuries had included fractured ribs, a punctured lung, and a broken leg that he still favored when he was tired.

It was late January before Tillie was well enough to return to active duty, and he had gotten back just in time for the lieutenant's breakdown, which was how Hentz thought of her extended leave. Tillie had soldiered on conscientiously during her absence; but of them all, he was the one who'd worked closest with her and he was the one who worried most about her well-being.

Now that she was back, he was also becoming the one most protective of her. Hentz wasn't sure if it was deliberate or unconscious, but Tillie was starting to remind him of his aunt Lizzie's golden retriever: always trying to put himself between the woman and whoever might be there to give her grief.

Reluctantly, Tillie now admitted that Lieutenant Harald was indeed still there. "I just finished typing up that Gottfried guy's statement, and I think she's working on her own. Want me to see if she's busy?"

"That's okay," Hentz said. "I'll do it."

Her door wasn't quite latched and when he tapped, it slid open readily. Inside, he saw that Harald was on the phone. He started to turn away, but she signaled for him to enter and handed him Gottfried's statement to read while she completed her call.

Instead, he took the opportunity to study her covertly as she jotted down notes on the conversation.

When she first transferred in, he assumed she'd gotten the job for reasons that had nothing to do with ability. She was a woman, and the grapevine had it that she was the daughter of a cop who'd been killed in the line of duty. When he learned that Leif Harald had also been Captain McKinnon's first partner, Hentz assumed he'd learned all he needed to know about why she'd been promoted in.

The one thing he hadn't assumed was that she'd slept her way up the chain of command. Not someone that skinny

and sexless. He briefly considered the possibility that she
was a lesbian even though nothing on the grapevine hinted
at it, but she didn't seem to cut the women on the squad any
more slack than the men. When squad room chatter had her
sleeping with some white-haired artist, it hadn't changed
his perceptions one iota. A guy old enough to be her father?
Probably all a woman like her could get, he had told himself sourly. No curves. Nothing feminine about her clothes,
no easy give-and-take in her personality.

As time went on, he'd grudgingly had to admit that she
was a savvy detective, particularly adept with the devious
puzzlers, but she wasn't much of a leader in his estimation.
Not that he himself was all that tight with the others on the
squad, but he'd seen icicles warmer than this woman.

Just because she hadn't rapped their knuckles the time
they let a perp slip through their fingers, Albee and Lowry
thought she was an even-handed administrator. They forgot
how Harald had come down hard on Urbanska over a case
that went south because the kid had lied to cover one of the
old-timers. Even gave her a command discipline when it
was that asshole Cluett who should have had his hide
stripped off.

Yeah, okay, the kid had to learn that favors carried price
tags, but Harald could've just chewed her out. She didn't
have to put anything in Urbanska's permanent jacket.

Fortunately for Harald, the kid was made of better stuff
and didn't hold a grudge. "No way," Urbanska had said
when he told her she could challenge the c.d. "She could
have had me transferred or suspended, Sam, but she
didn't."

No, except for Tillie, who got along with everybody,
Hentz couldn't see that Harald had established much rap-
port within the department. Just dumb luck that morale was
good here.

Still, in the past year, he'd watched her transformation
from an uptight, badly dressed, rather plain woman to
someone more at ease in her skin.

She would never be conventionally beautiful—and Hentz considered himself an expert on beautiful women—because her face was too angular, her mouth too wide, her chin too strong, and she was still built like a parking meter. Tillie kept insisting that she had a sense of humor, and even Lowry and Albee claimed to have seen her laugh a couple of times. For his part, he'd never seen more than a smile.

Nevertheless, her changeable gray eyes were okay. There were times when he could almost see a glint of intelligent amusement there. It was enough to make Hentz wonder if maybe that was what had attracted that artist.

And one thing he would hand her. He'd expected her to crawl back into her shell once her lover was no longer around to boost her confidence. It hadn't happened. If anything, she had become even more assured. Look how she'd blasted him this afternoon. And she was still keeping up her appearance: lipstick always in place, a hairdo that softened her face, bright colors.

Maybe, thought Sam, it's because she's inherited a fortune. Maybe it's because she's changed too much to change back. Or maybe it's because— Then her cool gray eyes met his and he quickly scotched the rest of that thought before it was fully formulated.

His own eyes dropped to Rudy Gottfried's statement, and when he got to the part where the murder victim's father had once screwed Gottfried royally, he became so absorbed that he barely heard the lieutenant say, "Thanks, Elliott. That fits with what he told me. . . . What reception? Oh. No, I don't— Do you think I really have to? Oh, all right. I'll think about it."

As she hung up, he finished reading and said, "Sounds like a pretty solid motive here."

She nodded.

"And opportunity."

"Yes."

"But you don't think he did it?"

She shrugged. "That was my friend on the phone. Elliott Buntrock."

"The guy who was supposed to meet DiPietro at the apartment."

"Yes. His version of the Macy's sale is even worse. According to one of the curators at the Museum of Modern Art, Rudy Gottfried punched out the senior DiPietro. Broke his nose, left him bleeding all over Macy's white carpet. Hal pulled him off his father and got a black eye for his troubles." She glanced at her notes. "I have names and dates if you want them."

"For twenty-odd years ago," said Hentz.

"That's the problem," Sigrid agreed. "If this is a motive for murder, why wait till now?"

"What if he got there early? Say DiPietro buzzed him in and, while they were talking, made a snide remark about the old days and Gottfried snapped?"

"And then calmly lugged those floodlights back downstairs to wait for me?" She shook her head. "I won't say it's impossible, but I'd certainly like a witness who could place him in the elevator or on that floor."

"Yeah, and I'd like a million ducks and a twelve-inch pianist."

"Excuse me?"

For a moment he'd almost forgotten who he was talking to. "Sorry. It's sort of a catchphrase. From my Aunt Lizzie's favorite shaggy-dog story."

"You must tell it to me one of these days," she said dryly. "In the meantime, did you locate DiPietro's next of kin?"

"Yeah. A wife who lives down in New Jersey. Out from Princeton. Horse country. No divorce. Not even a formal separation, she says. Twin girls. Twelve years old. She's supposed to meet me at the gallery at eleven tomorrow. Want to come?"

She lifted an eyebrow at the invitation.

"You've been there, you've met some of these people. They'll talk to you."

They both knew his overture was more than that.

"All right," she said.

"That reminds me." He got up and went out to his desk. When he returned, he was carrying the bag she'd given him two hours earlier. "The techies looked these over and didn't see any reason to keep them."

As he laid the bag on her desk, her slender hands reached out and circled it in a delicate caress. For moment he thought there might be tears in those wide-set gray eyes; then her chin came up, and for the first time he saw her wide mouth curve in a genuine smile for him. "Thanks, Hentz. But you're still not getting my job."

Her smile almost destroyed his earlier preconceptions about beauty.

Against his will he found himself smiling back, heard his own voice say, "Don't bet on it."

When Sigrid got home to her apartment an hour later, she expected to find Roman Tramegra at the stove stirring up something exotic. Instead, he'd left a note on the refrigerator door: *Home very late, so don't wait dinner. Cassoulet in the oven.*

She was not unhappy to have the apartment to herself tonight. It had been a long, tumultuous day, and Roman would have heard about the murder and wanted every detail, in case it was something he could incorporate into his mystery novel. Whether his book or his new computer, she was in no mood to answer more questions. She wanted only to be quiet and untalking. Perhaps even unthinking.

She fixed herself a tall gin and tonic and carried it to her bedroom where silence had to be put on hold because the light was flashing on her answering machine. Three messages from Anne in escalating degrees of urgency as she watched the evening news and reacted to the insinuations:

"How *can* they think this has anything to do with Oscar's death?"

Anne must have called her work number, too, because the last message was from someone working the evening shift. "Ah, Lieutenant? Your mother wants you should call her, okay?"

Sighing, Sigrid called and spent the next fifteen minutes erasing her mother's anxieties.

By then the ice was melting in her drink, so she went back to the kitchen, put Roman's cassoulet in the refrigerator, and added more ice and another splash of gin to her glass.

The discovery of a homicide in Nauman's apartment had aroused Anne's maternal instincts. She was upset over the media's reckless speculations, and she was worried about the fresh pain and grief this might inflict on her daughter.

Oddly enough, Sigrid realized that it was having an opposite effect. It was as if the apartment had somehow been purified and cleansed and made ordinary again by Hal Di-Pietro's death there. At Marcus Livingston's office day before yesterday, the very thought of subletting it till the lease ran out had been emotionally wracking.

Tonight it no longer bothered her. As soon as Hentz unsealed the apartment, she would tell Irene Bayles to put the artworks in storage, ship the books, papers, and photographs to Connecticut, and give everything else—clothes, furniture, housewares—to a charitable organization.

Thanks to Sam Hentz, she had the one thing, the only thing, she'd wanted from the apartment, and now she undressed and slipped it on. As she smoothed on face cream, her eyes fell on the framed silverpoint drawing Nauman had made of her at Christmas. Already the portrait's silver lines and crosshatchings had begun to mellow and darken against the light gray paper like those Dürer drawings that she loved.

She finished her drink, brushed her teeth, and got into bed with the blue terry-cloth robe wrapped around her thin body like Nauman's arms, comforted by the smell of him that permeated the robe's fibers.

His last message tape was still on the cassette inside her nightstand, but she felt no compulsion to play it tonight.

Instead, for the first time since his death, she slept straight through till morning and woke refreshed.

13

. . . always follow the dominant lighting; and make it your careful duty to analyze it, and follow it through, because, if it failed in this respect, your work would be lacking in relief, and would come out a shallow thing, of little mastery.

Cennino Cennini
Il Libro dell' Arte, 1437

By daybreak, Hal DiPietro's death was all over the early editions and the local newscasts. The commissioner had already been on the phone to him, said Captain McKinnon when he called Sam Hentz and Sigrid into his office for a briefing.

"He was killed in your friend's apartment," McKinnon told Sigrid. "*Is* there a connection?"

"So far as I know, it's a complete coincidence," she replied. "DiPietro's gallery was going to take part in Nauman's retrospective, so they did know each other, but the relationship was purely professional."

To the captain's further questions, Sam Hentz explained what they had so far—the stolen wallet, Rudy Gottfried's presence in the lobby and his possible motives, the taxi receipt that Urbanska was trying to trace in case DiPietro had brought someone along with him, the handy weapon, and no sign of struggle.

"The galleries open at ten," Hentz concluded. "Lieutenant Harald and I plan to question the decedent's colleagues, and then we're supposed to meet his wife at eleven."

"Fine," said McKinnon.

He glanced at Sigrid. "You okay with this?" he asked gruffly.

Sigrid flushed, knowing he and Anne had probably discussed her mental well-being.

"Yes, sir," she said.

"Just keep me informed," he told them.

After a session with the city directory and fruitless tries with four separate telephone numbers, Dinah Urbanska finally made contact with a Taxi and Limousine Commission clerk who was willing to run both numbers through her computer.

"If the last digit is a three, that medallion's owned by Shallcross Trans-City," said the TLC clerk. "They're a management group with a big fleet of cars. You'll have to contact them directly to find out who was driving yesterday."

She rattled off a Queens address and phone number.

"And if it's an eight?" asked Dinah, clutching at her notebook as it threatened to slide off the edge of her desk even as she scribbled furiously.

"If it's an eight, the owner-drivers are Nihat Zahir and Mohammad Palkhivala and those are the only two who should have been driving, but I see they've had at least one violation against them. Sometimes these owner-drivers pull in a ringer to drive a swing shift on shares so they can keep the car on the street twenty-four hours a day. They think we think they all look alike."

As the clerk began to give the two owners' Lower East Side addresses and phone numbers, Dinah tried to flip to a fresh page in her notebook and felt it walk right out from under her hand and crash into her wastebasket, where it immediately adhered to a half-eaten jelly doughnut she had discarded earlier.

"Oh, *jeepers*!" she wailed.

Across the room, Elaine Albee and Jim Lowry were also working the phones. When they got in that morning, they had found messages from both Dotty Vargas and a Richardson Whiteside.

Vargas wanted to let them know that an insurance agent would be calling about Todd Fong's death. She skipped her usual teasing come-on to Jim, and there was something odd about her tone that Elaine couldn't quite put her finger on, but her puzzlement was soon displaced when Jim dialed the local number that Whiteside had left.

"MidLantic Mutual of Delaware," caroled a professionally cheerful voice. "How may I direct your call?"

When Richardson Whiteside answered his phone, he sounded like a fifteen-year-old kid, chatty, breezy, and frankly surprised that no one would tell him officially whether or not Todd Fong had killed himself on March 17.

They, in turn, were equally surprised to learn that there was a sizable insurance policy on his life.

"Two years ago, on the thirtieth of March, about a week after their grandchild was born, I wrote up a sixty-thousand policy on Todd Fong for his parents," said Whiteside. "They wanted split benefits. Thirty thou to the kid, the other thirty to them. They filed a claim this week, so that's why I need to know."

"Why?" asked Elaine, who was on the extension. "What difference does it make? Dead is dead. Or is it a double indemnity policy?"

"Certainly not," Whiteside said. "We don't do those anymore. But there's a two-year waiting period on suicide, and he missed it by thirteen days."

"You don't pay off on suicide?"

"Not if it occurs within the first two years we don't. That's pretty much standard across the industry. So if he died by accident or was murdered, his beneficiaries split the full sixty thou."

"And if it's suicide?"

"Then we'll return the premium payments plus interest to his parents. They won't be out anything."

Only a screwed-up son whom they adored, thought Elaine, remembering Angie Fong's ravaged face.

"Did the Fongs know this?" asked Jim.

"No reason not to. It's all spelled out in simple English right there in the contract. We don't hide things in fine print anymore," he said virtuously.

"So if you wind up paying off on Todd's policy, does that mean Georgia Fong gets the use of the money?"

"Sure. The kid's a minor, and she's the legal guardian, but it's not the whole sixty thou," Whiteside reminded them. "She'd get the kid's half right away, but if I remember correctly, the Fongs planned to hold on to the other thirty thou for the kid's education. So which is it, guys? Does baby get new shoes, or do Mom and Dad get pocket change?"

They told him they'd get back to him as soon as they knew, and after they hung up, Jim said, "Wonder how many T-shirts you'd have to paint to make thirty thousand?"

Elaine nodded thoughtfully. "Telling us there was no insurance? Pretending all that surprise and anger when we suggested it was Todd that shot at her? Could be."

"Let's say she suspected him and figured out why. Say she went over to his apartment and told him he was a jerk because the policy had lapsed and he wasn't going to get doodly."

"Yeah!" said Elaine, seeing where he was going. "And then she remembers *his* insurance and knows his parents would have kept up the payments, so—"

"*Pow!*" they both finished together.

"I like it." Elaine grinned.

Jim did, too. "And don't forget that the baby's her only witness that she stayed in all evening."

Together they went and laid it out for Lieutenant Harald: the pristine gun and lack of contact between gun and skin as attested by Dotty Vargas; Fong's plan to shoot his estranged wife for the insurance, corroborated by drinking buddies and second wife; a still viable insurance policy that would net Georgia Fong thirty thousand dollars now and another thirty thousand for her daughter's education if Doug and Angie Fong made good on their announced intent; and finally, Georgia Fong's unsubstantiated alibi.

The lieutenant fished a silver puzzle ring from a small bowl on her desk and played with fitting the shining circlets together as she listened quietly.

Although most of Elaine's professional attention was centered on presenting their case, the subliminal woman automatically noted the lieutenant's appearance.

Harald had returned from her leave of absence even thinner than before, but in just these three short days, that haunted look had begun to fade from her eyes, those circles underneath weren't quite as dark, and thank God she hadn't reverted to last year's terminal dowdiness. Her boss might be job-smart and intellectual, but when it came to clothes and cosmetics, she was a total neophyte. Elaine had been astonished to realize that for the lieutenant, clothes were just something to protect one's nakedness from the elements, that cosmetics were a waste of time. So when she became involved with artist Oscar Nauman last fall and began experimenting with her looks, Elaine had felt an almost maternal interest.

First had come the haircut, then lipstick and touches of eye shadow, and finally, what looked to be a whole new wardrobe of brighter colors and more attractive fit, like to-day's dark red jacket and tattersall vest over tailored black slacks and white silk shirt.

"You're certain Georgia Fong knew about that policy?" the lieutenant asked, playing devil's advocate.

"She swore there was no insurance on his life," said Elaine.

"We'll check it out with his parents," Jim said, uncomfortably aware that it was something they already should have done.

"Assuming she did know, wouldn't she have wanted it to look like murder so her daughter could collect?"

"Maybe she didn't understand about the two-year waiting period on suicide," said Jim Lowry.

"I never read my car policy till I went on vacation last summer and somebody broke into the trunk and stole two suitcases and my new tennis racquet," Elaine argued. "Or maybe insurance wasn't even on her mind. He wouldn't pay child support, but now he's dead, and the baby's making out better on Social Security benefits."

"You've eliminated the first two wives and the possibility of a drug deal gone wrong?"

"The first wife's definitely clear, and it doesn't feel like drugs," said Elaine. "The blood-splatter pattern shows that he was lying on the couch when he was shot, shoes off, relaxed. If he'd been arguing with someone, it wasn't anybody he felt threatened by."

Jim leafed through the case file. "I'd say Randi Jurgen's clear on this. There are conflicting estimates as to when the shot was actually fired. It's an old building, thick walls, and you know how quiet a little twenty-two can be. The M.E.'s best guesstimate is between seven-thirty and midnight. When Eberstadt did the original canvass, he found a witness who saw Jurgen enter the building shortly before ten. A few minutes later the next-door tenant heard her banging on the door. He finally got tired of hearing it and went out and chased her away."

"What about his parents?"

"No way," said Elaine and Jim agreed. "They blame themselves for his screwups. They've been cleaning up behind him for forty years, and all accounts indicate that they were ready to go on for forty more."

"Besides," said Jim, "Whiteside said they only filed the claim last week. Almost like they forgot it was there."

"I wonder if their daughter-in-law reminded them of it." The lieutenant rotated the final silver circlet until it clicked into place and made one ring. She put it on one of her thin bare fingers, where it hung loose.

"Things certainly would have been a whole lot simpler if Eberstadt had done his job properly and tested the decedent's hands for powder residue," she sighed. "Okay. Check with his parents. If there's any possibility that Georgia Fong could have known about the thirty thousand, run it past the D.A.'s office and see if they agree that the cause of death should be changed."

"Then you think it's homicide, too?"

"Suicides don't usually take a chance on missing," she replied crisply. "If the barrel had been in actual contact with his head when the gun was fired, I wouldn't have let you waste two hours on it, much less two days. So let's not drag it out two more days."

The puzzle ring slid from her finger and broke apart, and she tossed it back into the bowl, where it landed with a jingle amid a dozen others.

Shallcross Trans-City's dispatcher sounded as if he wanted to be helpful. "But like I said, Detective, I got twenty-eight cars here running full-time. I'll have to check the time sheets, figure out who had that particular car. Tell you what, though. You say you're not even sure it's our medallion number?"

Dinah Urbanska explained again about the faint type.

"Doesn't sound like us," said the dispatcher. "We keep our meters inked up. But different meters print up different styles. Why don't you fax me a copy? That car should be back in around four, and I'll see if they're the same. That'll at least tell us if it's our receipt, okay?"

"We'd really like to get moving on this while there's still a chance the driver can remember," Dinah said. "Can't you radio him to come in?"

"Sorry, that one's got a busted receiving unit. We got a new one on order, but—"

Resigned, Dinah said, "I'll fax you the receipt, but it may be too faint to transmit."

"Just run it through your copying machine and use the darkest setting," he advised. "Sometimes that'll pick up light ink."

A few minutes later, Dinah discovered that he was right. Most of the digits still weren't clear enough to read, but at least those that were legible were now dark enough to make faxing Shallcross Trans-City worthwhile. She went downstairs to the station's one fax machine, punched in Trans-City's number, then pressed the send button.

Back upstairs at her desk, she called the owners of the other possible medallion number.

No answer at the Nihat Zahir residence, and the response at Mohammad Palkhivala's was only marginally better. A woman did answer, but her English was so poor there was no way Dinah could get through to her. She was reduced to yelling, "Taxi! *Taxi!*"

"He sleep now. You call later," said the woman and hung up.

"Now what?" Dinah asked Sam Hentz.

"If he's asleep now, he's probably the night man. The guy we want is probably out with the cab right now, but you might as well go over and roust this one out. Ask him if this is his receipt."

He read the names on her notepad. "Zahir? Palkhivala? Are they Turks, Pakis, or Arabs?"

Dinah shrugged.

Sam looked around the squad room. Lowry and Albee

were on the phone again; Gonzalez and Jackson weren't due in until much later.

"Hey, Tildon," he said. "Could you give Urbanska a couple of hours? Go check out a witness with her?"

Tillie looked up from his paperwork. "Sure. Just let me have ten minutes to finish here."

"I'll have to ask my husband," said Angie Fong's cautious voice when Elaine Albee called and asked if Georgia knew about the insurance policy.

From the muffled voices, Elaine thought she'd probably pressed the receiver to her thin chest.

A moment later, Doug Fong's voice came on the line. "What's this about, Detective?"

"Just routine," she said, and asked again if Georgia could have known.

Silence.

"Todd knew," he said at last. "We took out the policy the week Julie was born. We told him it was like an extra baby present, so that if anything happened to him, the baby would be taken care of."

Elaine persisted. "Is it possible that Todd told Georgia?"

"They were man and wife," he replied gently. "It would have been a natural thing to do, but she never mentioned it to us."

"Thank you," said Elaine and got off the line as tactfully as possible.

"Well?" asked Jim.

Her smile was gleeful. "Let's go find us a D.A."

14

. . . and this is an occupation known as painting, which calls for imagination, and skill of hand, in order to discover things not seen, hiding themselves under the shadow of natural objects, and to fix them with the hand, presenting to plain sight what does not actually exist.

Cennino Cennini
Il Libro dell' Arte, 1437

As Sigrid headed uptown with Sam Hentz, the sun disappeared and a thin April rain began to fall straight down.

Hentz had requisitioned one of the department's cars, and when the wipers smeared the windshield into an opaque mess, he activated the washer lever.

Nothing. Whoever had used the last of the washer fluid hadn't bothered to refill the tank.

He muttered an imprecation and Sigrid could sympathize. She was forever forgetting to fill the one on her car.

Before they'd gone half a block, however, the rain increased and the wipers began to contribute streaked bands of visibility.

"Here come the umbrella guys," said Hentz, gesturing to the stands that magically popped up along the streaming sidewalks. "Like those little pellets when you were a kid. Just add water. Instant flowers."

"And empty cabs are like the Wicked Witch," said Sigrid. "Sprinkle them with water and they instantly disappear."

On every street corner, stranded pedestrians huddled beneath inadequate umbrellas or sodden newspapers and frantically waved and whistled to cabs that whizzed by filled with luckier citizens.

"So who're these people we're likely to see up here?" asked Hentz, expertly threading the car through a narrow slice of daylight between a bus and a delivery van.

Briefly, Sigrid gave him the background on the plans for a major retrospective of Nauman's work at the Arnheim Museum and how he had agreed to the concept of a simultaneous four-gallery satellite show.

"All four galleries are in the same building?"

"Yes, but I haven't been in the Orchard Gallery yet, and Hester Kohn's the only dealer I've met more than once. Kohn and Munson were Nauman's gallery for years and years and Hester's the daughter of one of the founders. DiPietro Gallery's been there for years too, so we can assume that she knew him fairly well. Next door is the Germondi Gallery, and Orchard Gallery's on another floor."

She described Victor Germondi and Arnold Callahan for Hentz, the older man's civilized urbanity, the younger one's artsy edginess. "Germondi and DiPietro were extremely close, almost like father and son, but I get the impression that Callahan was included simply because his gallery is there in the building and specializes in works on paper."

As if on cue, a scrap of newspaper flung itself in April foolery across their windshield. Blinded, Hentz braked abruptly. By this time, though, the rain was coming down so heavily that the wipers soon shredded it to a pulp that quickly washed away.

"Who's this Anita Parsons I talked to last night?" he asked, when they were moving again.

"I think it's *Benita*," Sigrid corrected. "She hasn't been with the gallery very long. These part-time people seem to come and go rather frequently."

As she finished describing the staff she'd met, they came abreast of the building and Hentz slowed to a crawl, then stopped to let her out in front of the entrance.

"No point in both of us getting soaked," he said.

As she had no umbrella either, Sigrid didn't argue. "I'll wait in the lobby," she said and managed to sprint from curbside to sidewalk without stepping into the cascade of water rushing down to the corner drain.

Even so, her hair was wet and her clothes were damp by the time she made it inside. When Sam Hentz joined her, his salt-and-pepper hair was plastered down and the cuffs of his pants were sopping. He was always so fastidious about his appearance that Sigrid took pity on his discomfort.

"There's a men's room around the corner there," she told him. "Why don't you go get some paper towels?"

He reappeared a few minutes later with his hair nearly dry.

"That was quick," she said, pushing the button for the elevator.

He shrugged. "I stuck my head under the hand dryer."

"There they are!" one of the part-time assistants whispered excitedly as the tall woman and man tapped at the gallery's locked glass doors.

It was Hadley Jones's morning to be on duty and here she was, even though B'Nita Parsons had told her that Mrs. DiPietro did not want the gallery to open today.

But Hadley had missed the drama of Buck David's opening and she had no intention of missing anything else if she could help it. A couple of reporters had been waiting when she and B'Nita arrived at the same time, but B'Nita had refused to comment and had pushed her inside before she could say a word.

The phone had been ringing off the hook, but B'Nita wouldn't let her answer it. She'd switched the machine so that it would pick up on the first ring and waited until she was sure it was a legitimate call from a client or customer before she picked up. Most were from reporters.

Now Hadley hovered behind B'Nita as that young woman crossed the gallery and unlocked the doors.

A few minutes later, while B'Nita continued to screen the calls, she found herself back in the storeroom, sitting across the table from the two police officers.

"We'll take your statement first, Ms. Jones," said the sexy-looking man.

"Statement? Oh, gosh. That sounds so official," she said apprehensively.

But it turned out to be easy. They wrote down her name and address, asked her how old she was and where she was studying, and noted that her duties here consisted of light typing and covering the reception desk when the others were not there. Mainly they just wanted her impressions of Mr. DiPietro this week, especially yesterday.

"Well, it's always hectic before an opening and he kept forgetting stuff lately and that made it confusing." She described the mix-up with the catalogs and the last-minute printing errors. "But most of the time he was easy to get along with. He could get excited and fly off the handle when things went wrong." She hesitated, remembering the really sharp words he'd said to her over that price list.

"He couldn't stay mad at anybody long, and he always apologized afterward."

Was there anything different about him yesterday?

She shook her head. "Not that I could see, but then, I didn't see all that much of him. It was pretty busy all day yesterday because of the opening. I got here around twelve, and he was in the office finalizing a sale. Donny Levitz came back from lunch at twelve-fifteen, then Mr. D. went out to eat—"

Did she know where?

"Probably the deli next door, because he wasn't gone very long. Anyhow, he got back a little after one. Then he went down to borrow a key from Hester Kohn, and then he left. Must've been around one-twenty."

Alone?

She nodded.

And that was the last she'd seen of him?

Again she nodded, and this time she was a little teary-eyed. "It's so awful to think he's gone. He really was a nice man." She sighed. "Anyhow, Donny Levitz and I stayed till B'Nita got back from lunch—almost two-thirty. And then I had to rush out because I had a three-o'clock class."

"That's a late lunch," said Detective Hentz. "Did she leave before or after Mr. DiPietro?"

Hadley Jones concentrated. "Before. As soon as he got back from lunch, she left."

"Was there anything unusual about that?"

"You mean because she took more than an hour? Not really. After she ate, she went over to Fifth to exchange a book, but the store was too crowded, so she finally had to give it up and come back. It was okay, though. I made it to my class on time."

To Ms. Jones's dismay, Lieutenant Harald had heard a remark about the price-list fiasco and wanted all the details.

It wasn't *her* fault, Hadley Jones insisted. B'Nita would tell them that it was Mr. D. who mixed up the lists.

Every spring the gallery did a mailing to certain select customers, and it included a price-list insert prepared by Mr. D. himself, in his own handwriting, in his own brown ink. One sheet was for his own private records and had the prices he expected to pay the artist-owners; the other was for public consumption, and those prices included the gallery's hefty markup. Somehow the sheets had gotten scrambled and the mailing had gone out with the lower prices. She and B'Nita had taken deposits on several of the works before Mr. D. realized the mistake.

"God, he was mad!" she said. "Because these were his very best customers, and a couple of 'em? They were buying like bargain hunters at a January white sale. There was no way he could turn around and tell those people no, they had to pay forty percent more. Cost him a lot of money."

She paused, dimly aware that Lieutenant Harald was staring at her almost in disbelief.

"I don't care what he said," she told them sulkily. "I typed up the list he left for me. He's the one who messed up and left me the wrong list."

"Oh," said B'Nita Parsons. "I'm surprised she told you about that."

Her fingers, the color of light brown sugar, were quietly laced on the table before her. Her long fingernails were a cinnamon red that matched her long-sleeved sweater, and both echoed the natural reddish highlights of her soft brown hair.

Now *this* was a beautiful woman, thought Hentz. He had already ascertained that she was twenty-three, divorced, and had come north less than a year ago to take graduate courses at Columbia.

Her low voice was lightly inflected with a sweet Alabama drawl. "It was my first week here and I wasn't all that familiar with prices and procedures, so I honestly can't say which of them made the error. Mr. DiPietro swore he left the right price list in the folder for Miss Jones to type; she still swears she typed the one he left. All I know is that I proofread her work to make sure the prices she typed were identical to the ones on the sheet that she'd copied. They were, so I sent it on to the printer, and it went out with the mailing. It was a very costly mistake."

How costly? they asked.

"Thousands," she said succinctly. "Perhaps even tens of thousands."

Hentz whistled.

"A January white sale," Hadley Jones had called it. To Sigrid it sounded almost like a bizarre postscript to that long-ago clearance sale DiPietro's father had staged. Only this time it was a DiPietro who was the heavy loser.

"Do you know why Rudy Gottfried was so angry at the opening?" she asked.

Mrs. Parsons tilted her lovely head. "Something about a fight with Mr. DiPietro's father?"

Concisely, Sigrid recounted Rudy Gottfried's tale of the humiliation Henry DiPietro had inflicted some twenty-five years earlier.

Her brown eyes widened. "So *that's* why Mr. DiPietro was so—"

"Was so what?" Hentz prodded.

Slowly she described how she'd found Hal DiPietro on the telephone when she let herself into the gallery yesterday morning.

"The door was open to his office and he waved to me when I went past. That old man—Mr. Gottfried? You heard that he dumped his slides all over the floor?"

Hentz nodded encouragingly.

"Well, we picked them up and Mr. DiPietro had them on his desk, and it was Mr. Gottfried that he was talking to when I came in yesterday. I only heard his end of the conversation, of course, and he didn't talk about it afterward; but he had looked at the slides and he liked the work. Thought it was interesting, he said, and he wanted to discuss it with Mr. Gottfried. Now, most artists would jump at that sort of opening. Especially if they didn't have a gallery. In just the short time I've been here, I've seen at least two artists practically get down on their knees and beg for a show. But this was almost like Mr. DiPietro was begging Mr. Gottfried and Mr. Gottfried felt he was being insulted. Then he must have said something insulting to Mr. DiPietro, because before I could finish pouring my coffee, I heard him slam down the phone, and then the slides hit the wastebasket."

Knowing how expensive it could be for artists to have professional slides made of their work, Sigrid could only shake her head at the wastefulness.

Except for Gottfried, though, B'Nita Parsons remembered no other friction. "Unless you count that scene you saw with Buck David's girlfriend over the catalog," she told Sigrid. "And the champagne."

Sigrid rather doubted that someone would murder over a misprinted catalog and some warm champagne.

"These memory lapses," said Hentz. "Were they new or was he always forgetful?"

She gave a graceful palms-up gesture. "I've only been here less than two months, so it's hard for me to say."

Hentz glanced at his watch. Almost eleven. He moved to wrap things up by getting the name of the young mother who'd had the job before her.

Jessica Fay.

Hadley Jones implied that Donny Levitz had not left the gallery after he returned from lunch at twelve-fifteen. Would she confirm that?

Except for her own lunch break, certainly.

Her impression of DiPietro's state of mind when she last saw him?

Cheerful and preoccupied.

Her lunch or shopping companions yesterday?

None.

Many receipts these days have the time stamped on them. Had she bought anything?

Only her lunch, and she hadn't kept the receipt. She became wary. "Surely you don't think *I*—"

Nothing personal, Hentz assured her. They'd be asking everybody connected with her late boss. And that reminded him: could she supply them with a recent picture of him? "We hope to locate the cabbie who drove him to the apartment, and it would help us to refresh his memory."

The young woman thought a moment, then walked over to a file drawer and pulled out some head-and-shoulders shots of Hal DiPietro.

"He had to renew his passport a few weeks ago. They're not the greatest."

"They'll do fine," Hentz said. "And what about one of you?"

She recoiled. *"Me?"*

Again he soothed her by saying it was just routine. "We'll show it to the driver, he'll say no, and that'll prove you're clean, right?"

When she told him stiffly that she didn't carry pictures of herself, Hentz said, "That's okay. We'll probably be sending someone around with an instant camera anyhow."

Sigrid had wondered if he would need reminding that Gottfried had described one of the people who passed through the lobby as "a very attractive young black woman." Now she realized that he was right with her.

B'Nita Parsons wasn't very happy with this turn, but at that point, Mrs. DiPietro arrived.

Germaine DiPietro was as tall as Sigrid. A slender brunette in her early thirties, with very fair skin and full red lips, she should have moved with grace and poise. Unfortunately, she did not seem at ease with her height and had the rounded shoulders of a chronic slumper. The hand that she offered them was thin and boneless. Sigrid had held empty kid gloves that possessed more firmness than Mrs. DiPietro's handshake.

Even worse, the woman—presumably mature, known to be the mother of adolescent daughters—had one of those whispery little-girl voices that usually drove Sigrid up the wall.

Happily, she did not have to listen to it for long. With only a few deft questions, Hentz established her ignorance on anything to do with her estranged husband or the gallery since their legal separation two years ago, other than the fact that her daughters would inherit everything. She and the girls had lived on a horse farm in southern New Jersey ever since the twins were born. She had spent the middle of yesterday helping a mare give birth to "just the *darlingest* little colt you ever saw."

Sigrid could not imagine those limp hands doing anything so strenuous as birthing a colt, but "the vet said he could *not* have done it without my pulling on the forelegs."

She happily gave Hentz the vet's name with such glowing recommendations that Sigrid wondered if the woman thought he kept a stallion of his own pastured in Central Park. She also gave him a wallet-size photo of herself and her two daughters.

When asked if she knew who might want to kill her husband, she regretted to whisper that she did not. "He was a warm and generous man. We weren't separated because we didn't love each other," she assured them, wiping her eyes with a lace-edged square of batiste. "But our differences were irreconcilable. He was too urban, I'm too rural."

Was her husband absentminded? Sigrid asked. Prone to memory lapses?

"Oh, *heavens* no! He was the most organized person you could ever meet. He *never* forgot a birthday or anniversary or dinner engagement." Or, she added, any member of the Social Register on this side of the Atlantic or the other.

The blend of amusement and condescension in her finishing school tones made Sigrid suspect that this was a woman who could—and did—trace her ancestry back to the *Mayflower,* and that her social rank had been important to Hal DiPietro.

She had heard of that business between her late father-in-law and those unfortunate artists. "Poor Hal felt it so keenly that Henry was such a rotter. Too much of a money-grubber for my taste," she whispered.

In her whisper, Sigrid heard all the disdain of someone born with several trust funds.

For business details on Hal's work, Mrs. DiPietro suggested that they speak to Victor Germondi. "If he's up to it. *Dear* man! He was so *terribly* distraught when he called me last night. He's the twins' godfather, you know. Or Hester Kohn. She was almost like a sister to poor Hal. You *will* keep me informed, won't you?"

By that time Hentz, too, had had it with the wispy whispers. Victor Germondi and Hester Kohn sounded like bracing antidotes.

At the gallery next door, however, they found only the frail and scholarly assistant who told them that Victor Germondi had not felt able to come in today. Reluctantly, he gave them the suite number at his employer's hotel and asked that they respect Germondi's feelings. "Young Hal was like the son he never had. It's been a grievous blow."

Had he spoken to Hal DiPietro yesterday?

"Indeed, I may have been the last of his acquaintances to see him," he answered sorrowfully. "He stepped in here on his way out to see if Signor Germondi wished to go with him to meet Mr. Buntrock and examine Oscar Nauman's pictures. Unfortunately, Signor Germondi had left much earlier for a luncheon engagement and did not return until midafternoon."

Orchard Gallery was a pleasant, airy space. In addition to the framed prints and drawings on the walls, there were several waist-high wooden bins of various sizes scattered through the rooms. These held works on paper that had been matted and then shrink-wrapped in plastic. One long wall was devoted to file cabinets with wide shallow drawers for storing extras of various editions.

On this rainy weekday morning quite a few people had come in to browse among the bins and drawers. As Sigrid and Sam Hentz entered, a pleasant young woman came up to ask if she could show them anything in particular.

"Arnold Callahan," Hentz said.

"Lieutenant Harald!" Callahan exclaimed. More than

ever he reminded Sigrid of a friendly poodle as he bounded across the room to greet her with his topknot of stiff brown curls bobbing with every step. A sweeping wave of his hand encompassed his domain. "What do you think? Do you approve?"

It took her a moment to shift gears and realize he thought she was there to assess the space for showing Nauman's prints and drawings. She introduced Sam Hentz, who quickly disabused him of the idea that this visit was art-related.

Subdued, he led them past a back workroom where two part-time workers were cutting mats and shrink-wrapping prints, and showed them into his cluttered office.

"I really didn't know DiPietro very well," he said. "Except for some business dealings with Hester Kohn, I didn't know *any* of them until I opened here last summer."

They might have taken a more jaundiced view of his professed lack of involvement, but yesterday Arnold Callahan and his employees had ordered in lunch from the deli next door and all five of them could attest that he hadn't left the gallery from the time he arrived at eleven until he left at six.

"Poor old Victor," said Hester Kohn when they were seated in her sensuous office behind the exhibition rooms of Kohn and Munson. On the corner of her desk, the bright fuchsia throats of the dark red orchids Victor had brought her only three days ago glowed with a smoldering intensity against the green glass top. "He keeps thinking that if he'd been here to go with Hal, this never would have happened. I tried to tell him that he might have been killed, too."

Her words were directed at Sigrid, but her eyes kept flicking toward Sam Hentz as if she were a cat momentarily deflected from a particularly tasty dish of salmon.

"We haven't heard any of the details," Hester said. "Did Hal surprise someone inside the apartment, or was he mugged when he was unlocking the door?"

"Too soon to tell," Sigrid murmured. "DiPietro borrowed the gallery's keys to Nauman's apartment from you yesterday, is that right?"

Hester dragged her predatory hazel eyes back to Sigrid. "You didn't mind, did you? It was Elliott's suggestion."

"No, but you were one of the last to see him."

"Actually, it was my assistant who gave them to him. I was tied up on the phone in here till after two o'clock," she said, inadvertently supplying them with her alibi.

"Did he expect to meet anyone there?"

"Just Elliott. But then Elliott called back after Hal left. Said he wasn't going to make it after all." Her eyes narrowed. "You think Hal knew his killer?"

"We consider all the alternatives," Sigrid said. "Was there anything different about him lately? Was he under stress or worried about something?"

"No," she answered slowly. "Not unless you mean the way he seemed to be snakebit lately. He had more foul-ups this last six weeks than he'd had in the last six years. Did you hear how much money he's losing because he sent out the wrong price list?"

Sigrid nodded.

"What about possible enemies?" Hentz asked.

"Prince Hal was one of the sweetest guys in the business."

"Prince Hal," Sigrid mused. "Rudy Gottfried called him that, too. Why?"

"Because he was named for his father, and Henry DiPietro was a royal bastard who screwed everybody in his power. If you were his equal or his better, he was just a sharp businessman. But if you needed crumbs from his table . . . You heard what he did to Rudy Gottfried?"

Sigrid nodded.

"I was in high school by then and I remember my dad and Jacob trying to talk him out of selling those works at Macy's. That may have been the worst thing he ever did, but it wasn't the only thing. Hal spent the last fifteen years since Henry's death trying to prove that he wasn't the mercenary his father was. If he had a fault, it was that he was too easy on that broodmare down in Princeton. He was so tickled that his daughters had her blue blood that he let her get away with kicking him out of her bed after they were born."

She gave Hentz an intimate smile. Like a pheromone, the musky base of her gardenia perfume seemed to thicken in the air between them.

Sigrid was fascinated. She could tell that Hentz was trying to maintain an objective detachment, but he *was* male and things were happening on an almost primal, subliminal level. She wondered if Hester did it deliberately or if she was genuinely unaware of the undercurrents of raw sexuality that she exuded.

Deliberate or not, Hester gave him a gallery photo of herself as if she thought he wanted it for his personal collection, and Hentz was still breathing heavily as they told her they'd be in touch and went out to the elevator.

"Aren't you lucky?" said Sigrid when they reached the ground floor and could see through the glass doors. "It's still raining."

"Lucky?" Hentz gave her a sour look. "I'm about to get drenched again."

"Think of it as a cold shower," she told him heartlessly. "Weren't you feeling the need for one?"

Germondi's hotel was an attractive old-fashioned building a few blocks over from the galleries, right next door to the Museum of Modern Art.

When Sigrid phoned from the gracious wood-paneled lobby, Victor Germondi sounded as if he had been expecting her call and invited them up to a two-room suite that was modest in size but charming in atmosphere, with its sprigged wallpaper and Chippendale furnishings.

He was fully dressed in a dark gray suit, a white shirt,

and an understated silk tie of such a dark red that it was almost black.

"My associate told me you might come," he said after Sigrid introduced Hentz. "Such a terrible thing. Terrible."

He gestured toward a room service table that held a pot of hot coffee, cups, and more than enough assorted pastries for three.

Splashing in and out of the chilly rain had left the two detectives with damp clothes again, and they were glad to put their hands around a warm cup.

"If only I had gone with him," Germondi mourned again when Sigrid offered him her condolences, "but my luncheon engagement—it was set up before I left Milano."

Despite Germaine DiPietro's belief, he could offer no insight that might help them better understand Hal's final mind-set, business problems, or possible enemies. "Hal and I met in Rome recently. He came over for the ceremony to honor my father, and that was the first time I had seen him in several months."

He crossed to a small writing table beneath the window and showed them a framed five-by-seven candid photograph. He himself stood in the middle holding a jeweler's case in which a shining gold medal was clearly visible. On one side stood a silver-haired, laughing Hal DiPietro, on the other a man who smiled with solemn dignity.

"The president of Italy," said Germondi. "I brought this to give to Hal, but since I arrived in New York, there were always others around. Last night we planned to dine alone together for the first time. But if there had been problems, I think Hal would have found time alone to speak to me. Surely it was someone there to steal and not to kill him?"

Hentz gave a noncommittal shrug and asked if he might borrow the photograph, since it was so much more natural than the passport pictures B'Nita Parsons had given them. When Germondi reluctantly agreed, he carefully removed it from the frame and added it to the others in the manila envelope he carried.

"Rudy Gottfried thought Mr. DiPietro might have acquiesced in that Macy's sale," said Sigrid, setting her empty cup back on the tray. "Were you here when it happened? Did he?"

"No, I was not here," said Germondi. "And no, Hal did *not* consent. Like Jacob Munson, like Horace Kohn, like me when I heard of it, Hal tried to persuade Henry not to do this. It was a dishonorable act. Henry was a shrewd businessman in many things, but in this he was wrong and he hurt his own reputation in the art world for several years. It did not approve. Art is *not* lamps or carpets or furniture, things to be sold at discount to match a couch or wallpaper!" he said passionately.

"Hal felt this very deeply. He loved his father, but in the end, he did not respect him."

Explaining the need to cover all bases, Sam Hentz obtained the name of the restaurant and of the persons with whom Germondi had lunched.

As he and Sigrid rose to go, Germondi sighed and said to her, "Poor Hal. Tomorrow night is the Contessa d'Alagna's reception, and he was so looking forward to it. For me, I would gladly miss it if I could. You and Elliott Buntrock will be there?"

She had not yet fully committed herself to Elliott, but now that Sigrid realized this might be her last chance to see Hal DiPietro's colleagues interact with each other any time soon, she impulsively said yes.

"*Bene.* Then I will not say *arrivederla* till then."

"You're leaving?" she asked.

"Returning to Milano, yes. My plane reservations are for day after tomorrow. I will be back, of course, for Hal's memorial service."

Germondi glanced them to the window and a sad smile touched his lips.

"Look," he said. "The rain has stopped."

15

*If, after you have drawn with the style, you want
to clear up the drawing further, fix it with ink at
the points of accent and stress. And then shade
the folds with washes of ink; that is, as much
water as a nutshell would hold, with two drops of
ink in it; and shade with a brush made of miniver
tails, rather blunt, and almost always dry. . . .
Then, for the accents of the reliefs, in the greatest
prominence, take a pointed brush and touch in
with white lead with the tip of this brush, and
crisp up the tops of these highlights. Then proceed to crisp up with a small brush, with straight
ink, marking out the folds, the outlines, noses,
eyes, and the divisions in the hairs and beards.*

Cennino Cennini
Il Libro dell' Arte, 1437

As they drove back downtown, Hentz began to tick off aloud the people who knew that Hal DiPietro had planned to go to Nauman's apartment yesterday afternoon.

"You, of course. Hester Kohn and her assistant. Germondi and *his* assistant. B'Nita Parsons, Hadley Jones, and that Donny Levitz from his own gallery. Arnold Callahan. And this friend of yours."

"Elliott Buntrock," she agreed equably. "And for all we know, half the art world. Hester told me that Jacob Munson had a saying for DiPietro—'In his mind, in his mouth.' They say he loved to gossip, drop names, chatter about current projects. They never told him anything confidential because he absolutely couldn't resist talking about it if something triggered his memory."

"Do you suppose it was that simple? He mentions it to someone, they show up thinking to boost something valuable when he's not looking, he notices, so they smash him?"

"Nothing's missing, though," said Sigrid. "I checked before you and the others arrived yesterday. Nauman simply didn't keep that much here in the city. Every picture's still on the wall, the three small pieces of sculpture are still there."

"Except for our murder weapon. Is it really worth thirty thou?"

"I have no idea," she admitted. "I don't even know who Noguchi is. Or was. And I might not have been able to describe it in detail, but I would have known that a little stone *something* was missing."

She had arranged for Elliott to come down and give a statement, and as they pulled into the station parking lot, Hentz said, "You plan to sit in on this?"

"No, of course not. He's a personal friend, though, so I'll just say hello and then get out of your way. And if you like," she said, "I'll send Guidry back for pictures."

As they passed the front desk, the duty sergeant called,

"Detective Hentz? Guy here to see Urbanska, but she's not in."

The guy in question was a young, casually dressed Hispanic, who identified himself as a driver for Shallcross Trans-City.

"Dispatcher said for me to bring her a couple of meter receipts off the car I'm driving today," he said and pulled a ten-inch strip of paper tape from the pocket of his leather jacket. "These enough?"

"Perfecto!" said Hentz, after a quick glance for verification. "Thanks."

He did not need to compare the original receipt found in DiPietro's pants pocket. He could see that every digit on this one was clear and bright in crisp black ink; instead of I ♥ NEW YORK, the word LOVE was spelled out; and just below TLC's complaint number was the saccharine HAVE A NICE DAY, a phrase that the first receipt had lacked.

As they continued upstairs, he showed it to Sigrid and said, "If Urbanska or Tildon calls in while I'm with your friend, would you tell them the cab they're looking for's gotta belong to those Pakis or whatever over there on First Avenue?"

"Nonononono," shrilled the dark-skinned, sleepy-eyed man whose wife had reluctantly awakened him, at Dinah and Tillie's insistence. He hardly bothered to look at the meter receipt encased in its clear plastic evidence bag before handing it back to them.

"This is not being my ticket." His voice was now an octave higher and climbing. "Oh, no! You be looking some place else. Some other car."

"Your car," Tillie said firmly. "Where is it?"

With an impatient wave out toward the city, Mohammad Palkhivala said, "My sister's husband. He is driving all day. I am driving all night. You be coming back tonight."

"I have a better idea," Dinah said, speaking very slowly and distinctly as she printed her name and the address of the station house on a page from her notepad. "Your sister's husband will bring your car to this place before five o'clock or we will impound it."

"Oh, no! Oh, no!" *Two* octaves higher now, he ignored Dinah's outstretched hand and clutched at Tillie's arm. The male arm. "This is not the law. The law is not saying you can take my taxi."

With a polite smile, Tillie took the paper from Dinah's hand and placed it in Mr. Palkhivala's. "Five o'clock," he said, "or every cop in the city will be looking for your brother-in-law and that taxi."

Sigrid introduced Sam Hentz to Elliott Buntrock and left them to it in one of the interrogation rooms. Without any reason to think so, she subconsciously expected them to strike sparks of hostility. Instead, when Hentz escorted Elliott back to her office a half hour later, she was vaguely surprised to see them shake hands cordially before Elliott carried her off to a late lunch.

"Nice guy," he said.

"Hentz?" she asked.

"Yeah. Plays cabaret piano, he tells me."

"Hentz?"

"Yeah. So what are you in the mood for? East Indian or West?"

They ended up eating chicken soup with lemongrass in a tiny crowded Thai restaurant, then split an order of pla lad prig because a little chili-garlic sauce went a long way with Sigrid.

While they ate, Elliott repeated what he'd told Sam Hentz. As she expected, he'd been able to supply names of the people he'd been with constantly from morning till midafternoon yesterday. It did not seem to register that he might be a suspect. Instead, he saw himself only as one of Hal DiPietro's many associates, there to help flesh out their picture of Hal and to suggest possible reasons he'd been killed.

"Because it wasn't casual, was it?"

"Casual?" Sigrid parried.

"He was killed because he was Hal DiPietro, wasn't he? Not because he surprised someone in the apartment."

"We don't know," she told him honestly. "If this is a totally random and opportunistic act, then our chances of finding the killer are drastically smaller than if it's someone he knew, someone who killed him for spite or gain. Nothing was taken except his cash, and that could have been a ruse. The door wasn't forced, and whoever it was came without a weapon, so the killing probably wasn't premeditated. No struggle—his face and knuckles are unmarked."

She turned her hands up emptily.

"For spite or gain," Elliott mused.

Sigrid sighed. "Everybody talks about what a nice person he was."

"Ran his mouth a lot," said Elliott. "But he was bright and enthusiastic and overall, yeah, most people did like him."

"Rudy Gottfried's the only one we've found with a grudge, and even he admits it was DiPietro's father who crippled his career all those years ago. I suppose if Morris Wallender and Ben Slocum weren't both dead, we'd be taking a look at them. But they are, so cui bono?"

Latin was another of Elliott's languages, and he smiled. "Who benefits? His wife, one presumes. And his daughters. Or did he have a young mistress who—"

He abruptly flushed a deep red and looked at her in consternation. "Oh, hell, Sigrid! I'm sorry. You *know* I didn't mean that the way it sounded."

All Sigrid really knew at that moment was that her own cheeks were burning.

"Don't apologize," she said tightly. "I'm quite aware of what a clichéd situation Nauman left me in."

"I'm worse than Hal DiPietro ever was," he moaned. "I *swear* I never thought of you like that."

His distress was so palpable that she said, "Forget it,"

and poured the rest of her bottle of Thai beer into his empty glass.

"Sigrid—"

"Look, would you just let it go?"

"No!" he said doggedly. "Just this one time and then never again, okay? From where I was standing, what you and Oscar had was very real and very special."

"Don't do this, Elliott," she said. "Please."

"On the plane out to California, he was thinking of his own mortality. He didn't expect to die, but he did think that you were his last love."

The restaurant was crowded and noisy, but silence held their table. She sat very still, eyes down, and her fingers were clenched so tightly around the empty beer bottle that her knuckles were white.

Very gently, Elliott said, "He did not think he was your last love."

She lifted her eyes to him then. "He was wrong."

"No. He was realistic. 'She makes me young,' he told me, 'and I make her beautiful. And everything else is gravy for both of us.' "

He lifted his glass, drained it, and set it down with a bang. "And one more thing," he said firmly. "Love, wherever it's found, is too rare and precious to *ever* be a cliché, so there!"

She shook her head, but her lips curved in a reluctant half smile.

"Furthermore, I think you should let me escort you to Lucia d'Alagna's reception for Victor Germondi tomorrow night."

"All right."

"Really?" Pleased, he tilted his bony head toward her. "I shall go home and practice being mute."

Nihat Zahir lived one street over and two blocks down from his brother-in-law. His apartment was on the second floor directly above a single-car garage where Zahir and

Palkhivala kept the cab during the relatively few days a year it was not out on the streets twenty-four hours a day.

When Tillie rang the ground-level bell, a dark-skinned, black-eyed woman raised a window upstairs and called down, "Yes?"

"Mrs. Zahir?"

"Yes?"

"Police officers, Mrs. Zahir. We'd like to talk to you about your husband."

Mrs. Zahir's English was much better than her brother's, and she did not automatically assume that they had come to give grief.

Dinah Urbanska showed her the receipt and explained why they were there. Once they made it clear that they had no connection with the Taxi and Limousine Commission and couldn't care less about minor violations of the hack laws, she admitted that her husband wasn't quite as committed to the twelve hours a day, seven days a week work ethic as her brother. Occasionally he wanted to take three hours for lunch, enjoy an afternoon card game with his friends, go out with her and the kids on a weekend. When that happened, he would let a friend drive on halves.

"My brother's wife will be a rich widow someday," she said. "But for my husband and me, time can be more valuable than money."

"Was yesterday one of those days?" asked Dinah.

"Maybe. I think yes, but not today."

She did not know the last names of the two or three men her husband allowed to substitute for him or where they could be found, she told them. Nor, when they showed her the meter receipt, could she say if it came from their cab.

"For these things you must ask Nihat," she told them. As for the five-o'clock deadline they'd given her brother, she shook her head doubtfully. "Sometimes my husband comes home for supper, most times no."

She promised that if he came in before five, she would send him right over to the station. If not, then surely first thing tomorrow morning would be all right, please? Otherwise, her brother . . .

Reluctantly they agreed.

"Honest to God, I forgot all about it," Georgia Fong said. "Todd did tell me Doug and Angie took out insurance for Julie, but I thought it was for when they died, not if something happened to Todd. Although, now that I'm thinking about it, it makes more sense like that. Angie used to worry about the kind of friends Todd had, always afraid he was going to get hurt."

With nothing else pressing her after lunch, Sigrid had decided to sit in on Albee and Lowry's questioning of Georgia Fong. She was too experienced to think she could always tell whether or not a witness spoke the truth. Too often she saw lies spoken with wide-eyed candor, heard truth from the lips of uneasy people who could not meet her eyes. But if Georgia Fong was lying, she was pretty smooth about it.

As the questioning became more pointed, the young mother became indignant first, then scared. "What're you people saying? I left my baby by herself and went over and shot her daddy? Jeez Louise!"

"Can you prove you didn't?" they asked. "If you didn't see anyone, if no one spoke to you—"

"My sister!" she exclaimed. "I called my sister. About nine-thirty. She'll tell you."

"No good," said Albee. "You could have been calling from the phone at your husband's place. Now, if she'd called *you,* that'd be different."

"But I *did* get a call!" Her face was suddenly brighter. "Two calls." Then her shoulders slumped. "Oh, jeez, though. They won't count."

"Why not?"

"Because I hung up on 'em both times."

"Obscene calls?"

She grinned appreciatively. "Not that interesting. Telemarketers. The first was about eight-fifteen. I was in the middle of giving Julie a bath and it was a lady wanting me to buy some of those twenty-dollar light bulbs from the handicapped, you know? I said I couldn't afford them and she started to hassle me, so I hung up on her. The other one was right before I called my sister, and that wasn't even a person. It was one of those recorded messages—'Hello! We're offering cable hookup in your neighborhood for a special introductory price.' I hung up on that one, too."

She threw up her hands in appeal to Sigrid. "Who knew? I should've bought from both of 'em, huh?"

For Sigrid, the telephone had always been a means of communication, not a form of entertainment in and of itself, but she knew there were people who felt otherwise, so she said, "When you called your sister, how long did you talk, Mrs. Fong?"

"Not long. Maybe a half hour. Forty minutes, maybe."

It was not a question that would have occurred to Jim Lowry, and he gave Elaine Albee a dejected glance. Instead of doing a quick wrap-up, they would now spend the next few hours on the phone. Their fingers would do a lot of tedious walking through the book, but eventually, after they called a zillion numbers, they'd probably find both the charity that hawked light bulbs and the cable company that had targeted Georgia Fong's neighborhood. Because while lots of wives kill their husbands, damn few of them call up from the scene of their crime and launch into extended conversations.

"Tell us your sister's name again," he said.

And Elaine added, "Can you remember which charity the woman was calling for?"

By late afternoon, Paula Guidry, their in-house photographer, was able to give them pictures of everyone connected with the art galleries. She'd even made extra copies of the photographs Hentz and Sigrid had collected that morning. If and when Nihat Zahir arrived, the pictures would be ready and waiting. If they were lucky, he would identify Hal DiPietro as one of his fares. If they got really lucky, he might even pick out someone who had ridden over with him.

Sigrid shuffled through a set of the photographs.

"Rudy Gottfried's not too far from my place," she told Hentz. "Want me to see if he recognizes B'Nita Parsons?"

"Sure," said Hentz, "but even if he fingers her, I gotta tell you—to me, he's looking more and more like our grand prize winner."

As the sun slid down the sky behind the twin towers of the Trade Center, it became increasingly apparent to Urbanska and Tillie that Nihat Zahir was going to be a no-show.

"You got his license number?" asked Hentz.

Dinah nodded.

"So give him till midmorning tomorrow and then put out a pickup on the cab."

For Elaine Albee, the day did not end on an up note.

To begin with, Georgia Fong's sister confirmed their lengthy conversation. "I remember because it was the night after somebody shot at her and Julie. And Georgia and me, we were talking about a little baby getting shot right through his bedroom wall over on the West Side."

At least the next confirmation came quickly. The very first cable company they called routed them to its marketing division where an efficient person punched up the numbers on his computer and said, "Yep! We did target that neighborhood that night. There's no way to tell you who answered, but I'm showing that our tape was activated at nine thirty-eight P.M., so someone did pick up the receiver at that number."

They hadn't yet pinpointed the charitable light bulb woman, but surely it was only a matter of time.

"So here we are," Jim griped. "The D.A.'s willing to call

it murder and take it to the grand jury and our best prospect's down the tubes. Back to square one."

He looked rumpled and tired and in need of diversion.

"So we'll come at it fresh tomorrow," Elaine said. "There's a Jeanette MacDonald–Nelson Eddy movie playing uptown. Want to grab a bite and catch the early show?"

For a moment he looked interested, and then he looked— embarrassed? Dismayed? She couldn't quite categorize his expression.

"I've—um . . . The Knicks are playing tonight."

"Oh," she said, a little disappointed.

"Another time?"

She smiled. "Sure."

That would have been the end of it except that Urbanska got up to leave about that time, then gave one of those little distressed yelps that meant she'd goofed up again, and turned back to say, "Hey, Jim, I almost forgot. Dotty Vargas called while you guys were out, and she said be sure and tell you she'd meet you at the box office."

And that look on his face Elaine *could* categorize.

Driving over to Gottfried's apartment, Sigrid suddenly remembered Nauman's yellow sports car and wondered where it was. Garaged here in the city or parked in the driveway up in Connecticut?

Nauman had been a cavalier driver, so his MG was marked with dints and dings. Half the time he couldn't get the top to stay up, and even when it did, the interior was always drafty in winter and stuffy in summer. Yet even though he'd heard all the jokes about sports cars and men over fifty, he loved that car. It probably didn't have much resale value. Maybe she would put out the word at Vanderlyn. Have a raffle or a drawing for really needy grad students or teaching fellows who might like to own it, who would enjoy zipping around the city the way Nauman had.

The thought pleased her and she was still smiling as she pulled her sensible sedan into a parking space across the street from Gottfried's place. As she got out and locked the door, she was startled to see him crossing toward her.

Yet he had almost passed on down the sidewalk before her face registered.

"Lieutenant Harald! Were you coming to see me?"

Sigrid nodded. "I had some pictures I was hoping you would look at."

He hooked his thumb toward the corner diner. "Any reason we can't do it over a bowl of lentil soup? It's not fancy, but it's good."

Sigrid realized that lentil soup was exactly what she was in the mood for, and she followed him willingly into the brightly lighted eatery.

16

*Your life should always be arranged just as if you
were studying theology, or philosophy, or other
theories, that is to say, eating and drinking moderately, at least twice a day, electing digestible
and wholesome dishes, and light wines.*

Cennino Cennini
Il Libro dell' Arte, 1437

The glass-fronted diner was not a place Sigrid would
have chosen on her own. Too new and too basic, the interior was utilitarian minimalism at its coldest, with harsh
white lighting, bare walls, narrow Formica tables, tubular
steel chairs, and chrome holders for paper napkins.

What warmth there was came from the staff. Rudy Gottfried appeared to be a regular customer, and the waiter and
counterman both greeted the burly artist with jocular famil-
iarity. At this time of day there were only three other customers, and minutes after Gottfried and Sigrid walked in,
two thick pottery bowls of hearty lentil soup appeared on

their table. Without asking if they wanted it, their waiter spooned a dollop of sour cream into each steaming bowl and set a red plastic basket of crisp saltines between them. He poured beer for Gottfried and coffee for Sigrid, then left them with the cheerful reminder to yell if they needed anything.

The coffee was as hot and robust as the soup, and both felt good going down.

As they ate, Sigrid laid out the pictures across a bare space on the table.

"Did you see any of these people in the apartment lobby yesterday afternoon while you were waiting for me?" she asked Gottfried.

He put down his spoon, wiped his thick fingers on a couple of paper napkins, and immediately lifted Hal DiPietro's passport picture. Ocher paint rimmed his cuticles, and his hair was so badly barbered that Sigrid wondered if he had cut it himself with a pair of dull scissors.

"You ever see a picture of Henry DiPietro?"

She shook her head.

"This could be him. Hard to believe." He touched the one of Hal with Victor Germondi and the Italian president. "They never looked that much alike when he was a kid. Probably the beard."

Beside it lay the picture of Germaine DiPietro and her daughters. Gottfried was interested that Hal had fathered identical twins. "Must take after their mother's side," he grunted, staring at their girlish faces. "Nothing of Henry here. Hal either, for that matter."

Irresistibly, Sigrid was reminded of her grandmother Lattimore, a woman congenitally unable to look at a person of known lineage without cataloging the forebears from whom that person had inherited each feature—a father's eyes, a mother's strong nose, a grandfather's shiftlessness. Family legend enshrined the time Jane Lattimore beamed down at a toddler after church services and remarked to every Sunday morning worshiper in earshot, "Well, no mistaking what pod that little pea popped out of. He's a Campbell through and through, isn't he?" Which made everyone suddenly realize that he was. Unfortunately, the child's mother was married to a Johnson at the time of his conception.

Rudy Gottfried seemed to have the same sharp eye for inherited family likenesses.

When he came to Hester Kohn's picture, he asked, "Horace Kohn's kid? She's got his eyes and mouth. Looks like a hot number. She couldn't have been more than eight or ten the last time I saw her. Even then you could tell, though. I knew she was going to turn heads. Bet she gave old Kohn a few cold sweats before she got past puberty."

He scanned the Polaroids of Arnold Callahan and the assistants from all three galleries without pausing. "Sorry, Lieutenant."

"Are you sure?" Sigrid tapped the photo of B'Nita Parsons. "You said one of the people was a very attractive young black woman."

Gottfried cocked his head and his eyes abruptly narrowed.

"Who'd you say she is?" he asked, frowning.

"I didn't."

"She wasn't at Oscar's place, but there *is* something familiar about her."

"Maybe you saw her at the gallery night before last. She worked for DiPietro. B'Nita Parsons."

"Benita? That's a name you don't hear much anymore."

Sigrid demonstrated the unusual spelling on her napkin.

"She from here?"

"Alabama. Studying for a graduate degree at Columbia."

He laid the Polaroid on top of the pile and picked up his soup spoon again, but Sigrid noted that his eyes kept flicking back to Mrs. Parsons's face as he ate.

It was not a particularly flattering picture. Judging by the hostility in her level eyes and tight, unsmiling lips, she was still resentful when Officer Guidry returned with the camera this afternoon. Even so, resentment did little to obscure her beauty.

For an instant, as Sigrid gazed at the picture from this oblique angle, B'Nita Parsons's likeness almost triggered a memory, yet she couldn't think of what. She stared hard and let her mind go blank. Sometimes that would trick her subconscious into giving up its secrets, but not this time. With a mental shrug, she let it go. Things that were important eventually bobbled to the surface. If not, not.

Appetite sated, she nodded when the waiter came over to top off her mug of coffee and asked if he could take her bowl. After he returned to the kitchen, she said, "According to this Mrs. Parsons, Hal DiPietro called you yesterday morning."

"Yeah?"

"She also said the call ended in angry words."

His coarse and raggedly cut gray hair seemed to bristle when his head came up, and he looked at her pugnaciously. "So?"

"Could you tell me what it was about?"

"You still trying to get me involved here?"

"You *are* involved, Mr. Gottfried," she said quietly. "How much or how little is what I need to know."

Gottfried leaned back in the tubular steel chair with a weary sigh, and his spoon clattered in his empty bowl. The waiter started over, but Gottfried waved him off.

"He phoned me. Prince Hal. Said he'd looked at my slides. Said retro abstract was *deliciously* hot right now." His voice dripped acid. "Said he wanted to let bygones be bygones. Maybe represent me again. I told him where he could stick it. End of conversation."

He picked up the picture of B'Nita Parsons and set it down next to Germaine DiPietro's. "Wonder if they'll keep the gallery going."

Sigrid shrugged. "The Parsons woman's only been there six or eight weeks, and Mrs. DiPietro doesn't seem too interested in it. Besides, it's lost a lot of money lately. They had an unintended bargain sale less than a month ago, and this time the gallery took a beating."

"Yeah?" Gottfried took a swallow of his beer and looked interested.

Sigrid seldom gossiped about information uncovered during an investigation and certainly not with a principal; but the coincidence was too strong not to share it with the man who'd been destroyed by the gallery's first bargain sale.

Rudy Gottfried listened intently as she described the two price lists Hal DiPietro had compiled and how a part-time assistant had somehow typed up the wrong list, which was then sent out to the gallery's best customers.

"Her?" he asked, tapping B'Nita Parsons's picture. "She the one that screwed him?"

"She's the one who had it printed up and mailed," Sigrid said, "but she hadn't been working there long enough to know the prices were off. No, the one who typed it up wrong—" She sorted through the pictures till she came to the part-time assistant's. "This one. Hadley Jones."

Gottfried gave the picture a cursory glance and laid it aside.

Sigrid was puzzled by his response. She hadn't expected gleeful cheers, but surely it would have been only human for him to say "Serves them right" upon hearing that the gallery had taken a serious financial blow?

Instead, he seemed preoccupied, as if working out some sort of mathematical equation in his head.

She finished her coffee and began gathering up the photographs.

Abruptly, and apropos nothing that she could name, he murmured, "The sins of the fathers . . ." and gave a deep sigh.

"Excuse me?"

"Nothing. Just—"

He broke off, shook his head, then seemed to gather up his thoughts and refocus. His broad face became almost cheerful. "I've been thinking about the piece Buntrock wants me to write, about when Oscar first came over to New York, just a kid from Pittsburgh. He knew my sister, and she told him how I had this loft on Prince Street. In those days, it was against the law to live in lofts, so we slept on old couches we lugged up from the Salvation Army, and we had to be careful not to let the building inspectors catch us cooking."

Fascinated, Sigrid listened for over an hour as Gottfried spoke of his and Nauman's early years in the city. The friendships and feuds. The yeasty ferment of ideas and theories in endless, passionate bull sessions. Living life on the margins at times, skimping on food and clothing when they had to come up with the rent, and always holding to the one basic premise: that art not only mattered but mattered enough to make almost any sacrifice worthwhile.

Later, as she drove up Sixth Avenue with her windows cracked, enjoying the cool night air, she decided that if Rudy Gottfried could write half as well as he talked, his piece would probably be the liveliest part of the show's catalog.

"I suppose you ate already?" Roman Tramegra asked in exasperation when she let herself into their front hall.

"Only soup." She sniffed the kitchen's entrancing aromas. When her housemate stuck to the basics, he was a wonderful cook. "What smells so good?"

Mollified, Roman smoothed his thin strands of hair across his high-domed head and said, "Lemon roasted chicken. With tiny spring potatoes and julienned zucchini."

Sigrid said, "Ummm! Want me to set the table?"

Hopeful relief swept over him as she moved between kitchen and dining room with plates and utensils. Nor did she argue when he suggested wineglasses and candles, too. Without staring, he noted that she'd eaten off her lipstick, but the windy April night had tousled her dark hair and given color to her cheeks.

For too long she had only picked at the food he prepared for her, not caring what it was, wanting only to be left in silence. Sometimes he thought that if he hadn't *bullied* her until she snapped at him to leave her alone, she would have just gone to bed and *never* gotten up again.

Tonight she ate with returned appetite, asked about his book, and seemed genuinely interested in his continuing struggle with the computer.

"But I *do* think I'm beginning to master it," he told her in his deep bass voice as he spooned tangy lemon sauce over her serving of crisply roasted chicken. "I've signed up for a two-week crash course that starts on Monday, but *today* I figured out how to transfer all my notes onto a disk. Such a *marvelous* invention! Six months of work on one little piece of plastic."

Happily he plunged into a synopsis of the murder mystery he'd been working on almost from the moment Sigrid first met him.

Down in his SoHo studio, Rudy Gottfried sat with his pen in hand, too lost in speculation to concentrate on those earliest years with Nauman, those halcyon days before he'd ever heard of Henry DiPietro. A great sadness was growing inside his burly chest, a sadness that had nothing to do with the beers he'd drunk. He hoped he was wrong, but he could still see the photograph in his mind's eyes and he knew the name was no coincidence.

The sins of the fathers bloody the children, he thought, muddling the half-forgotten Bible verses from his youth. From generation unto generation.

17

When you want to do the head of an old man, you should follow the same system as for the youthful one; except that your verdaccio wants to be a little darker, and the flesh colors, too.

Cennino Cennini
Il Libro dell' Arte, 1437

Jim Lowry was totally average, Elaine Albee told herself dispassionately. Average height, average looks. His hair was a nondescript sandy brown, his eyes an ordinary hazel, his smile lopsided and downright goofy at times. It was a face that could probably be found on a hundred Pennsylvania apple farms.

Nihat Zahir, on the other hand, was probably the best-looking man she'd ever seen up close and personal. Dark curly hair he had, smoldering black eyes, and teeth that flashed pure white against clear olive skin. There was even a dimple in his left cheek that looked deep enough for her to bury her fingertip in. His features should have been smiling out of billboards or million-dollar movies, not stuck on a hack license on the back of a taxi seat.

He was sitting at Urbanska's desk only a few feet away from Jim, yet all she could think about, all she'd thought about last night each time she turned over, was Dotty Vargas running her fingers through Jim's hair, Dotty Vargas smiling into Jim's eyes. Dotty Vargas inviting him into her bed?

It was totally illogical that those images should have kept her awake half the night. It wasn't as if Vargas was poaching on her territory. Jim was her friend. Her colleague. Partner. Nothing more. Her choice. Was she now going to start growling like a dog in the manger because he had finally taken no for an answer and started looking elsewhere?

What did she expect, for God's sake? That her vows of departmental chastity were binding on him, too?

Get real, she berated herself.

And yet . . . *Oh, damn,* something inside her moaned. *Dotty Vargas?*

She gave Dotty Vargas a mental boot and tried to concentrate on the Todd Fong case while Jim eavesdropped on Nihat Zahir's interview with Dinah Urbanska. Whenever she looked up, Jim's eyes met hers and then guiltily bounced away.

Zahir was Urbanska's witness, but he'd arrived right on Jim's heels, before Urbanska got in this morning; and the cowardly hound had seized the opportunity to avoid having to make natural-sounding small talk with Elaine over their coffee.

Elaine was equally reluctant to talk to him, but Lieutenant Harald would be calling them in this morning for a status report, and she was going to want to know where, if anywhere, the Fong case was going. Unable to sleep, Elaine had been in for over an hour, and she'd read through the entire jacket without spotting any loose threads to unravel.

"Let's ask his parents in, get them to list all of Todd's

known acquaintances," she suggested to Jim glumly. "Maybe it'll trigger some memory for them."

He reached for the phone with an expression equally glum.

The receipt Nihat Zahir had torn from his meter this morning exactly matched the one found on Hal DiPietro, but Dinah Urbanska's elation quickly turned sour when the driver looked at the pictures of the dead man and said, "Maybe I am driving him, but he is not strong enough in my head to say for sure yes."

"You probably picked him up at Madison and East Fifty-seventh," she said, and told him the cross streets nearest the East Side apartment building where he'd probably let DiPietro out, but nothing seemed to strengthen his memory of the gallery owner.

"Wait a minute," said Tillie, who had wandered over to hear what Zahir had to say. "I thought your wife said you didn't work that afternoon shift."

The man shrugged good-naturedly. "What can I tell you? My wife, she is wrong."

"Look," Urbanska told him. "We don't care if you let someone else drive. But this man was killed, and he had your receipt in his pocket. All we want is to talk to the person who gave it to him, okay?"

"Is me," said the cabbie, pointing to the faded time. "One fifty-two. Is me!"

"Then how about these?" she asked, thrusting into his hand the pictures of DiPietro's wife and gallery associates.

He smiled at the picture of the twin daughters, but if his memory of DiPietro was dim, it was clearly nonexistent for these faces.

"Sorry. I drive many, many peoples. Sometime I am not remembering if that person is lady or gentleman, you know? I am looking in the mirror to see is which, you know?"

Sighing, they agreed that they knew.

Sigrid picked up on the tension between Albee and Lowry almost as soon as they entered her office, but she marked it down to their frustration over a case that seemed to have dead-ended for them.

She listened with growing puzzlement as they summarized what they'd learned so far:

That Todd Fong had been screwing up since he was a teenager.

That he couldn't or wouldn't hold a steady job.

That his elderly and overindulgent parents kept bailing him out of trouble.

That he consorted with known criminals and was a user of drugs and alcohol.

That he was a bully and quick with his fists.

That he'd risked killing his own daughter in an attempt to shoot his estranged wife for insurance that no longer existed.

That a hefty insurance policy on him would pay off for his daughter and his parents if it could be proved that he had not died by his own hand.

"Mr. and Mrs. Fong are in the interview room right now trying to come up with more names for us," said Lowry, "but I don't know."

He glanced at Albee, who shook her head. "We can keep digging, Lieutenant, but Georgia Fong's the only one with a strong motive, and between all the phone calls, she's pretty much out of it."

"Am I missing something here?" Sigrid asked. "Why are you giving the parents a free pass? Are they independently alibied?"

They looked at her blankly.

"Well, no," said Albee, tucking a lock of blond hair behind her ear. "But the Fongs adored that creep. They've rationalized and justified and cleaned up behind him for forty years. Why would they suddenly kill him?"

"And even if they did," said Lowry, "why would they

start yelling murder when it was going to go down as a suicide?"

"Perhaps like you, Albee, they finally read the policy," Sigrid said crisply. "Look at what's here."

She ticked the points off on her fingertips. "You have an elderly couple now on a fixed income and a son who keeps needing financial help, with no end in sight. The son punches out his wife and is known to have shoved his own mother at least once. But why is he killed now?"

It was her favorite question and the one she always tried to answer: Why now? Why not last week? Why not next month?

She flipped through the gory pictures in the case jacket. "Look at him. He's lying on that sofa, no sign of a struggle, and you think close friend or lover? I see Mom or Dad. She did his laundry and mended his clothes, right?"

Lowry nodded reluctantly.

"So maybe one of them went over to take his things, saw the gun, and somehow pieced it together that he was the one who took a potshot past the granddaughter. Isn't this a reasonable motive for murder? The Fongs may have adored their son as much as you say, but I'll bet that baby's not exactly chopped liver."

Elaine Albee stood up purposefully. "Which one do you want?" she asked Lowry.

"I'll take the father."

It didn't take very long.

Within the hour a weeping Angie Fong broke down and told them everything. The second time through was by the book and with both her lawyer and someone from the D.A.'s office in attendance.

Sigrid sat in on the session, but it was no satisfaction to see her suppositions confirmed by that ravaged old woman.

As she'd thought, Angie Fong had indeed walked the few short blocks to her son's place. While she was there putting away his laundry and tidying up the efficiency apartment, Randi Jurgen had called. Todd had been drinking and was just tipsy enough to tell his ex-wife that he'd missed.

Instantly his mother realized everything.

"And then he laughed!" Angie Fong wailed. "*Laughed!* He could have killed Julie and he *laughed*. I knew where he kept the gun and I waited till he lay back down on the couch to watch TV and then I just walked up from behind him and did it. I had to. Anyhow, it was my right, wasn't it? I gave him life and I took it back again. For Julie."

Her thin wrinkled hand reached out to her attorney. "The insurance company will have to pay now, won't they?"

18

[In casting a life mask] have some plaster of Paris ready. . . . And bear in mind that if this person whom you are casting is very important, as in the case of lords, kings, popes, emperors, you mix this plaster with tepid rose water; and for other people any tepid spring or well or river water is good enough.

Cennino Cennini
Il Libro dell' Arte, 1437

The Contessa d'Alagna's New York pied-à-terre occupied the top two floors of a Fifth Avenue apartment building overlooking the park. The elevator required a key and a white-gloved attendant; but when the polished brass doors slid back, Sigrid and Elliott Buntrock stepped directly from the elevator into a formal open archway that flowed into an enormous room decorated like a spring garden, complete with stone fountains, flowering azaleas, and white wicker tables and chairs softened by bright silk cushions. At the far end, a string quartet played beneath mature dogwood trees in full bloom.

"I don't think I've ever been in a private ballroom before," Sigrid confided to Elliott as they waited for the receiving line to begin moving again.

"Just think of it as your grandmother's living room with the rugs rolled back," he murmured. "Only bigger."

She smiled. "Someday you'll have to meet my grandmother."

Amusing to picture her grandmother here. She would not be one bit intimidated by Lucia d'Alagna's fortune, her position in international society, or her penthouse apartment.

Although the Lattimores were comfortable, they were by no means wealthy. But Jane Lattimore was one of the South's natural aristocrats who believed that should a lady extend or accept hospitality, it mattered not if the invitation came from a mansion or a mobile home. ("Only parvenus judge one another by possessions.") When it came to entertaining, Mrs. Lattimore judged—and judged quite severely—by one simple standard: a guest must always be offered the best that one had; without apology if the offerings were necessary humble, and certainly without boast if one were more financially blessed.

"Fresh water in an honest jelly glass is always to be valued over inferior wine in Baccarat crystal," she told her grandchildren. "Unless, of course, they have no palate and don't *know* it's inferior," she would charitably add.

Grandmother Lattimore would probably approve the contessa's style. She must have staggered the times on the invitations because the receiving line ahead of them was blessedly short. Her ash blond hair appeared to be going gray with an artful naturalness. Her gown was a rich midnight blue ornamented only by a large pearl-and-diamond brooch on the bodice. More pearls and diamonds clustered on her ears.

Sigrid had no idea whether the contessa possessed a photographic memory and had studied her guest list for hours, or if she simply relied on the young woman who stood slightly behind her and murmured softly in her ear as the guests approached, but she greeted each one by name and even held Sigrid's hand an extra moment as she expressed her regret for Oscar Nauman's death.

"We met perhaps twice or three times," she said. "And I attended one of his gallery talks six years ago. He seemed to me both brilliant and unpretentious. Was he truly so?"

"Yes," Sigrid said. "He was."

"A rare combination."

She passed them along to Victor Germondi, resplendent in white tie. His smile expressed both pleasure in seeing them and continuing concern about Hal DiPietro's death.

"Is there not something you can tell me?" he asked Sigrid. "My plane departs at five tomorrow afternoon and I do not like to leave without knowing."

Sigrid shook her head regretfully, remembering Sam Hentz's resigned air that afternoon when he reported the dead end on the cab driver and the failure to turn up witnesses on their second canvass of the building. Hentz still liked Rudy Gottfried for it and hoped to find someone who could put the burly artist (and his portable floodlights) in the elevator or on the fifth floor before Sigrid arrived; but after hearing Sigrid's account of her meeting with Gottfried over lentil soup, he wondered if they ought to take a closer look at B'Nita Parsons.

"No alibi," he'd said, "but no apparent motive, either. I mean, how much can you hate a guy you've worked with for less than two months?"

"Oh, I don't know," Sigrid had said, and both of them had abruptly remembered Hentz's hostility from the get-go.

"Ah, well, Hester has promised to keep me informed," Victor Germondi said now, as he in his turn introduced them to the Italian ambassador and senior officials of the Italian Mission to the UN.

The formalities over, Sigrid and Elliott strolled through the crowded ballroom-cum-garden. Uniformed maids circulated with silver trays of excellent white wine and hot canapés. Sigrid at first saw no one she knew, but like Nauman whenever she'd gone with him to similar events, Elliott was greeted every few minutes by associates in the art world. Whether they were influential critics, museum people, or serious collectors, he was punctilious about introducing her.

She was amused by their reaction when they realized she was the "COP TO INHERIT ARTIST'S WORK WORTH M$$$!" as headlined in the *Post* back in February. One portly gentleman betrayed the interest he'd taken in those stories when he exclaimed, "Heavens! You look nothing like your pictures."

No disputing that, she thought, willing herself not to appear as self-conscious as she felt under the man's appraising stare. The *Post*'s only file pictures of her were candid shots taken by Rusty Guillory during various investigations before she began to take an interest in her looks. Since then she'd had her dark hair cut and styled, had taken a couple of makeup lessons, and had even gone with Anne to have her colors done. As a welcome-home-from-California present for Nauman, she had been in the process of revamping her wardrobe to weed out the drab and shapeless beige and olive clothes he disliked, in favor of the clear, bright colors he preferred. Now that the terms of his will were public knowledge and her name was irrevocably linked to his, she felt it was almost her solemn duty not to give people newly meeting her an obvious reason to question Nauman's taste.

That was why she had left work early today to have her hair and makeup done professionally, and that was why she wore the sapphire gown Grandmother Lattimore had sent for her birthday last year, a deceptively simple raw silk sheath. The cut of the gown flattered her thinness, and the rich color turned her gray eyes blue. Her only jewelry was a pair of long earrings that gleamed like liquid silver whenever she moved her head.

Eventually they wandered through one of several open

French doors onto the wide penthouse terrace, which continued the spring garden decor with flowering pears, forsythia, and more azaleas massed in reds and pinks. A dozen pink-and-white garden umbrellas gave extra color and charm to the terrace and added warm air as well, since each umbrella contained a small heater that helped take the edge off the cool night air.

In addition to the people Elliott knew personally, he had pointed out to her a famous drama critic, a Booker and two Pulitzer winners, and an actor who had probably been invited not because of his superstar status but because of his impeccable art collection.

They found Hester Kohn by the railing with a dazzled Arnold Callahan, who loved the night view of the park, but was afraid he'd miss a celebrity if he took his eyes off the passing parade. "Look!" he whispered. "Is that Barbra Streisand?"

"Poor Hal," said Hester to Elliott. "Wouldn't he have loved this party?"

Sigrid gave an inquiring look, and Hester said, "I'm sure it's not speaking ill of the dead to say it. Hal loved mingling with the rich and famous, and this reception would have given him enough names to drop for six months."

"Oh, my God!" Callahan croaked in quiet hysteria. "There's Caroline Kennedy!"

He darted away in the direction of a young woman in black silk, and Elliott's bony face lit up with a rueful smile. "Another Hal in the making."

With a sigh, Hester said to Sigrid, "I don't suppose you've caught his killer yet?"

"No."

"But surely you must have strong leads?"

"I really can't talk about it," Sigrid demurred.

"Sorry to sound callous, but this really screws up our plans for Oscar's show," Hester told them. "Victor's willing to continue, but Germaine DiPietro's talking about selling out, and without Hal's gallery . . ." She shook her head.

"I'll try to get Germaine to keep it going for the rest of the year anyhow. That B'Nita Parsons doesn't have Hal's contacts, of course, but she's a quick learner and she's got a good eye. In fact, if Germaine does close down, I may offer the kid a job. Now that Jacob's gone, I could sure use someone with her potential."

A maid came by with more wine, followed by a waiter who collected empty plates and glasses.

"Where did you get your plate?" asked Elliott, who was beginning to feel the need of sustenance with his wine.

"Go past the string quartet," said Hester, "and hang a right at what I swear to God has to be a Donatello. And if that's not a Cellini in the middle of the buffet, I'll eat it."

Elliott pronounced the wonderful bronze statue by the dining room door a Donatello indeed, but he was less sanguine about the enormous silver bowl piled high with apples and pears and bunches of grapes. Half as big as a washtub, it was elaborately decorated with rearing horses, lounging gods, and dancing nymphs. All in solid silver.

"Even if it's not Cellini, it's certainly of the period," he said when they had worked their way through the crowd to the buffet. He filled his plate with puffs of savory pastries, stuffed mushrooms, and paper-thin prosciutto wrapped around slices of melon and mozzarella. "Imagine actually using it as a fruit bowl."

Sigrid was delighted. "My grandmother would," she told him. "She said she wouldn't have something she couldn't use if she wanted to, and after all, isn't that what it was designed for?"

"I really must meet this grandmother of yours," he said.

They joined the director of the Arnheim, his wife, and Irv Coats, an antiquarian book dealer turned syndicated bridge columnist, at one of the tables near the string quartet, and the conversation turned to the difficulties of funding cultural events in the new era of stringent cuts in government programs.

"This current rage for branding government the enemy

drives me up the wall," said the Arnheim director. " 'Get government off our back,' they yell, but every time the vaunted private sector falls flat on its face and can't tie its own shoes, it's the government that has to pick up the pieces. I'm not just talking about the savings and loan industry either, or every time there's a flood or an earthquake or an airplane falls out of the sky. I was a kid in Brooklyn in the thirties. My dad was making about eighteen dollars a week, but every month or two it seemed something new was opening up—playgrounds, libraries, the zoo at Prospect Park, public beaches and the roads and bridges that led to them. I remember my dad piling the neighborhood kids into the old 'twenty-nine Studebaker every weekend and off we went, running boards scraping the ground. New York was the most generous place on earth when I was coming along. It supported five *free* four-year colleges. I could never have gone otherwise. And all the free concerts and art exhibits! I owe my life to that civic spirit, and it grieves me that these so-called private-sector advocates keep fattening themselves at the public trough while denying our children and grandchildren the enrichment that we had."

Irv Coats nodded. "The Carnegies and the Mellons built libraries and museums with the money they gouged. The Donald Trumps build casinos."

They had almost finished eating when the string quartet fell silent and Lucia d'Alagna drew their attention to the other end of the hall where panels slid back to reveal a large television screen. For those who had missed the ceremony in Rome last week, the contessa explained that she would now run a tape of the part where Leo Germondi was honored and Victor Germondi accepted his award.

Sigrid had not been present when Hal described the ceremony, but Elliott provided a whispered translation for her benefit.

Afterward, as the lights came up again, the contessa called for Victor Germondi to come forward.

"What Leo Germondi did for Italian art, his son did for

my family," she said. She was an entrancing storyteller and soon had the room on the edge of its collective seat as she verbally re-created those confused and dangerous weeks near the end of the war when the teenage Victor stole a truck loaded with art treasures, many of them belonging to her family, almost from under the Nazis' noses, and suffered bullet wounds that could have killed him in the act.

"In token," she said to Victor, her voice breaking. "In very small token, *amico mio,* I wish you to have this."

"Oh, my," said the Arnheim director as everyone stood to clap. "Oh, my!"

"What is it?" asked Elliott, clapping so furiously that his angular elbows gave him the appearance of a stork flexing its wings.

"Unless I'm very much mistaken, she has given him her Andrea del Sarto drawing of Aeneas bearing Anchises on his shoulders."

Elliott was impressed. Del Sarto was a follower of Raphael and many today considered him the finer artist.

Sigrid was more impressed with the symbolic significance of the drawing itself. The Trojan hero who carried his aged father to safety from the burning city of Troy surely paralleled Victor Germondi's saving of Lucia d'Alagna's patrimony.

In a few heartfelt, emotional words, Victor Germondi expressed his deep gratitude to the contessa, to his country, and to his fellow guests tonight. He assured them that he would never forget this moment.

As the string quartet broke into a jaunty Italian rondo, the contessa began her grand sweep around the ballroom.

"A very generous gesture," Elliott told her when she reached them. "But then, it *does* stay in your family."

"Pardon?" The contessa looked puzzled.

"Victor Germondi is your cousin, isn't he?"

"Why, no. Whatever gave you that idea?"

"I had the impression that he was part of your Cedronio branch."

"Ah, no! The last Cedronii were killed in the war when my uncle's estate took a direct hit from two bombs."

"That's right. I remember now. One of the great art tragedies of the war. An Etruscan mosaic *and* a da Vinci mural were destroyed, weren't they?" he asked sympathetically.

"Everything," she said. "Smashed to dust. I was only a little child, but I remember going there with my mother after the war. She was weeping, and we picked up a handful of red and blue tesserae. I have them yet."

She turned to Sigrid, murmured that the pleasure was hers when Sigrid thanked her for a pleasant evening, and then swept on to the next group.

In the cab on their way downtown to Sigrid's apartment, she asked him why he'd thought Germondi was kin to the contessa.

"It was that book that Hal gave him, remember? With a picture of Leo Germondi's Madonna? Hal said the photograph was taken while the Madonna was still in the chapel of Victor's grandmother. I must have misread the caption underneath. I could have sworn that it said the Cedronio family chapel, and I remembered that the contessa's mother was a Cedronio."

"Were they an important family?" Sigrid asked. "She came very close to haughtiness when you suggested Germondi might be related."

"The Cedronios were even more ancient and noble than the d'Alagnas," he assured her. "Land, money, tons of artworks that were destroyed in the bombing."

Sigrid had drunk just enough wine to loosen her inhibitions. "Oh, my protoplasmal ancestor!" she said wickedly.

"Pooh-Bah?" He smiled and searched his memory of *The Mikado*.

She leaned back and softly warbled, " 'But family pride Must be denied And set aside And mor-or-or-tified.' "

They spent the rest of the taxi ride home trying to sing the trio with only two voices. The cabbie, one Christophe

Baudelocque, professed himself unable to take the part of Pish-Tush.

After letting himself into his hotel room, Victor Germondi laid the leather portfolio on the table. He realized that he should have put it in the hotel safe when he passed through the lobby, but he was too exceedingly weary to call down and go through the formalities now. With one hand he tugged at his white tie, while with the other he began to undo his pearl shirt studs. The chambermaid had turned down his bed, and it took great willpower not to drop his clothes on the floor and crawl in.

Instead, he hung everything in the closet, put on pajamas and brushed his teeth; and these actions refreshed him enough that he undid the portfolio and propped up the matted del Sarto drawing against the brass lamp base.

It was an absolute beauty. No question. It had occupied a place of honor in Lucia d'Alagna's Milan palazzo, and she had given it sincerely and with no motive but to honor him.

And yet just looking at Aeneas staggering under the weight of his father brought back his own great weariness. All his life, he had borne his father's reputation upon his shoulders.

Hal, too, he reminded himself.

Yet Hal had envied him, never realizing that, in many ways, a shining reputation can weigh even more heavily than a besmirched one.

He sighed, returned the drawing to the protection of the leather binder, and turned out the light.

Waiting for sleep to come, the wine no longer fuzzing her brain, Sigrid let her thoughts drift to Hal's murder. Random bits of information lay in her brain like pieces of a mental jigsaw puzzle, and she lazily fitted this piece next to that one until it suddenly dawned on her that she was asking herself that same old question: Why was the murder committed *now*?

Not only was she asking the question, but enough pieces now fit together to give her an answer. It might not be the correct answer, but it seemed to her as convincing as anything Hentz had come up with.

Her clock showed long past midnight, but she switched on the light, found Elliott's number, and dialed it.

When he answered groggily, yawning and protesting, Sigrid said, "You knew him better than I did, so tell me. If Hal DiPietro had gone to the reception tonight thinking that Germondi was a Cedronio and kin to the contessa, would he have dropped the subject as quickly as you did?"

"Oh, hell, no," Elliott answered grumpily. "He'd have run back and forth between Victor and the contessa all night. He'd have quoted the book, insisted on talking about the Madonna, and . . ."

His words trailed off and Sigrid could almost hear his mind working across the telephone wires.

"My God!" he said slowly. All sleepiness left his voice, and she knew he had reached the same conclusion. "I didn't misread that caption, did I? Do you suppose Leo stole it?"

"As I recall," said Sigrid, "Victor Germondi said his father would have sold his soul to keep it."

"And if he stole one Cedronio picture, that probably means he stole all of them. Say the Cedronios gave him their family treasures for safekeeping. The Cedronio line was totally wiped out in the war. No direct heirs, so who would know if he just kept the stuff? Let the relatives assume it was bombed to smithereens or disappeared into the maelstrom. Before the war, old Leo was an art professor and small-time dealer. Ten years later he was one of the wealthiest dealers in northern Italy. People assume his fortune was the result of shrewd trading on his part. But what if his money came from a discreet disposal of his Cedronio holdings?"

"All except the Madonna?"

"All except the Madonna. So many were painted, and

often the differences were minute. The ancients had a different take on 'originality' than we do. If someone was a master, the others gladly imitated him, so that Madonna was safe enough to keep."

Abruptly he realized where their suppositions were leading and he was profoundly shocked. "*Victor* killed Hal?"

"At the moment there's not a shred of proof," Sigrid warned. "But after all the fuss that's been made over his father these past few weeks, could he simply ask DiPietro to keep his mouth shut and trust him not to talk?"

"No," said Elliott. "Not Hal."

19

To paint a wounded man, or rather a wound, take straight vermilion; get it laid in wherever you want to do blood. Then take a little fine lac, well tempered in the usual way, and shade all over this blood, either drops or wounds, or whatever it happens to be.

Cennino Cennini
Il Libro dell' Arte, 1437

"It fits," said Sam Hentz. "The way he was struck from behind while he was looking at the pictures? We've thought all along it had to be someone he knew and didn't feel threatened by."

One thing about Hentz, Sigrid thought approvingly, was that you didn't have to run things by him more than once. He had heard enough about Hal DiPietro's character that he could follow her line of reasoning and even explain it in greater detail to Dinah Urbanska, who was so open and uncomplicated that she didn't quite understand why someone like Victor Germondi might kill a good friend over a picture that had been stolen fifty years ago.

"I mean, he wasn't even the one who stole it, for Pete's sake. He was just a kid. So what if DiPietro told? Nobody could blame *Germondi* for what his dad did."

"But they wouldn't praise him, either," Hentz told her. "The Italian government would probably want its medal back, and last night's fancy party would have been canceled. Instead of calling him and his father heroes, people would be calling them thieves and cheats. He'd have to give back that valuable painting—"

Hentz glanced at Sigrid. "I assume it's pretty valuable?"

"Extremely."

"More than that Nooji thing that killed DiPietro?" asked Urbanska, mopping up the coffee she had dribbled on her pale green sweater.

"Noguchi." Sigrid moved her own coffee away from Urbanska's immediate reach. "A masterpiece like that Madonna could very literally be priceless."

"Wow!"

"And there might even be lawsuits if they could prove his father stole all that other stuff," said Hentz.

Sigrid sighed. "Proof. We could use something concrete ourselves. Everything's circumstantial."

"Not everything," Hentz said. "We've been checking alibis. Germondi said he didn't go with DiPietro because he had a lunch appointment, right?"

Sigrid nodded. "His assistant said he left early and didn't get back till midafternoon."

"He might've stayed away till three, but according to the men he had lunch with, the meal was over by one o'clock. I say we get Germondi down here and have a talk."

Accordingly, Sigrid phoned Victor Germondi at his hotel. She apologized for the inconvenience, but since he planned to leave the country that afternoon, could he oblige them by first coming down to answer a few questions about Hal DiPietro? She would send a car if he liked.

His attorney? Oh. Well, certainly if he felt an attorney was necessary. . . . In a half hour, then?

"I just wish we had something stronger to hit him with," she told Hentz and Urbanska.

The interview played out not as they hoped but as they feared.

The only bright spot in all this was the attorney himself. Hentz and Sigrid instantly recognized that the white-haired Robert Schimmer had spent his entire career on the civil side of the law. No doubt he was a tiger on contracts and fine print and the ins and outs of dealing in international art across foreign boundaries; but when it came to criminal procedure, he was out of his depth and didn't seem to realize it.

With his attorney there, however, Victor Germondi was prepared to be urbane and courteous. A two-hour gap between lunch and his return to the office?

He had taken a long walk up and down Fifth Avenue, enjoying New York on a spring day.

And the Duccio Madonna that had once belonged to the Cedronio family. Could he explain that?

A misattributed illustration in a seventy-year-old book, nothing more.

Hoping to slide a knife edge under his shell, Sigrid kept her voice gentle and sympathetic. "That first evening in your office, Mr. Germondi. You were so eloquent when you talked about your Madonna that it made me wonder. You love that period as much as your father did, don't you?"

"I deal in modern," he said stiffly.

"You deal in it, but do you really love it or are you expiating your father's crime?" she asked. "As a vulnerable teenage boy, you saw firsthand where too passionate an obsession with Italian primitives could lead. Did you decide then that modern art was safer? That it would never tempt you into stealing? You said your father would have sold his soul for that Madonna, and he did, didn't he? And along came poor Hal DiPietro. He gave you that book as a memento of your father's award, and he was doubly excited because it had a picture of your Duccio."

Hentz decided it was time to play tough cop. "What happened, Germondi? You meet him on the street when he was leaving for Nauman's apartment? He ask if that countess was your cousin? Is that when you knew he'd never shut up about it and you'd have to kill him?"

"Really," said Mr. Schimmer, dimly aware that perhaps he should be objecting to this line of questioning. "These accusations are insulting and child's play to refute. The Duccio Madonna has been in the Germondi family's possession for two hundred years."

He turned to Germondi. "Are the papers here or in Milan?"

"Milano, of course." Instead of erupting in anger, indignant bluster, or even fear, Victor Germondi seemed to become more detached and uninterested as they tried to close the net around him.

"There, you see?" said Mr. Schimmer. "Now then, Victor, tomorrow morning, as soon as you get home, send me a certified copy of the documentation, and I will bring it down and show it to these officers and that will be that."

"Don't bet on it," Hentz told him. "I think you're bluffing, Germondi. There aren't any papers because your old man was no better than—"

He glanced to Sigrid for help. "What's the name of that Nazi who liked art so much?"

"Goebbels?" Robert Schimmer flushed an angry red to the roots of his white hair. "You dare equate Leo Germondi with Goebbels?"

"Not exactly," Hentz said coolly. "From what I've read, Goebbels took what he wanted and bragged about it. He didn't sneak around and pretend to be a national hero."

At last Mr. Schimmer remembered the laws of habeas corpus and stood up stiffly. "This has gone on quite long enough. I think we should go now."

The shadows under Victor Germondi's eyes were darker than Sigrid remembered from last night, and although he seemed tired as he pulled his portly body from his chair, his manners were as courtly as ever while he took his leave of her.

"We'd prefer that you delay your flight home," she said to him.

"Don't be absurd!" Schimmer snapped. "If you think you have grounds to detain my client, do so now."

The two detectives exchanged looks, and Schimmer gave a satisfied nod. "I thought not. Come, Victor."

Although Hentz told her it wouldn't do any good, Dinah Urbanska rushed off to hunt up an assistant district attorney she'd made friends with.

"He's an Italian citizen and he'll be leaving the country in a few hours," she pleaded when she'd caught up with the older woman at the courthouse.

"So? Don't worry, kid. We've got an extradition treaty with Italy. It might take a little red tape, but you bring me something I can take to the grand jury and I'll get him back for you. Right now, though," the woman said bluntly, "you ain't got shit."

"Then I'd better go get you a shovelful," Urbanska said hotly.

The A.D.A. shook her head as the young detective slammed out of the room. God, she hated spunk!

Back out in the April sunshine, Urbanska grabbed a hot dog from a corner vendor and sat down on the courthouse steps to think what she could logically do next. Get pictures of Germondi and go back to the apartment building? See if someone remembered seeing him?

Her watch said one-thirty. Victor Germondi would be

heading for the airport soon. Checking out of his hotel. Getting into a cab—

Cab?

Yes!

It took longer than she'd expected. First she had to convince Mrs. Zahir that police detectives really didn't give a damn if the hack licensing regulations got bent a little. Next, she had to get Mrs. Zahir steamed with a feminist interpretation of Nihat Zahir's condescending the-little-wifey-doesn't-know-what-she's-talking-about routine that he'd pulled on them yesterday. Then, when the woman was ready to go chop off her husband's balls, get her to blurt out a name. Finally, go find the guy's social club and drag him out of it.

Which is why it was five after four before Dinah Urbanska walked into the squad room with Fahri Esenbel.

To her disappointment there was no sign of Sam Hentz, and the lieutenant's office was empty, too, but she was too excited to let that slow her down.

"Hey, where've you been?" asked Tillie as Urbanska rummaged in Hentz's desk for the photographs.

"Out finding the cabbie who really drove DiPietro to that apartment building," she said with a triumphant grin.

"Yeah? Well—"

"And he's about to confirm it! Come and witness, okay?"

Tillie started to speak, then said, "Okay." He was favoring his leg as he pushed his chair over to her desk and was introduced to Fahri Esenbel, a handsome young man who could pass for his cousin Nihat—or rather, could pass for the photograph on his cousin Nihat's hack license.

Without dropping more than one picture as she thumbed through the pack, Dinah Urbanska laid out the three photographs of Hal DiPietro.

Esenbel studied them carefully and nodded judiciously. "Is him. This is the man who is paying me."

Then he looked closer at the picture taken during the ceremony in Rome and pointed to Victor Germondi. "And this is his friend who comes with him."

It was all Urbanska could do not to hug him, and she said to Tillie, "Be a pal and take his statement, would you, Tillie? I've got to find Sam. Get a warrant. Germondi's plane will be taking off in—" She glanced at her watch and wailed, "Oh, jeepers! In less than forty minutes."

"Relax," said Tillie. "That's what I've been trying to tell you. His hotel called about twenty minutes ago."

"He checked out at two forty-five," said the hotel manager, who accompanied them upstairs. "And everything was in order."

"Did he seem normal then?" asked Hentz.

"Oh, no one actually *spoke* to him," the manager explained. "It was all done electronically. On closed-circuit video. One reviews one's bill, and if everything's in order, one clicks the appropriate numbers, drops the key card off at the desk as one leaves, and everything's billed to one's credit card. No standing in line in the lobby."

A uniformed officer stood by the open door of the hotel room. More uniforms milled around inside where an EMS team waited for them.

"We expected to be nearly full tonight," said the manager, "so the room number was immediately entered on Housekeeping's list to be cleaned. We always wait at least thirty minutes to give our guests time for any last-minute adjustments to their toilette or in case the bellman is held up. But at three-fifteen a chambermaid entered this room and found him in there."

He did not seem to feel the need to escort them further.

Paula Guidry was there before them, taking flash picture of the scene, and she stepped out so they could see inside.

The bathroom was tiled in slabs of dark green marble, accented with shiny brass fixtures and lots of mirrors. The tub was standard white, however, and filled with red water that was probably still warm. Victor Germondi's ashen image was reflected endlessly in the polished mirrors.

Except for his jacket, he was fully dressed, and he had carefully removed the gold links from his French cuffs and rolled up the sleeves of his white batiste shirt. A gray brocade hassock had been brought in from the bedroom so that he could sit at the right height without wetting his clothes; and his head was cushioned by a goose down pillow that lay on the edge of the tub.

"Filled the tub, got himself all comfy, then slit his wrists and stuck them in the warm water to drain," said Hentz.

"Razor's probably on the bottom of the tub," said the EMS team leader.

Looking down at the body and remembering Victor Germondi's earlier air of detachment in her office, Sigrid felt a great sorrow and wondered which potential loss had impelled his self-destruction. Was it the thought of having to pay for Hal DiPietro's death, or did he have a greater fear of public humiliation when the art world learned that the much-honored Germondi reputation was a shabby hollow sham?

As she and Hentz stepped back into the bedroom, she asked, "Did he leave a note?"

"Yeah, but it's not exactly a confession," said a crime-scene technician. He gestured toward the leather portfolio on a nearby table. On top of the portfolio lay one of the hotel's scratch pads:

Please return this to the Contessa d'Alagna with my apologies.

V. Germondi

20

*. . . take liquid varnish, a little white lead and
verdigris . . . And then work these ingredients up
together very finely. Take the pieces of your broken dishes or goblets, and, even if they are in a
thousand fragments, fit them together, putting
this cement on them thinly. Let it dry . . . and you
will find these dishes stronger, and more fit to
stand water, where they are broken than where
they are whole. . . .*

Cennino Cennini
Il Libro dell' Arte, 1437

Someone on the hotel staff had leaked to the media, and
Victor Germondi's suicide made most of the local five
o'clock news shows on both radio and television, with all
newscasters promising fuller details on the late news.

Rudy Gottfried immediately turned off his radio, un-
zipped his overalls, put an envelope in his jacket pocket,
and caught the Q train uptown.

When he got to the gallery, a television van was parked in front, but he barely hesitated before taking the elevator up to the seventh floor.

As he expected, the Germondi Gallery to the right was lit up like Christmas for the camcorders and several people were clustered in the hallway to look through the glass doors while a well-known city reporter taped an exclusive interview with Victor Germondi's elderly assistant.

Gottfried turned to the left, to the DiPietro Gallery. The doors were locked, but lights were still on here, too.

He rapped on the glass sharply.

Eventually a slender young black woman stepped out of the office and signaled that the gallery was closed.

He continued to rap until she came close enough to recognize him.

"We're closed," B'Nita Parsons said. "Sorry."

"I have something to show you."

"What?"

"I can't tell you from out here."

She started to argue, then shrugged and let him in. "Actually, I have something for you, too," she said. "Your slides."

He had almost forgotten about them, but he followed her back to the office and was touched when she opened the drawer and handed them back.

"Thanks. I assumed Hal threw them out."

"He did."

"And you rescued them? I'm indebted. It was a gesture I could ill afford."

"So what do you want to show me?" she asked, leaning against the edge of the desk as if making the point that this was not a social visit and he would not be asked to sit down.

He sat down anyhow on a nearby chair. "You heard that Victor Germondi killed himself?"

"Yes." She looked at him warily.

"They're saying he's the one who killed Hal. Why?"

"How should I know?"

"You didn't help him?"

"Now, just a minute here." She came to her feet and her soft southern voice went hard. "Who the hell do you think you are to come talking stuff like that?"

"I know who *I* am," he answered pointedly. "The question is, my dear, who are you?"

Before she could answer, he drew a frayed and yellowed envelope from his coat pocket and handed it to her. Inside were several photographs.

"You're Ben and Anita Slocum's daughter, aren't you? You're very like your mother."

The young woman barely seemed to hear him as she hastily flipped through the pictures and then went back again more slowly. "Which is Ben Slocum?" she asked, fanning them out on the table in front of him.

"This one," he said. "And here. And here. You never saw a picture of him before?"

"Never. My grandparents burned almost every trace of him after my mother died."

"Ah," said Rudy feeling dreadfully disappointed. "I hoped she was still living."

"She wasn't strong," said B'Nita. "After my father died, my mother took me back to her parents in Alabama. I don't know if it was postpartum depression or pure-out grief, but she overdosed on sleeping pills and slept herself to death. And for the next sixteen years, not a day went by that my granny didn't tell me if it hadn't been for me and my white daddy, their sweet little Anita would still be alive."

"They shouldn't have blamed you and Ben," said Rudy. "If Henry DiPietro hadn't—"

"Yes!" she said. "That's the only thing that kept me going. Knowing that someday, some day, I was going to get even with him for what he took away from me before I was even a year old."

Rudy cocked his scraggly thatched head at her. "How did you know about Henry?"

"My dad's notebooks. Two of them. My grandmother kept them for some reason, and it was all in there. I didn't understand it at first, but eventually, as I grew older, I realized that Henry DiPietro had cut y'all's legs off and blighted my life, too."

As she talked, she paced up and down, gesticulating angrily. "My grandparents weren't just poor in material things. I could've lived with that. But they were narrow-minded and poor in spirit, too. They crippled Mother's spirit and they crippled mine as well. I got married at sixteen just to get out of there, but the marriage was over before I could finish high school, and since then I just seem to keep on picking losers. And it's all Henry DiPietro's fault. I swore I'd get him back."

She looked at Rudy and her brown eyes shone. "And I almost did it, too, Mr. Gottfried. If Hal DiPietro hadn't been killed, I could have put this gallery out of business all by myself."

"Like you did with the mailing list?" he asked.

She was instantly on guard. "Who told you about that?"

"Lieutenant Harald. Oh, don't worry," he reassured her. "She doesn't suspect it was anything but an accident."

"Then how did *you* know?"

He rubbed the back of his thick neck and gave a sardonic smile. "Because I recognized you when I saw your picture, and I knew there was a fox in the henhouse. One of Buck David's pals told me about the catalog mix-up and about champagne served at room temperature. Was that you, too?"

She nodded. "And if Mrs. DiPietro tries to keep the gallery going, I think I can help her lose a bundle."

"No," he said.

"What?"

"Let it go."

Her lovely face was both puzzled and mutinous. "I don't understand. You ought to be glad that I'm getting even."

"I am. You have. Now let it go." He held up his hand to stop her protest. "When I realized who you were, I was afraid you were the one who'd killed Hal. And I thought I knew why. God knows I wanted to kill Henry enough times myself, and I got drunk for a week when he finally dropped dead. He ruined my life. He ruined Morris Wallender's life, and hell yes, he ruined your parents' lives and blighted your youth. But it would have been a hundred times worse if you'd killed Hal. My life may be in shambles, but yours is still in front of you. You don't want to let it eat on you another twenty-five years the way I've let it eat on me. Let it go, B'Nita. Let it go."

She stared at him silently. He didn't realize he was holding his breath until he saw the anger and tension begin to leave her slender body, and suddenly he relaxed, too.

As he stood up to leave, she returned the photographs to the ragged old envelope and started to hand them back to him, but he shook his head. "No, you keep them. They mean more to you now than to me."

At the doorway, he paused. "And I'll tell you something else. I've got a sketch I did when you were about two weeks old. Ben was painting you and Anita, and I made a sketch of him painting you. Come over sometime and I'll show it to you."

Before he knew what was happening, she stood on tiptoe and lightly kissed his cheek. "May I come tonight?" she asked.

With Hentz still officially in charge of the case, Sigrid was off the hook early enough to make her dinner engagement with her mother at Gus' Place down in the Village. Anne's treat. It was one of Anne's favorite restaurants, but a little pricey for both of them as a rule.

Unbidden came Hal DiPietro's gibe that she no longer had to count the cost of anything.

"What's the occasion?" she asked as the waiter departed with their order.

"No occasion," Anne said guilelessly, patting her hand. "I'm just pleased that it's spring and that you're working and . . ." Her voice trailed off and she gave a happy little shrug of her shoulders.

Sigrid had never seen her in quite this mood.

"What are you up to, Mother?"

"I don't see why you can't just accept what I say when I say it, Siga. You always—" She hesitated, then took a deep breath. "Okay. *Newsmonth* is sending me to Mexico to do an in-depth story on the Zapatistas down there."

"And?"

"And Mac is going with me." She flushed a bright rosy red that Sigrid found endearing. "Separate bedrooms, of course. No strings."

"Hey, who's the mother here?" Sigrid tilted her head and smiled. "I don't do bed checks, okay? And I think it's great that the captain's going with you." She would not spoil her mother's happiness by letting her know how awkward this could make things when McKinnon returned.

As if reading her mind, Anne touched her hand again and said, "Now you must *not* repeat this, honey, but there's a good possibility that Mac may be retiring soon."

"*What?*"

"Well, there's no reason for him to stay on, is there? He's put in thirty years, he's as high as he's going to go unless he gets a lot more politically active, which he doesn't want to do, so we—*he* thought he might as well leave now. Maybe travel a bit."

"Starting with Mexico?"

"Mexico's to see if he can leave the job for ten days. Ah," she said happily. "Here's our wine. Can grilled trout be far behind?"

When Sigrid got home that evening, it was nearly ten, but the door was still open to Roman's quarters beyond the kitchen and she found him in his small sitting room. He sat at his L-shaped desk with a glass of wine in his hand, and from the looks of the nearly empty bottle in front of him, she assumed it was not his first glass.

On the short side of the desk's L, colorful tropical fish swam across his computer in his own personalized screensaver program, but he seemed mesmerized by the gas logs ablaze in the fireplace.

"Roman?"

"Oh, hello, my dear. I thought I heard the door. Did you have supper? No, that's right," he reminded himself in his deep bass. "You were going to meet Anne. That's good, because I'm afraid I didn't cook anything."

"Are you all right?" Sigrid asked.

"All right?" He considered the question gravely. "Yes. I do believe I *am* all right. At the moment, that is. Had you asked me earlier—aye, there's the rub. Or do I mean scrub? Rub out, scrub out, both clean up the disk, don't they?"

"Sorry," said Sigrid. "You've lost me."

"No, no," he corrected. "I've lost *me*. Would you like some wine?"

"Will it help me understand what's going on?"

His laugh was like the distant rumble of heavy thunder. "Probably not. In a nutshell, my dear, I thought I had copied the outline and all my notes for my book onto one of my magical little diskettes, so I went ahead and erased all of the original material from my hard disk. Four hours ago I put my diskette in the proper drive, booted my computer, and guess what? Zilch! There's absolutely nothing on the diskette. Six months of work off in electronic limbo."

"And you can't get it back?"

He shook his large domed head. "I fear not. My computer instructor informs me that I could pay an enormous sum and perhaps recover half of it fairly intact. The other half is probably scattered all over the hard drive in hundreds of disconnected phrases."

Sigrid was appalled and distressed for him. "Oh, Roman. All that work. All your emotional investment. That's dreadful."

But Roman had passed from despair into philosophical acceptance. "Maybe it was for the best," he said, pouring himself the last of the wine. "I learned an awful lot doing this first book. It taught me pacing, structure, motivation. Who knows? Maybe the next one will be even better."

They talked for a few minutes longer till Sigrid was reassured that he really was all right; then she went down to her room at the other end of the apartment and began to get ready for bed. Nauman's robe lay on the pillow as she undressed. First her outer clothes, then the silky lingerie that gave him such endless delight.

"So buttoned up on the outside," he used to tease her. "So sexy underneath," and his hands would trace the curves of lace.

The things he had given her in their few short months together! She couldn't begin to number the things he had taught her to see.

The things he had taught her to value.

She put on his robe and belted it tightly around her naked body, then opened the drawer of her nightstand. Her fingers found the play button of the cassette and pressed it.

Once more Nauman's voice flowed up and over her, as warm and alive as he himself had been that final February day: *"I hated to walk out of the room, Siga . . . it was like I might never see them again. . . . Never had that feeling before."*

His voice filled her ears, and she leaned back against the pillow, breathing in the ghostly fragrance that emanated from his robe.

She couldn't quite remember which early saint it was who had been blessed by the smell of roses whenever he prayed to the Madonna, and she smiled to think how Nauman would have snorted at any similar comparisons. Nevertheless, the faint aroma of his aftershave and pipe tobacco wreathed her now like a spiritual benediction, and she knew that this feeling would endure after all that was physical had inevitably faded into the air around her.

The tape came to an end and she rewound it.

When it clicked off, she hesitated for a long moment,

then reached over, turned the volume all the way down, and pressed the record button.

As the tape began to record silence, she quietly closed the drawer.

> *Praying that God All-Highest, Our Lady, Saint John, Saint Luke the Evangelist and painter, Saint Eustace, Saint Francis, and Saint Anthony of Padua will grant us grace and courage to sustain and bear in peace the burdens and struggles of this world. . . . Amen.*
>
> *Cennino Cennini*
> Il Libro dell' Arte, 1437